The Uist Girl Series Book 2

HIS BITTER SEED

A tense and emotional historical novel

MARION MACDONALD

Cover designed by Get Covers

In memory of my Mum and Dad

Mary (Mallon) Macdonald and John Macdonald

Beware lest there be among you a root bearing poisonous and bitter fruit.

Deuteronomy 29:18
The Holy Bible, English Standard Version

CHARACTERS

The Macdonald Family

Chrissie Macdonald	Our Heroine
Roderick Macdonald	Her husband
Roddy Macdonald	Son of Chrissie and Roderick
Donald Donaldson	Son of Heather and Colin
Heather Macdonald (deceased)	Daughter of Roderick and Lily

The MacIntosh Family

Marion MacIntosh	Chrissie's mother
Angus MacIntosh	Chrissie's father
Johnny MacIntosh	Chrissie's brother
Lachlan MacIntosh (deceased)	Chrissie's brother
Morag MacIntosh/Hamilton	Chrissie's sister

The Adams/Hepworth Family

Bunty Adams/Hepworth	Our Antagonist
Mary Hepworth	Bunty's daughter
James Adams (deceased)	Bunty's Father (killed in Canada)
Frederick Adams (deceased)	Bunty's stepfather and brother of James
Grace Adams	Bunty's mother
Harry Hepworth (deceased)	Bunty's husband
Charles Adams	Bunty's brother

Other Characters

Flora McAllister	The Housekeeper
Sir Arthur	The Laird
Colin Donaldson (deceased)	Former Factor and Donald's father
Victoria Donaldson	Colin's Sister
Janet McLeod	Johnny's Fiancée
Aunt Katie	Angus's Sister
Maude	Solicitor/friend of Aunt Katie
Michael Hamilton	Morag's husband
Reverend Macaulay	The Minister
Elizabeth Macaulay	Minister's wife
Shona & Alex McIver	Shopkeepers
John McInnes	Doctor
Dr Graham	Doctor in Long Island Poorhouse
Morag Campbell	Island Gossip
Mairi Campbell	Morag Campbell's daughter
Archie Campbell	Morag Campbell's son
Annie Nicolson	Rural Member
Mr Abernethy	Island Solicitor
Murdo Mackenzie	The Postman
Ian and Sarah Fraser	New Postmaster and wife
Archie Morrison	The Constable

GAELIC WORDS USED IN THIS BOOK

I am not a Gaelic speaker but have used some words to indicate when characters are speaking in Gaelic. My apologies if I have used any of them incorrectly.

An droch-shùil	The evil eye
Athair	Father
Dadaidh	Daddy
Ciamar a tha thu?	How are you?
Cromag	Shepherd's crook
Gorach	Silly
Leanabh	Baby
Machair	Low-lying coastal grazing land
Mamaidh	Mummy
Mathair	Mother
Mo graidh	My darling
Murt	Murder
Priosan	Prison
Seanair	Grandfather
Seanmhair	Grandmother

PROLOGUE
Lochmaddy, North Uist, August 1923

It's a fine summer afternoon when I return to North Uist. The gulls whirl and screech enthusiastically overhead, as I watch the familiar toing and froing on Lochmaddy pier, alive now with locals soaking up the drama of the ferry's arrival. I release a deep sigh of contentment, mixed with some anxiety. As well as the locals, there are also passengers waiting to embark and family and friends gathered to meet their loved ones. My sons Roddy and Donald are there with my mother and father, and they wave enthusiastically when they see me. I wave back eagerly, but my stomach flutters as I wait to get off. It isn't so much meeting my family that's causing me anxiety, but the fear of bumping into Shona McIver, the local shopkeeper or Morag Campbell, the local gossip, with their curiosity and questioning. I wasn't sure I was ready for that yet.

It takes a while to get off the ferry, as I have a pram and a baby to offload and am grateful that my sister Morag is with me to help. I don't know what I would have done without her these past few months. It's several years since Morag has been back home and three months have passed since I last saw my family, so mother and father approach us eagerly, each of them taking it in turns to pull us into their arms. But I notice the boys hold back and feel a pang of guilt for leaving them. At least I'm back in time to see Roddy off to school in Portree and Donald off to school in Glasgow.

Tears form in my mother's eyes as she looks at me and then at the baby in the pram. Gazing inside, she coos at her new granddaughter and little Heather rewards her with a smile as she draws up her legs, crumples her little face, and blows tiny bubbles from her cupid bow lips.

'It's a pity Roderick never got to see her,' *Mathair* whispers, looking at me as the tears spill over and slide down her wrinkled cheeks.

My eyes nip in sympathy, but my husband Roderick comes to me, his presence supporting me from the other side of life's veil.

1

Just the way he had done that day I walked into the sea at Clachan Sands, when I felt I had nothing left to live for. So, my tears don't fall. I've done what he wanted and hope that everything I've needed to do has been worth it. Roderick died knowing I was going to have a child, and I wonder what he thinks as he looks down from heaven. She isn't his, although my friends and neighbours in North Uist assume differently. After Roderick died, I was troubled, and everyone thinks I went away because I was afraid I would end up in Long Island Poorhouse, the place where the insane share accommodation with those too poor to rent a house. But that wasn't the reason.

Respectability is such a precious thing still, just like it was back in 1914 when Roderick and I forged a birth certificate, saying we were Donald's parents. We wanted to save him from the shame of being illegitimate, but it didn't work because of Colin Donaldson's determination to have an heir. Some would find it hard to understand why I was covering up another illegitimate birth, but I thought it was the right thing to do and prayed to God that my little Heather and my boys would never find out the truth.

Standing again on Lochmaddy pier, my thoughts went back to that day three years ago when we had stood on this same spot, watching as the undertakers carried Colin's body onto the ferry for the trip to Glasgow and his funeral. I had an overwhelming sense of relief that all our troubles would be over now he was dead and out of our lives. How wrong I was. Although that man could cause trouble, even from the grave, it wasn't just Colin's legacy that brought us misfortune. The legacy Roderick had created in Canada was to bring even more suffering to our doorstep. I could hardly believe it had only been three years. So much had happened in that time and it all began the day Bunty Hepworth came into our lives.

CHAPTER ONE

Lochmaddy, North Uist, August 1920

As Roderick and I made our way outside, while the undertaker closed the coffin, I could hear Flora McAllister scolding the boys, so I looked through the window to see what was going on.

'Roddy, Donald, stop that laughing. Have some respect,' she said, in that stern voice of hers. 'Your father has just died, Master Donald. You shouldn't let that Roddy lead you astray the way he always does. Look at the state of your new trousers. They're covered in muck.'

Donald stared at the ground, but Roddy dug him in the ribs with his elbow while replying to Mrs McAllister.

'I didn't lead Donald astray, did I Donald? *Mathair* told us to go outside and play and that's what we did.'

'Is that so, young Roddy? Well, whatever has happened, it will soon be time for Donald to leave and he can't go with trousers in that state. Come away inside, Donald, and I'll sponge them down.'

I quickly went outside. These were my boys, and it was my job to chastise them if they needed it. But I felt hesitant to put Mrs McAllister in her place, as she had been the housekeeper when I worked here before I married Roderick and went to Canada. But I would need to get over my fear of her now that I was to become mistress of the big house. I took a deep breath and put a hand on each boy's shoulder, hoping to show they were my responsibility and not hers.

'Thank you, Mrs McAllister. If you would sponge Donald's trousers, that would be helpful. The undertaker will leave soon, and Donald needs to be ready, or they will miss the ferry.'

She nodded and went inside with Donald.

'Roddy, tell me what was going on there. You know you shouldn't talk back to your elders.'

'But *Mathair*, she was making out it was my fault that Donald's trousers were dirty, but we had only done what you told us to do. You know I wouldn't lead Donald astray.'

He looked up at me innocently, but I knew from his expression that he was lying to me. He had changed so much since he had found out that Donald wasn't his brother.

'Will she still be working here when we move in?' he continued. 'I don't like her very much.'

I didn't like the woman very much either, but I didn't tell Roddy that. There was little I could do about it. Although Roderick would be the Factor and I the mistress of the house, the Trust employed her, not us. As we would both be living in the house and our roles reversed from what they were, I wanted to get on with her. I would find it uncomfortable if there was constant hostility between us. My mother couldn't understand why I didn't like Flora, as they had gone to school together and were close friends. But she hadn't worked under her the way I had when I was companion to the Factor's daughter, Victoria. She had always been so disapproving of me, like I was a silly young lass with no common sense. When I thought back to that time, it occurred to me she was probably right.

'It doesn't matter if you like Mrs McAllister, Roddy. I will not have you being rude to an adult. Do you understand?'

He smiled cheekily and nodded, but I could tell my words were like water off a duck's back and feared he would go astray or get into more serious trouble. Everything had changed for my two boys when Colin Donaldson, the previous Factor, had claimed Donald as his son two years ago. Colin encouraged Donald to consider himself a cut above the rest of us by feeding him stories about the Laird being his cousin and hinting that the Laird was a relation of the King. He also lavished Donald with clothes and gifts and even gave him a pony of his own. It was difficult for Roddy, who had always been the big brother that Donald looked up to. But once Donald started going to visit Colin, all that changed. It was Colin he looked up to and not Roddy. Roddy had retaliated by refusing to play with Donald when he was at home, and they gradually grew apart. Roddy also became more difficult. He had always been confident, but he seemed to be full of bravado all the time, testing Roderick and me to see how far he could go. It had been a difficult time, and I was pleased to see the two boys playing and laughing together as I had asked them to do, but it looked like things hadn't changed.

Just then Mrs McAllister brought Donald outside, his trousers cleaned and pressed. I kissed his cheek and took his hand, trying to comfort and reassure him on what, for him, must be another terrible day in the series of terrible days he had suffered over the past couple of years. I remember how upset and angry he was when Roderick and I had to tell him we were not his parents and showed him a photograph of Heather.

'I don't want another *mamaidh*,' he had said, throwing Heather's photograph to the floor. 'She's funny looking, and she doesn't even look like me. She can't be my *mamaidh*.'

Although he shared some of her features, it was his skin tone that made the difference. It was a darker shade than his brother's, just as Heather's skin had been darker than Roderick's Scottish pallor. Heather was half Cree and half Scottish, but Colin had made us promise never to reveal Donald's heritage to him or anyone else. I think it had embarrassed him to admit that he had fathered a child with a woman of mixed race, but he said it would be an added burden for Donald to carry if people found out. Roderick and I agreed to his terms as it was the only way we could get him to set up a trust approving shared custody of Donald with us. Heather died after giving birth to Donald. I had tried everything to save her, but I couldn't and when she had given him into our care on her deathbed, we had promised we would do whatever it took to protect Donald and keep him safe from harm. My thoughts were brought back to the here and now when I heard the undertaker and Callum, the stable hand, coming down the stairs with Colin's coffin.

CHAPTER TWO

Mrs McAllister, Jeanie the scullery maid, Catriona the housemaid, Roddy, Donald, and I stood with our heads bowed while Roderick and Calum helped the undertaker to put Colin's coffin onto the cart that would transport it to the ferry. Although he would go to his grave in a proper hearse drawn by a black stallion with a black plume on its head in Glasgow, the undertaker could not bring it over to the island and there was nothing so grand on North Uist. We were crofters and shopkeepers with very little money to spend on fancy burials, and yet it was the one thing that each of us faced, irrespective of how much money we had or our station in life.

Our family rode in the buggy behind the cart to the pier at Lochmaddy, where Roderick, Donald, and the undertaker would catch the ferry to Glasgow. The vessel was there when we arrived, and people were already boarding, so I said a quick goodbye to Roderick and Donald and stood watching as they went on board. Calum drove the cart back home, but I lingered a while. I had always loved the rhythms of the ferry coming and going into Lochmaddy pier and, as always, a sense of excitement filled the atmosphere.

As Roddy and I stood waving to the departing ferry, my thoughts moved again to how Donald would cope. How does a seven-year-old come to terms with losing a father who had only come into his life two years ago? Although Colin had been the bane of my life and was ill thought of by the local crofting people, somehow, in those two years, he had formed a close relationship with Donald. I knew his passing would be hard for Donald, so I would need to give him special attention when he returned from Glasgow after the funeral.

I was so busy thinking about Donald that at first I didn't hear the woman's voice and it was Roddy who told me that someone was speaking to me.

'Oh, I'm sorry,' I said, turning to see a young, well-dressed woman with a hat covering her shiny brown hair cut in a short,

6

modern hairstyle and a little girl with pigtails. There were two suitcases at her feet.

'Can I help you?'

'I hope so,' she said apologetically in an English accent. 'My name's Mrs Hepworth, the new schoolteacher for Lochmaddy and this is my daughter, Mary. I'm wondering where the schoolhouse is and I'm afraid I haven't been able to understand anyone I've asked.'

'They'll have been speaking the Gaelic, that's why. You'll find, despite being forced to learn the English at school, most of us still prefer our own language.'

I laughed lightly but noticed a spark in her eyes. It made me think of the evil eye and the misfortune that might befall me if someone took against me. Although I tried not to be superstitious, the age-old beliefs of the islands still wormed their way into my mind sometimes.

'I didn't realise English wasn't the language used up here. That wasn't explained to me when I took the job.'

She looked around doubtfully, obviously wondering what she had let herself in for. Feeling contrite for what I'd said, I offered her a lift, hoping to put her at her ease and make up for causing any offence.

'Why don't you and Mary put your bags in our buggy, and we'll take you along to the schoolhouse? It's not too far.'

'That's very kind of you, Mrs...?'

'I'm Mrs Macdonald.'

'That's very kind of you, Mrs Macdonald. But I don't want to put you to any inconvenience. I couldn't help noticing you seem to have suffered a bereavement. I hope it wasn't anyone close.'

'It's a long story, Mrs Hepworth, which I won't go into today. But it really is no problem for Roddy and me to give you a lift.'

'Roddy? I haven't heard that name before.'

'Yes, he's named after his father, Roderick. It was him you saw going on the ferry with our other son, Donald.'

She looked thoughtful for a moment, then smiled at me.

7

'You have two boys that I'll be teaching then?'

'Yes, that's right.'

The sound of the horse clip-clopping along the road for the brief journey to the schoolhouse sounded louder than normal as we all sat without speaking. Mrs Hepworth and Mary gazed around them, soaking up this place that would become their new home, and I didn't want to disturb them with trivial chatter. She hadn't said where they had come from and, for all I knew, she was used to a small island or rural village. But if she had come from a town, Lochmaddy might feel strange in comparison with towns on the mainland.

Lochmaddy was more of a large village than a town. However, it was the major settlement in North Uist with its own courthouse, post office, church, school, hotel, and shop, as well as the major ferry port, so hopefully, it wouldn't be a step too far for them. But there was a whole other island world beyond Lochmaddy, and I wondered how they would take to its lonely expanses of bleak peat bogs punctuated here and there with small settlements. Getting around was difficult if you didn't have a horse or a bike, and we locals walked miles sometimes and thought nothing of it. But it would be a pity if she and Mary didn't venture out of Lochmaddy.

The island was beautiful with its white sand beaches and fertile machair carpeted in wildflowers in the summer. The light was remarkable, and in summer we had daylight almost all the time. But the weather could also be wild and unpredictable. As there was nothing between us and America, whipping winds assaulted our coasts from the Atlantic ocean irrespective of the season, although sometimes that was a blessing, as it kept the midges at bay in the summer. All that and our habit of speaking in Gaelic might take a bit of getting used to by English city dwellers.

When we reached the schoolhouse, Roddy and I helped them in with their bags. I thought it wasn't much to bring, but there were several trunks sitting in the middle of the main room that had obviously been delivered earlier.

'Well, I hope you settle in okay. At least you'll have a few weeks before the new term begins. If you need anything, you'll find me at the post office.'

'Oh, you're the post mistress? That must be an interesting job.'

'Well, post office assistant, but yes, it is an interesting job, although Roderick and I won't be there for much longer. The Laird has appointed my husband as the Factor, and we will move into the big house on the outskirts of town as soon as we can arrange the move.'

'So, we will both be moving into a new house and into a new role. I hope we can become friends, Mrs Macdonald. It would be such a comfort if we could support one another through the changes we're about to face in our lives.'

I agreed with her. It would be good to have a friend and I returned to the post office feeling lighter in spirit than I had in a long time.

CHAPTER THREE

On the journey from the mainland to North Uist, Bunty Hepworth wondered if she had done the right thing coming to this place in the far north of Scotland, separated from the world by an expanse of murderous waters. She and her daughter Mary had both vomited violently as the stormy sea heaved the ferry through the crashing waves, carrying them to North Uist on what another passenger told her was the Minch. At several points on the journey, she had wondered if they would ever make it to dry land. But here they were, and she relished the soft fresh wind caressing her face and the feel of the warm sun on her back.

As she stood in the unfamiliar port of Lochmaddy holding her daughter's hand, she gazed round at the strange-looking people in their rough clothes speaking to each other in their strange language and wondered if Roderick Macdonald was like them or was he more sophisticated. She had found out he was the postmaster in this remote place through private investigators she hired after her stepfather died. As good fortune would have it, the man who had murdered her father lived on an island where a suitable job had become available and so it was easy for her and Mary to make their escape from the dirt and stench of Manchester where she had been brought up.

Bunty could never forget her early life when indeed she had lived among the squalor of Manchester, when her stepfather was building up his rag and bone business and she was the butt of his angry temper. Later, he had built his business and his wealth, making armaments and machinery for the war effort and her family now lived in one of the most affluent areas of Manchester, far removed from any dirt and grime. But it was the bad times she remembered. Living in a comfortable home with servants to take care of her every need didn't make up for the void left by the absence of her real father. He had gone to Canada, promising to come back and marry her mother, but he never had. It was only because her uncle had stepped into the breach and married her mother that Bunty had avoided the stigma of illegitimacy. But she was sure life with her uncle had been much worse than any stigma she might have suffered.

She hated her uncle and what he had done to her throughout her life, but especially when her husband Harry died in the war and she found herself pregnant with Mary. He insisted she come back home to live with him and her mother, but when she suffered a breakdown after Mary was born, he put her into a sanatorium and her mother had looked after Mary for the first six months of her life. By the time Bunty recovered her health and returned home, Mary had become more her mother's child than hers.

Bunty had put up with taking second place in her daughter's life while her stepfather was still alive. But when he died from the Spanish Flu, she decided to take Mary and make another life for her and her daughter somewhere as far from Manchester as possible. It turned out North Uist was just the place. Her thoughts went back to when her uncle caught the flu and how much she wished he would die from it. She had watched him lying in bed, his breathing laboured, his clammy body signalling imminent death, and had imagined what it would be like to put a pillow over his head to hasten his end. When she discovered the truth about her real father, she wished she had.

She couldn't believe her luck when the woman she approached on the pier turned out to be Roderick Macdonald's wife. It really must be a small world on an island such as this. Although she had smiled and said she hoped they would be friends, she didn't like the woman. That remark she had made about the islanders being forced to speak English and preferring to speak their own language was rude. The woman must have known from her accent that she was English. Having grown up in a family where she was the odd one out, a cuckoo in the nest, she was oversensitive to what she saw as a slight against her.

11

She had an anxious moment that she might be too late when she asked the woman about her bereavement, but she had quickly dispelled Bunty's anxiety by pointing out her husband, who was boarding the ferry with a young boy. She still had time to plan her revenge.

CHAPTER FOUR

While Roderick and Donald were away, I asked Roddy to be extra kind to Donald when he came home.

'But why *Mathair?* He doesn't seem upset about Colin dying. I've never seen him crying. He just reads his books and comics like he always does.'

'People don't always show their feelings, Roddy, so he might be upset, but isn't showing it. And even if he is okay, it doesn't mean you shouldn't be extra kind to him. He's your wee brother, and it's up to you to look after him. We'll soon move from the post office to the Factor's house and that will be strange for Donald because he's used to going to see Colin there.'

He looked down at the floor and then squinted up at me.

'He's not really my wee brother, and he's not really your son either, is he *Mathair?*'

His words and the look on his face made me uncomfortable.

'He might not be your wee brother by blood, but you've been raised together and as far as I'm concerned, you are brothers, so don't let me hear you saying that again.'

'That's not fair. Why can't I talk about it? I bet you would never have told me Donald wasn't my brother if Colin Donaldson hadn't forced you to. For all I know, I'm not your son either.'

'For goodness' sake, Roddy. Don't be *gorach*. Of course, you're our son.'

'I'm not silly *Mathair* and don't expect me to be nice to Donald.'

He turned on his heel and stomped out of the room, leaving me feeling angry and inept as a mother. How could he talk to me like that and expect to get away with it? Roderick brooked no nonsense or cheek from the boys, but Roddy seemed to be always pushing the boundaries nowadays.

When Roderick and Donald came home from the funeral three days later, and we were chatting after the boys had gone to bed, I told him what Roddy had said.

13

'I don't know what's going on with that boy lately. He's a bit too full of himself, if you ask me.'

'Don't you think it might be a way to cover up his fears? He was never like that before. It's been a tough couple of years for the boys, but hopefully now you're the Factor, we can settle down and just live a normal life.'

'I hope so, Chrissie, but you know not everyone is happy that I got the job. The Factor's always been someone from the outside, someone related to the Laird, not a crofter's son.'

'Why do you say that? Has someone said something?'

'Well not directly, but I was talking to Reverend Macaulay, and he told me that Jimmy and Morag Campbell had been complaining in the shop to Alex and Shona McIver and, anyone else who was happy to listen about it, when they were in collecting their paraffin and herring.'

'I hope the reverend stood up for you, Roderick. They're lucky they're getting one of their own to be Factor, ignoramuses that they are.'

He laughed.

'I love when you get angry. You should do it more often.'

I made a face at him and then smiled, my anger leaving me as suddenly as it had come.

'So, tell me about the funeral. Was it a grand affair?'

'It certainly was. The Laird himself was there. He told me the school board had appointed a new schoolteacher and asked if we would do our best to make her feel welcome. He told me it didn't look good that the island kept losing teachers at the rate they had done in the past couple of years.'

'Oh, I've already met her. She arrived off the ferry that you and Donald went on. Roddy and I gave her and her daughter Mary a ride up to the schoolhouse. She's English and seems very nice. By the looks of her, she's younger than me.'

'No husband?'

'Doesn't seem to be. I didn't like to ask her why, but there'll be a good reason she's on her own. I don't think the school board

14

would appoint a woman with an illegitimate child to teach the children of the island, do you?'

'I'll go round and see her when I'm in Lochmaddy tomorrow and invite her to afternoon tea the week after we move into the big house, shall I?'

'Yes. Good idea. Our first ever guest as Factor and Mistress. Oh, I'm so looking forward to this new stage in our lives, aren't you, Roderick?'

He rose from his chair and pulled me into his arms.

'You're such a snob sometimes, Chrissie. Don't be lording it over people. We still have to live here when our job as Donald's trustees is at an end.'

'How was Donald? Was he really upset?'

'It's hard to tell with him. He's so quiet now, so different from how he used to be before Colin Donaldson got his claws into him. I think it frightened him more than upset him. He grasped my hand like a vice when the coffin was going into the ground, and I could feel him shaking.'

'Och poor wee lamb.'

Little did I know then how frightened Donald had been by the funeral rituals he had seen and how his brother had taken advantage of that fear.

CHAPTER FIVE

Bunty was surprised when she heard a knock at the door. She had only been on the island for a week and knew no-one except the Minister's wife, who had called on her the day after she arrived.

'Hello. Mrs Hepworth?'

'Yes.'

'I'm Roderick Macdonald, soon to be the new Factor.'

Bunty took his outstretched hand and felt herself tremble slightly. She couldn't believe the man himself was here on her doorstep.

'Come in, Mr Macdonald. It's kind of you to call.'

'Well, thank the Laird. It was he who asked me to call to make sure you were settling in okay.'

She smiled.

'The Laird? I must be a very important person for him to worry about how I'm settling in.'

'Well, I think you are. We've lost quite a few teachers over the last couple of years, and he wants us to do everything we can to make you feel welcome and encourage you to stay.'

'And what made the other teachers leave? Do you have a lot of unruly children who are difficult to teach?'

'Och no, nothing like that. It can be difficult though for a teacher with no Gaelic as that's all some children speak when they first start school, but I think the reason some of them left was more to do with the weather. The few days you've been here have been mild, but sometimes it's wild with wind and rain.'

'Probably not much different from Manchester where I come from. I met your wife the day I arrived. She was very kind and gave Mary and me a lift to the schoolhouse.'

'Well, that brings me to the reason I'm here. Mrs Macdonald wonders if you and Mary would like to come to tea when we move into the Factor's house. I could send Callum our stable hand to pick you up.'

'That would be lovely, Mr Macdonald. So, what does a Factor do, if you don't mind me asking? Can I get you a cup of tea, by the way?'

'That would be grand, Mrs Hepworth, thanks.'

'Please call me Bunty. Mrs Hepworth is so formal.'

He looked a little uncomfortable and she wondered if she was being too forward.

'Okay. Bunty it is.'

As she busied herself making the tea, she thought about the man in the next room. He must be a good twenty years older than his wife, probably not much younger than her father and stepfather. Poor woman, being married to an old man like that, although she grudgingly admitted he was quite handsome in a rugged way. She wondered how that marriage had come about. What an opportunity this was to get to know him and work out a plan of action to destroy him. She had to admit she had been quite reckless coming up here without a plan, but when she saw the job vacancy, it was too good an opportunity to miss.

Roderick picked his cup up and slurped loudly. The sound made her feel sick, but she continued with the conversation they had begun earlier.

'So, you were going to tell me what a Factor does.'

'Basically, it's looking after the land for the Laird. He owns the island, you see.'

'Owns the entire island. My goodness.'

'The crofters rent their crofts from him, so part of my job is to make sure they pay their rent on time and don't get into arrears. I also need to make sure the Laird's guests have good game and fishing opportunities and to make sure I get the constable to prosecute any poachers.'

'Sounds like you're a kind of policeman yourself. I can't imagine a Factor is very popular with the local people.'

'Not normally, no, as it's usually someone who doesn't come from the island. But I'm hopeful being local will make me a better Factor.'

17

'Why has the Laird chosen a local person to do the job this time?'

'Och, well, it's a long story, Bunty and I'm sure you'll find out about it soon enough, so I won't bore you with it just now.'

That's what his wife had said, so it only made Bunty even more curious to find out what the story was, but she decided to find out if he would admit that he had lived in Canada.

'Have you always lived in North Uist?'

'No, not always. I lived in Canada for a while.'

'What made you leave?'

'I was ill and couldn't manage my farm any longer. Also, my wife was homesick and wanted to come home. She hated the sound of the wolves howling at night.'

Bunty shuddered theatrically and told him she would hate that, too.

When he had left, she sat and thought about him and what would hurt him most. He was obviously quite pleased with himself for getting the Factor's job, so losing that might be a way of getting at him. But was it enough? An eye for an eye was what the bible said but killing him like he had killed her father would be a step too far as she wouldn't do anything that would separate her from Mary. Unless she could do it without being caught. As she contemplated this solution, she decided it was too risky and she would just need to be more creative about the ways she could cause him harm.

CHAPTER SIX

Bunty paid a visit to the local shop. She needed some provisions, and it might give her the opportunity to find out more about the Macdonald family. When she went into the shop, there was a woman of about forty behind the counter. She was on the plump side, wore a coarse cloth overall wrapped beneath her ample breasts, and had her sleeves rolled up over her dimpled arms. She was busy counting something in a notebook, but looked up when the little bell on the shop door rang as Bunty and Mary entered.

'*Halo. Ciamar a tha thu?*' she said, smiling at Bunty.

Bunty smiled back, but inside was cursing the woman for using that damn foreign language all the locals used.

'Hello. I'm Mrs Hepworth, the new schoolteacher, and this is my daughter, Mary. I'm afraid we don't speak your language.'

'Och, well now, that's a pity as quite a few of the children who will join your class next week don't speak your language yet. Anyway, it's grand to meet you, Mrs Hepworth and you, Mary,' she said, nodding her head at Mary. 'I'm Mrs McIver. My husband and I own the shop. How can I help you on this fine morning?'

It was anything but fine. The warm weather that had welcomed Bunty to the island had left and in its place was a gale-force wind that almost swept her and Mary off their feet as they made their way to the shop.

'It's a pleasure to meet you too, Mrs McIver,' she said, holding out her hand, which the woman grasped firmly in her podgy one. 'I don't really know very many people yet. Mrs Macaulay, the Minister's wife and Roderick Macdonald, the new Factor, are the only people who've called on me. Oh, and Mrs Macdonald gave me a lift to the schoolhouse on the day I arrived, and she's invited me and Mary for afternoon tea next week.'

'Och, I'm sure it won't be long until you get to know people once the school starts back next week.'

'Do you think I should try to learn some Gaelic, Mrs McIver?

I feel a little worried that the children won't be able to understand me or I them.'

'Och, I think that's a grand idea Mrs Hepworth. None of the other incoming teachers ever bothered trying to understand our mother tongue. But it's part of our culture and one we treasure.'

'I'm sure it is Mrs McIver. Can you recommend anyone to teach me Gaelic?'

'Well, the Factor's wife, Chrissie, was always good at picking up the English, so maybe she could help you pick up the Gaelic.'

'Do you think she would have the time to do it? Being the Factor's wife must be quite an important job, I think.'

'Och, well, she thinks it is for sure. Chrissie likes to think she's a cut above the rest of us because she's lived in Canada and works in the post office.'

'Roderick told me that normally the Factor's job goes to an outsider, so the crofters must be pleased that a local person got the job Mrs McIver.'

'Yes, normally the Factor is a relative of the Laird.'

'And Roderick Macdonald isn't related to him?'

'No. He's only a crofter's son, the same as most of the other people on this island, but he seems able to land himself a good job. He had no sooner come back from Canada than he got the job of postmaster when war broke out.'

Bunty nodded. This conversation was going precisely where she wanted it to go.

'He only got it because there was no-one else to take it on. Everyone was away fighting in the war or working on the crofts to supply food, so he didn't have to try very hard to get the job. And he only got the Factor's job because of Donald.'

'What do you mean, Mrs McIver, because of Donald?'

Although the shop was empty, Mrs McIver looked round, making sure no-one else was listening in on the conversation.

'Well, although Chrissie and Roderick made out that Donald was their son, it turned out his father was actually Colin Donaldson, the previous Factor. He set up a trust, making

Roderick and Chrissie Donald's guardians if anything happened to him. He died of the Spanish Flu. Such a terrible thing and him so young.'

'My stepfather died of the Spanish Flu too. It was a bit of a relief when he passed away as he was so ill with it.'

Bunty made a sad face at Mrs McIver, but smiled inwardly as she remembered her stepfather's last days of pain.

'I'm sorry for your loss, Mrs Hepworth. What can I get you this morning?'

After she had made up Bunty's order and stowed it in a box, Mrs McIver turned to her again.

'This is heavy, so I'll get my husband to drop it along to you this afternoon. Will your husband be joining you soon, Mrs Hepworth?'

'My husband died at Ypres. It's just me and Mary.'

'Och, I'm sorry to hear that. We lost a lot of our young men in that hellish war. In fact, Chrissie's brother Lachlan died out there, too. He was a very sensitive boy – wrote poetry and journals. I believe she's been trying to get someone to publish them.'

Bunty's ears pricked up. Her father-in-law was a printer. Perhaps that would come in handy to gain Chrissie's trust if she needed.

'It's very brave of you coming away up here to a strange place on your own,' continued Mrs McIver. 'I hope you and Mary settle in well.'

As Bunty made her way back to the schoolhouse with Mary, she thought of all that Mrs McIver had told her. Roderick and Chrissie Macdonald were obviously not the most popular people on the island, so she thought it would probably be quite easy to cause mischief for them. She also wondered what the story was behind the boy Donald belonging to the Factor's son and why Chrissie and Roderick had told people he was their son when he clearly wasn't. Perhaps she would find out when she went to tea.

CHAPTER SEVEN

The weather was still warm, and I could see swarms of midges hovering in wait for unsuspecting passers-by as I looked out of the window to see if Bunty and Mary were here yet. These were my first guests for tea, and I wanted everything to be perfect. I had been harassing Mrs McAllister all morning, and I deserved it when she snapped at me.

'Chrissie Macdonald, I've been the housekeeper here for twenty-odd years. I think I know how to make an afternoon tea.'

'Yes, sorry Mrs McAllister,' I said, and retreated to the small drawing room where we were going to have the tea. I liked this room as it was more homely and comfortable than the large drawing room where we were expected to entertain the Laird's guests. There was a group of family photographs on the mantlepiece, one of which was a photo of Heather with Donald in her arms.

My thoughts drifted back to when Roderick had taken the photo. It was the night Heather died. She and I had started out confident that between us we could deliver her baby, so weren't too worried when the doctor couldn't make it through the snow to our homestead. That all changed when we realised the baby was not lying in the correct birthing position. No matter how much I tried to massage the baby round, it remained in the same place. We had telephoned the doctor, and he had told me I would need to cut her to get the baby out. I'll never forget her screams and the blood that poured from her young body.

We had known she wouldn't last the night and when I placed Donald into her arms to hold; she had asked Roderick to take a photograph of them together on the Brownie camera he had bought when Roddy was born.

'I would like to think that one day he might know the truth about his birth and that it would bring him comfort to know what I looked like,' she had said.

Roderick and I took it in turns to sit with her throughout the night, burning special herbs, the Cree tradition to help the dying on their journey into the next world.

The sound of the buggy's wheels scrunching over the driveway transported me back from that horrible night to Scotland. I realised my face was wet with tears and quickly wiped it with my handkerchief. Fixing a smile on my face, I went to greet my guests. But the sadness aroused by my memories took the shine off the excitement of being a hostess at the big house for the first time.

After tea, Roderick and the children went out for a walk while Mrs Hepworth and I chatted.

'Can I ask what brought you to North Uist?'

'Well, I'm a widow. My husband, Harry, was killed in the war, and I needed to find a job that would supply a house for Mary and me.'

'I'm so sorry for your loss, Mrs Hepworth. It must have been very hard for you. You're so young to have such a responsibility.'

'Yes, it was hard. Harry and I hadn't a home of our own, so when I became pregnant I moved in with my in-laws, but I felt that wasn't a long-term solution when Harry died. I wasn't too well after I had Mary and I moved back in with my mother and stepfather.'

'I'm sorry to hear that. I hope you made a good recovery.'

'Oh yes, I made a full recovery and when my stepfather died recently, I decided it was time to find a place just for Mary and me. So, when I saw the job advertised for Lochmaddy school, I applied and here I am.'

'How did you become a teacher?'

'My stepfather sent me to boarding school, and I became a pupil teacher there. That's where I met Harry. I liked him straight away. He was very bookish as his father was a printer and he helped me a lot with my studies. He was such a kind person.'

I felt quite envious and wished I could have gone on to higher education. Maybe I could have trained to be something more than a servant. I also thought Mrs Hepworth was truly brave, not only looking after Mary on her own but moving to a remote Hebridean island so far removed from her family and the life she knew. It made me wonder if I would have her resilience if anything happened to Roderick.

'But what made you choose North Uist? It's so far away from Manchester and although I love it here, it's remote, and the weather is unpredictable.'

'Oh, but that's why I love it. It's so clean and fresh compared to the grime of Manchester. I think I might happily settle here forever.'

She glanced over at the photographs.

'Are these your family photographs?' she said. 'Do you mind if I have a look?'

'No, of course not. Mr Macdonald takes photographs on a Brownie he bought in Canada, so they're less formal than the ones taken in a studio. You'll see one of them is of my brother, Lachlan. He died in the war too.'

I went over and gave his picture to her. He had looked so handsome and eager in his uniform that day he had left the island to go to war, but he hadn't coped well at all.

'He had a difficult time and wrote about it in a journal. He's already had some poetry published but I've been trying to find someone to publish his journals too, but so far haven't been successful.'

'I might be able to help you with that, Mrs Macdonald. As I said my father-in-law is a printer and might have contacts who would publish them. If you like, I could write to him with a sample of your brother's work.'

'Oh, Mrs Hepworth, that would be the best thing you could do for me. I could never thank you enough.'

I was smiling from ear to ear and felt like hugging her. I couldn't wait to tell my mother and father. They would be so pleased.

'Please call me Bunty, Mrs Macdonald.'

'Well okay, if you call me Chrissie.'

We smiled at each other, and I felt we had taken the first step on the road to friendship.

CHAPTER EIGHT

The wolf's eyes are shining yellow against the white of the snow, its teeth bared, ready to pounce. My baby screams in fear, knowing the wolf will savour sinking its teeth into his tender, sweet flesh. But his screams only encourage the wolf to move in closer. I hear Roderick's voice calling my name. He's come to save us at last.

'Chrissie, Chrissie, wake up, wake up. Can't you hear Donald?'

I surface from my dream and realise that the screams are real, part of what has become a living nightmare. Even though I'm sleeping next to Donald, Roderick has had to come through and shake me awake as I'm so tired with the constant interruptions to my sleep. Ever since Donald went to Glasgow for his father's funeral, nightmares had plagued him. He was five when he found out his real father was Colin Donaldson. Colin Donaldson, who had done nothing but bring trouble to my life since the day he had come into it back in 1905. I had hoped that now he was dead, our lives would settle down and we could live a normal happy life, but even in death, he seemed to have a hold over us.

'Donald, Donald, it's alright *mo graidh*. It's only a dream.'

'But I saw *Dadaidh*. Maggots were crawling all over him and eating him. Why did they have to put him under the ground? He will be all alone there. Why couldn't he stay here with us?'

He was cowering back against his pillow, holding the sheets in front of him, staring straight ahead at this horror.

'And that woman Heather keeps coming into my dreams too, *Mamaidh*. She says it's my fault she's dead.'

This almost nightly routine had begun shortly after his father's funeral. We had called in the doctor, and he said Donald would get over it in time and gave us medicine to help calm him. We believed him, but Donald hadn't got over it. No matter how much we tried to reassure him that Colin was safe with God in Heaven and that Heather would never blame him for her death, the nightmares

25

continued. We asked Roddy to sleep beside Donald, the way they used to do when they were little, to see if that would help, but Donald wasn't for it and begged us to keep Roddy in his own room.

'I don't want Roddy in here, *Mamaidh*,' he screamed, after one of his nightmares.

'But he's your big brother. He'll protect you,' said Roderick.

'He's not my brother. I don't want him in here. Please don't make me have him in beside me, please.'

He was sobbing hysterically, and I could only look at Roddy, feeling sorry for his brother's rejection of him, but he just shrugged his shoulders.

'If he doesn't want me in here beside him, then it's not fair to force him, *Mamaidh*.'

'Perhaps you should go in with him, Chrissie,' Roderick said. 'Just for a week or two until he settles.'

'Would you like that, Donald?' I asked.

He nodded.

'Right, that's what I'll do, starting tonight. Roddy, you go through to your own bed now *mo graidh* and I'll stay here with Donald.'

'He's just a big cry baby looking for attention,' said Roddy, nearly taking the door off its hinges as he stormed out of the room. Roderick and I had looked at each other helplessly, wondering that a nine-year-old could display such anger.

CHAPTER NINE

It was now two months since Colin's funeral and, although the nightmares were less frequent, they still caused regular disruption to our sleep. I found out why soon after, when the boys and I went for a walk on the beach at Clachan Sands one Friday after school. It was a beautiful autumn day, and they enjoyed going to the beach as the tide sometimes washed interesting things up on the shore. Although it was normally shells, stones, or driftwood, we had also found bottles and once a jar of jam. The boys ran on down to the beach and quickly disappeared.

I was thinking about some clothes I had seen in that month's magazine and wondering if I could make them myself or order them from the catalogue where we bought our clothes. I made most of my own dresses as my mother had done before me and I wasn't too bad at it, but it would be nice to go into a shop and look around. My Aunt Katie had told me about the big shops in Glasgow like Copland and Lye and the House of Fraser, which had assistants who helped you to choose new outfits. What a luxury!

It was then I heard screaming and knew straight away it was Donald. I had become used to the sound of his screams from the nightly terrors he suffered.

'Stop, stop, please, please,' he cried.

My heart was beating fast, and I scanned the machair to see if I could see him and Roddy, but all I could see were the sheep grazing peacefully in the pasture. There were sand dunes nearby, so I moved towards them. Who could he be screaming at? Although you heard about children being taken away by strangers in the big cities, no strangers came to North Uist without us knowing about it. Word always got out somehow when anyone new arrived on the island. That's why it had always amazed me that Lachlan had arrived home and hid in my parents' croft, with no one knowing.

'Donald,' I called. 'It's *Mamaidh*. Where are you, *mo graidh*?'

27

But the only reply was the sound of the wind whistling through the marram grass and the bah of a sheep annoyed at being disturbed in its grazing. I made my way over to the dune and it was there I heard a voice that was unmistakably Roddy's.

'Shut up Donald. You're such a mummy's boy. If you fall into this quicksand, you'll be in big trouble. You'll sink and choke to death, you know. But then maybe you'd like that. You would be with your precious *Dadaidh* if that happened.'

I could hear Donald whimpering.

'I don't want to go into the ground, Roddy. Heather will get me.'

'Yes, she will, so you mind and do what I tell you. Do you hear? And no blubbering to *Mamaidh*.'

I was finding it hard to breathe. I couldn't recognise this boy. It wasn't my Roddy. What had happened to him that he could speak so cruelly to his brother? I didn't know how to deal with this and called out again as if I hadn't heard them. I needed time to think about what to do.

'Hello, Donald? Are you here *mo graidh*? Are you okay?'

Roddy appeared from behind the dune.

'Why is Donald screaming? Is he all right?'

'Yes, he's fine. Aren't you Donald?' he said, leaning down and pulling his brother up. 'He fell when we were climbing over the dunes and thought he was going to fall into the mud.'

Donald pulled away from his brother and rushed into my arms. I cuddled him and shushed him quietly.

'My poor *leanabh,* there, there. Let's get you home.'

While I was comforting Donald, Roddy strode off across the machair, kicking the flowers as he went. I didn't bother calling to him to wait for us. I needed time to compose myself and take in the full implications of what I had heard. Poor Donald gripped my hand all the way home.

I was on tenterhooks the whole afternoon, wondering what to do. This was too much to deal with on my own, but I feared what Roderick would do to Roddy when he found out. It already annoyed him I was still sleeping beside Donald, and we weren't sharing our normal marital closeness. So not only did I have a disturbed child scared to go to sleep, but I had an angry child and an unhappy husband who was jealous of the attention Donald was getting. It was a mess, and I was struggling with a lack of sleep and anxiety about how to deal with it. How I wished I had a friend I could talk to about it. Although Bunty had come to tea with us a couple of times, I hadn't really got to know her yet and didn't feel I could confide in her. So, I only had my mother and when I talked to her the following day, she said I was being too soft.

'What Roddy did was just terrible, and I can see why you're so worried, but at the end of the day, your responsibility is to your husband and your own son, Chrissie. You need to look after their needs first. Donald will never get over the death of his father if you keep mollycoddling him the way you're doing. He's not even your own son.'

'How can you say that, *Mathair?* Donald has been with me since he was born, so he's as much my son as Roddy is. I also promised Heather I would look after him as if he were my own, and I would never break that promise. Are you telling me you don't see him as your grandson?'

She looked wary and took a breath before answering.

'I can see by the anger in your eyes that my words have upset you, Chrissie, but I'm only speaking the truth. Of course, I consider Donald to be my grandson, but I'm not the one who is important here. It's your husband and your own son. So, you need to find a way of giving more of yourself to them *mo graidh* and less to Donald.'

'But what am I going to do about Roddy? Roderick will take the slipper to him when he hears what he's done.'

'Sometimes, it's the only way for children to learn their lesson.'

CHAPTER TEN

When I returned from talking with my mother, as it was Saturday, I prepared for the Sabbath the following day. There was always a lot to do, as it was traditional to rest as much as possible on a Sunday. Luckily I had Mrs McAllister, Catriona, and Jeanie to do all the cooking and household preparations, so my Saturday night was making sure the boys had a bath, that Roderick's razor was ready for his Saturday night shave and that our Sunday clothes were ready for church in the morning.

Donald took longer than normal to settle to sleep when we had finished saying our prayers, so by the time I joined Roderick by the fire, he was relaxed and reading the paper. Conversation was the last thing he wanted when I told him I needed to have a chat about the boys.

'Chrissie, I'm reading the paper. Can't we talk about the boys tomorrow? Your magazine arrived with the mail today, so I'm sure you're eager to see all the latest fashions and read the love stories.'

'Och Roderick, there's nothing I would like better, but this can't wait. Please put your paper down.'

He sighed and put his paper on the table at the side of his chair, then poked the fire before turning grumpily to me.

'Well? What's so important it can't wait?'

I took a deep breath and began my sorry tale.

'The boys and I went for a walk on the machair up at Clachan Sands yesterday and I heard Donald screaming for me.'

'That boy. He'll be the death of you. You can't even go for a walk, but he's screaming for you.'

'He sounded terrified, Roderick. He and Roddy had run down to the dune so I couldn't see them and wondered if someone had been hiding and was hurting them.'

I had his full attention now.

'And was there?'

'No, but what I heard was terrible, Roderick.'

'Don't keep me in suspense, woman. What happened, for goodness' sake?'

'It was Roddy. He was being so cruel to Donald; I couldn't believe he was our son.'

'What was he saying that was so bad?'

I could tell from the way Roderick said this he thought I was over-reacting, but when I repeated what Roddy had said, his face changed. Doubt, disappointment, and anger surfaced across his face as he rose from his chair and strode up and down the room.

'So now we know why Donald's been having nightmares. His brother has been feeding him stories. But why?'

'He's obviously jealous.'

'Jealous of what?'

'The attention Donald's been getting. You understand that, surely. I mean, haven't you been a little jealous of him yourself?'

He looked shamefaced.

'You're right, but the only reason you're sleeping with Donald is because of his nightmares. You don't think it was Roddy who set that off by frightening him, do you?'

'After what I heard today, I do, Roderick. Remember how Donald begged us not to move Roddy in beside him at the beginning of all this?'

'Yes, I do now you mention it, and I wondered why. Now we know.'

'What are we going to do? We can't let Roddy keep tormenting his little brother.'

Roderick stood up and moved towards the door.

'No, we can't, and by the time I've finished with him, he'll regret that he ever did.'

I rushed over and stood in front of the door.

'Roderick, you can't do anything tonight. He's in bed. Please take some time to think about what we're going to do. We need to understand what's going on in his head and help him if we can.'

'I'll help him understand the difference between right and wrong, Chrissie. It doesn't take a genius to understand what's going on inside his head. His nose is out of joint because he thinks Donald is better off than him.'

'What do you mean?'

'Remember how he reacted when he found out Donald was Colin's son? He hated that Donald was now related to the Factor who could put his grandfather off his croft if he didn't pay his rent.'

'Yes, and he was annoyed when Donald said he was a distant relation of the King.'

'Exactly. He was never the same with Donald after that.'

'If that's the case, then what can we do about it?'

'I don't know, but I know that all the talking in the world won't work. He needs to be taught a lesson, but I'll wait till Monday. It wouldn't be right to do it on the Sabbath.'

I thanked God for the Sabbath, although not the way I used to thank Him when we lived in Canada. Back then, it had been a blessed respite from the hard work of the homestead when I had been so busy, but now it was just a long day that dragged by for me and the boys. Everything was very bleak on Sundays - no cooking, no playing, no socialising, only bible readings and church. Roderick still appreciated it, as did others on the island. It was part of our tradition. And today I was grateful that it gave a breathing space for Roderick to calm down before he tackled Roddy.

CHAPTER ELEVEN

When Monday morning arrived, I told Roddy his father and I wanted to talk to him when he came home from school. He frowned but didn't ask what about which I was thankful for, as I didn't want to send him off to school upset. Hearing him speaking to Donald on Friday in such a cruel way, I wondered how he was behaving in school. It would be awful if he was the school bully. When I dropped the boys off, I asked Bunty if she would mind Donald for me for an hour after school.

'Of course, Chrissie. Is anything wrong?'

She looked so sympathetic, I wanted to tell her everything, but of course the other children were arriving at school, so I couldn't.

'I'm not sure, but I need to talk to Roddy on his own and it will be easier if Donald is here with you.'

When Roddy got home from school, he had tea in the kitchen with Mrs McAllister as usual and didn't mention the chat his father and I wanted to have with him. Perhaps he was hoping we had forgotten, so he looked a little apprehensive when I called him into the drawing room.

'We want to talk to you about why Donald was so upset at the beach on Saturday.'

'What has Donald said to you, *Mathair*? Whatever he's told you, don't believe him. He's a liar.'

'We haven't spoken to Donald yet, Roddy. I heard what you said to your wee brother when you were in the dunes. You were deliberately trying to make him frightened. Why would you do that?'

'He's so easy to kid on. I was only joking with him about the maggots and things.'

'So, have you been trying to frighten him since he got back from his father's funeral? Is that why he's been having nightmares all this time?' Roderick's voice was like thunder.

'It's not my fault it gave him nightmares. Anyway, he thinks he can lord it over me because he's the Laird's great nephew or something. When he went to visit Colin, he was always telling me how good it was to have his own room and his own toys.'

'I knew it,' roared Roderick, picking up one of his slippers which was sitting in front of the fireplace. 'You're jealous. You feel he's got more than you. Envy is a sin Roddy and to terrorise your baby brother because of it is a worse sin. Come here.'

When I realised he was going to hit Roddy, I felt sick, and my knees buckled. I flopped down onto the couch and watched as Roderick put Roddy over his knee and struck him with his slipper over and over. Neither Roderick nor I had ever hit either of the boys before and Roddy's cries broke my heart. I couldn't bear it, but I dared not interfere with Roderick's way of dealing with his son. He was my husband and Roddy's father, and his decision was final.

When Roderick had finished skelping him, Roddy stood in front of him, gulping pitifully and wiping his face with the back of his hand to get rid of his tears.

'I'm ashamed of you, Roddy. I thought you were better than that.'

Roddy glanced down, away from his father's icy stare. He was trembling, and so was I. Unable to stand by and do nothing any longer, I went over and sat beside him.

'Yet if you think about it Roddy,' I said. 'What does Donald have? He's an orphan without a *Mamaidh* and *Dadaidh* of his own. You have us. Isn't that worth more than all the toys and clothes in the world?'

He turned and fell into my arms, murmuring that he was sorry for all the trouble he had caused. At nine, he was still a child, and he needed to be comforted after being beaten. I turned him to face me.

'It's not good for brothers to be cruel to each other. I remember when you were younger, you and Donald got on like a house on fire. You were his hero, and he ran after you all the time wanting to play with you.'

His face became sad, and he looked over at Roderick.

'I know it's a sin to hate my brother, *Dadaidh,* and I'm sorry I was bad to him. I won't ever do it again.'

'I hope you really are sorry, Roddy,' said Roderick, unwilling to let him off so easily. 'You need to shed more than a few tears to make things right with Donald.'

'I know I'm lucky to have you and *Mamaidh,* but sometimes I worry you'll die and then what'll happen to me and *Mamaidh?* Where would we live? Who would look after us?'

It shocked me he was worrying about these things, and yet was it so strange? His father was much older than Colin, so was it any wonder he was worried that Roderick might die too. I shivered at the thought of being left a widow and wondered how he would answer this question.

'One day you will grow up, get a job and make your own way in the world without the benefit of anyone else. You're smart. I know you'll go far, so long as you lose this envious streak you seem to have.'

Roddy looked shamefaced, but I thought he was pleased that Roderick had said he was smart and would go far.

'Nothing's going to happen to me and even if it does, your mother is a clever woman and could earn her own living if anything happened to me. Look at Mrs Hepworth, your teacher. She's doing okay without a husband. So, I don't want you to be worrying about any of this. Okay?'

Roddy looked at his father and nodded.

'I'm sorry, *Dadaidh.* I promise to be kinder to Donald.'

I prayed to God he would be kinder to Donald and to me. I was finding him quite a handful to deal with and hoped this talking to from Roderick would sort things out.

CHAPTER TWELVE

When I collected Donald from Bunty, she looked at me expectantly, so I knew I couldn't just pick Donald up without giving her an explanation.

'Thanks for looking after Donald, Bunty. He's been having problems sleeping recently, and it turns out it's because Roddy's been teasing him about what happens after you die. He didn't realise how bad it would affect him.'

'Oh, I'm sorry to hear that. Is it to do with him going to Glasgow for his father's funeral that day I arrived in North Uist?'

So, she already knew who Donald's father was. I wasn't surprised. Everyone on the island knew and probably couldn't wait to tell the new schoolteacher.

'Oh Bunty, we've had such a difficult time over the last few years, and it's been so hard on my boys.'

To my surprise, I burst into tears and realised I was still shaken from watching Roderick hit Roddy with the slipper.

'There, there Chrissie,' she said, patting me on the back. 'Come and sit down and I'll make you a cup of tea. Tea always makes the world seem a better place.'

While she was making the tea, Mary and Donald came in. I was sitting, blowing my nose and feeling rather foolish.

'What's wrong *Mummy*?' said Donald, coming over and looking at me fearfully.

'Nothing pet. I just took a fit of sneezing and it's made my nose run. You and Mary play for a little while longer while Mrs Hepworth and I have a chat and then I'll take you home.'

He looked as if he might cry himself, but Mary came over, took his hand and off they went to the bedroom to play a game.

'Here's some tea, Chrissie. Would you like to talk about what happened?'

So, I talked.

'As you'll probably find out from the island gossips, Colin Donaldson, who was Factor on the island before Roderick, was

36

Donald's father. I won't go into it all, but when he alleged Donald was his son, everything changed for our family. Can you imagine what it must have been like for my two boys? Donald found out that we weren't his parents, and Roddy found out that Donald wasn't his brother. Donald was only five and Roddy seven.'

'I can imagine. I didn't know my stepfather wasn't my real father until I was six years old.'

'How did you find out?'

'Sorry Chrissie. You're telling me your story, please go on. I'll tell you mine afterwards.'

'Well, after Colin Donaldson died, I thought everything would change and we would be a happy family again, but we aren't. It's been a terrible time. Donald started having these awful nightmares following his father's funeral, so I moved in to sleep with him, thinking it would help, but it hasn't.'

I looked at her and felt the tears beginning again. I was so ashamed of what I was about to tell her about my son.

'And the reason it hasn't is that Roddy's been deliberately frightening him. I just couldn't believe the things he was saying Bunty. To talk to his brother and scaring him like that was just too awful. So, I told Roderick, and he said he would talk to Roddy today. That's why I asked you to mind Donald for me.'

She nodded, and I took a gulp of my tea.

'But he didn't just talk to Roddy. He took his slipper to him. He was so angry. I felt sick watching my son being beaten, but Roderick is his father and may chastise him, but it was so hard to bear.'

'I remember my stepfather taking his belt to me and my mother doing nothing to stop him. It was the worst day of my life.'

Bunty was staring at the wall, no doubt reliving that awful time, but somehow she had managed with those words about her mother to make me feel how much I had let Roddy down by not intervening. I sobbed uncontrollably.

'You think I'm a terrible mother? You think I should have stopped Roderick?'

37

She came over and knelt beside me.

'Oh Chrissie, don't be silly. I understand what it's like in the world we live in; that wives must obey their husbands' wishes and decisions. We may have the vote, but nothing much has changed in that way. My stepfather was a cruel man, but I'm sure Roderick felt it was the only way to get through to Roddy. He wasn't doing it just to be cruel, was he?'

I clung to these words.

'Of course not. Roderick's a good man. He would never deliberately harm anyone, least of all his son. From what you say, your stepfather was a different man altogether.'

She rose from her knees and sat down in her chair again.

'Yes, he probably was a different man from your Roderick. He liked to be cruel to me just for the sake of it. When I was six years old, he locked me in the cellar and made me sit in the dark. I could hear rats scuttling about and screamed and kicked the door to be let out. When eventually he let me go, I asked him why he was so cruel to me. How could a father be like that to his own child? And that's when he told me I wasn't his daughter. Although I hated him for telling me, a part of me was relieved as it made sense of why he was so bad to me.'

I felt myself grow cold. How could someone lock a child in a dark cellar? She had suffered just as my boys had suffered, but much, much more at the hands of that monster of a man.

'I'm sorry, Bunty. I didn't mean to bring up painful memories for you. What happened to your real father?'

She looked at me.

'He went to find work in another country and never came back because someone murdered him.'

Silent tears slid down her cheeks.

'Oh Bunty, I'm so sorry.'

This time, I went to kneel beside her.

'My mother told me he had promised to send for her, that he was a kind and generous man and would never deliberately have abandoned her. He didn't know she was pregnant with me when

38

he left, or he would never have gone. She knew something must have happened to him when he didn't come back or reply to her letter telling him about me. But it wasn't until my stepfather died we found paperwork that told us the truth. After I found out my father was really my uncle, I used to dream that my father would come back to save me from my stepfather, but of course he couldn't as he was already dead, murdered in cold blood.'

I shivered again. What a terrible thing to happen to her father. I could only imagine how she must have felt when she found out why her father couldn't come back to save her.

Just then, the door creaked open and two little faces peaked round it. I had forgotten all about the children. Goodness knows what they must have thought, seeing both their mothers red eyed and sniffing into a handkerchief.

'Sorry for taking so long, Donald. You get your jacket on and I'll just say goodbye to Mrs Hepworth.'

I turned to Bunty and gave her a hug.

'Thanks so much for the chat.'

'No problem Chrissie. I'll keep an eye on things between the boys and let you know if there are any difficulties.'

I left Bunty's house in a much better state than when I had gone in and knew that ours was now a special friendship. How could it not be with the sharing of so many confidences? But I found it hard to stop thinking about the horrors she had told me about her own life.

CHAPTER THIRTEEN

Bunty found she was enjoying her life in North Uist. Although she was used to living in a large comfortable house with gas lighting, running water and servants to do the housework in Manchester, the little house with its large kitchen, two bedrooms and a bathroom was perfect for her and Mary. There was no gas or electricity on the island, so candles or paraffin lamps still provided lighting, but she found it cosy when the nights drew in and loved the smell of the peat that everyone used for heating their homes. But she especially loved the weather. Like her, it was quite unpredictable.

She felt free for the second time in her life. The first time was when she had gone to grammar school as a boarder and later trained as a pupil teacher. She had made friends there, and it was where she had met Mary's father, Harry Hepworth. Now she had made a friend again and smiled when she thought about Chrissie Macdonald and how they had exchanged such personal information. She knew it was necessary to tell Chrissie things about her stepfather to gain her sympathy and to get her to confide in her. Becoming friends with the wife of her father's murderer would allow her to become closer to him, and it would help her firm up her plan for ruining him.

She had found out quite a lot about the family in the short period she had been here, so it was time to take some action. The first thing she had found out was that Roderick getting the job as Factor was not popular amongst the locals, that he had only got the job because he was Donald's guardian. There was some kind of scandal behind all this, and she would need to find out what it was before she could use it to her advantage. If Roderick was not Donald's father, then it was unlikely that Chrissie was his mother, so she would need to find out who was.

There was trouble between the two boys she knew from her conversation with Chrissie, so could work on that to cause even more disharmony. She knew Chrissie was a loving mother, but she

40

wasn't so sure about Roderick. Although Chrissie thought he was a concerned father, she was sure the opposite was true. Anyone who could kill another person in cold blood couldn't be a caring person. But, if he were, what better way of harming him than through his children?

She also wondered about their financial situation. Since they had come back from Canada, they had lived in houses attached to their job so they had no property of their own. Chrissie's family had a croft, but she wasn't sure what Roderick's situation was. So, if his job depended on his guardianship of Donald, then she would need to do something about that. What that something would be, she didn't know now, but was confident she would come up with a plan.

CHAPTER FOURTEEN

Roderick suggested that only I should have a meeting with the boys so that they could talk things through. He felt I could handle them much better than him, but I would have appreciated his support as I knew I could become over emotional. I so wanted them to get back to being the friends they had been before Colin had upset our lives. The thing that most worried me was that Donald seemed to be haunted by the images of Heather blaming him for her death. We all knew who was to blame for that, but I couldn't come out and say that to Donald about his father as much as I wanted to.

Both boys were quiet as I sat them down and told them I wanted to clear the air.

'What does clear the air mean, *Mamaidh?*' asked Donald.

'Well, it means we all talk openly about how we feel, so there's nothing hidden away for us to be upset about. Roddy told us last week that he'd been teasing you about what happens after we die, and I wondered if that was why you were having nightmares.'

'No,' he said, looking over at Roddy.

'But he said some things that upset you, didn't he? I heard him.'

He looked at Roddy again.

'Yes, but I know he was only kidding me on.'

'You know I'm sorry Donald, I won't do it again,' said Roddy, looking at Donald and then at me. I smiled encouragingly at him.

'You said you've been dreaming about Heather. Was that because of something Roddy said?'

'No. It was somebody at school. I can't remember who. They said she was only dead because of me and would come back to haunt me.'

He looked over at Roddy again. Was he lying because he was still scared of him? I couldn't tell.

'You weren't responsible for your mother dying, Donald. God decided it was her time, just as He does with all of us.'

42

He looked frightened

'Does that mean He could decide to take you as well, *Mamaidh*?'

I hesitated. How should I answer? I could see Roddy watching me closely, waiting for my reply. Wasn't it just the very thing he had been frightened of, only about his father? How could I reassure them? How I wished Roderick was here.

'I suppose He could, Donald, but I think God has other plans for me. He gave you into my care when Heather died, and I think He will let me be on this earth until you and Roddy have grown up and can take care of yourselves. Why don't we pray together asking God to keep us safe and well and thank him for looking after Colin and Heather for us in heaven?'

Things seemed to improve between the boys after this and gradually the nightmares stopped. It was such a relief when they did, as I could move back into bed with Roderick, get a full night's sleep and resume my marital duties. Roderick and I were both much happier and relaxed because of this. Bunty told me she had noticed Donald didn't seem to have many friends, and she was right. That was because of Colin Donaldson, who was very strict about crofters paying their rent on time. He would also report any of them he found snaring a hare or catching a trout to the constable. He enjoyed riding around the island, showing off what a big man he was, and often took Donald with him. Most of the islanders disliked Colin and, by association, Donald and gradually the other children stopped playing with him. So, when Bunty suggested he could stay after school on a Wednesday to play with Mary, if I thought that would help, I jumped at the chance.

Although I was disappointed she had not included Roddy, I wasn't too worried, as Roddy was popular with the other children and had lots of friends. It obviously bothered Roddy, however, as he complained that Mrs Hepworth didn't like him and was much stricter with him than Miss Cooper, his previous teacher. I was glad Bunty seemed to like the weather in North Uist as Miss Cooper hadn't stayed long as it was 'too dreich for her', she'd said. I realised I would hate Bunty to leave the island now, as I had grown fond of her and had started to depend on her friendship as well.

To make up for Donald going to visit Mary, I suggested to my father that Roddy might go to the croft on a Wednesday to help him and then he wouldn't feel so left out. So that's what we did. It worked for a while, but it wasn't long before he had something else to complain about against Mrs Hepworth.

CHAPTER FIFTEEN

Roderick had become a regular visitor to the schoolhouse. He himself or Calum often brought her a creel of peat for the fire, for which she was grateful. She loved the sweet smell of it and the cosy glow it produced in the hearth. She had also asked him if he would help her learn some words of Gaelic so that she could understand the children better and he had readily agreed. It meant he had been over at her house several times recently, a matter which, as she had hoped, Mrs McIver remarked on.

'You and the new Factor seem to be awfully pally, Mrs Hepworth,' she said, when Bunty called in to do her weekly shop and told her that Roderick Macdonald or his stable hand would pick it up for her later.

'He's a very kind man,' she'd said with a dreamy look on her face. 'He's helping me learn a few Gaelic words so that I can understand the children better.'

'And what does his wife have to say about that? I thought she would have been the one to teach any Gaelic you needed to learn.'

'She's got her hands full with those two boys of hers. I think they run rings round her, poor soul, especially that Roddy.'

She could see Mrs McIver was itching to ask more, but just then, the doorbell tinkled and Morag Campbell came in. She was as thin as Shona was fat, had black hair with wisps of grey in it and a stern expression on her face.

'*Ciamar a tha thu,* Shona. Hello Mrs Hepworth. How are you settling in? I hear Roderick Macdonald has been helping you out with the Gaelic. Can you say anything yet?'

'*Ciamar a tha thu*, Mrs Campbell,' said Bunty, smiling at her, but she just frowned back at her.

'Not bad, I suppose. I hear your Mary's friendly with Donald and he comes over to tea every Wednesday now.'

'Yes, that's right, Mrs Campbell. It gives Chrissie a break.'

'I'm surprised she needs a break. She's got Flora and the two girls to do all the cooking and cleaning. What does she do all day?'

Bunty shrugged her shoulders and bade the women a good day.

She was pleased with the way things had gone. The two women were the biggest gossips on the island, so she was sure word would get round about Roderick visiting her. She had already begun her plan to undermine the family by inviting Donald and not Roddy to tea every Wednesday. Although he had friends in school, it warmed her heart to see him trudging home on his own with his head down on the days Donald stayed for tea. She also hoped Donald would give her more information about the family's background. She wanted to find out who Donald's mother was, but, in the meantime, putting around the notion that Roderick was behaving inappropriately by visiting her would help to further undermine him.

CHAPTER SIXTEEN

It was coming up to the beginning of December and I asked Donald what he would like to do for his birthday. When it was one of the boys' birthdays, Roderick would take them out with him, perhaps to go fishing or just to walk along the sands and I would make a nice tea with their favourite food. Normally, both boys loved this, but this time Donald said he didn't want to do anything special.

'Why not Donald? Normally you love spending time with your *dadaidh* and I was going to get a hen from the croft for your birthday supper.'

'I know I do, *Mamaidh*, but I don't think it's right.'

'What do you mean, not right?'

'It's not right to celebrate on the day that my real *mamaidh* died.'

It surprised me to notice a little knot of pain when he said 'real'. Didn't he think of me as his real *mamaidh* anymore?

'Are you still having bad dreams about her?'

'No. I try not to think too much about her, but Mrs Hepworth got us to do a family tree.'

'A family tree? You never said.'

'She only got us to do it today, and I just copied what Roddy had written. He knew you and *Dadaidh's* birthdays and *Seanair* Angus and *Seanmhair* Marion's birthdays, but I know nothing about my family except for when Heather and Colin died.'

He looked away from me as if he were ashamed.

'Did you have to hand it in to Mrs Hepworth?'

'Yes, she said it would help her get to know us children better and which families we belonged to.'

'And did she say anything to you about copying Roddy's?'

'She hasn't read them yet, so I'm dreading going to school on Monday. If she asks us to read it out in class, the other children know Colin was my *Dadaidh,* and they'll tell on me.'

He was becoming agitated, biting on his nails as he thought about it.

'She'll make me do it over. But how can I do that, *Mamaidh*? I don't know who my mother is except that her name is Heather or who my granny and grandpa on her side are. And it means I've got to go over all that stuff about Colin being my real *dadaidh*. I don't want to do it.'

I felt cold. Raking up the past would only bring misery to us all. Bunty already knew that Colin was Donald's dad, so she wouldn't need the other children to tell her.

'I bet she's doing it deliberately to embarrass us.'

'Why would she do that, Roddy? Bunty's my friend, and she's encouraged Mary's friendship with Donald.'

'She's not a friend to me, *Mathair*. She deliberately ignores me in class when I put my hand up to answer a question and she never invites me to tea with Mary the way she does Donald.'

I was at a loss for what to say. Perhaps Bunty wasn't as fond of Roddy as she was of Donald.

'Don't be upset Donald. I'll see Mrs Hepworth and explain things so that she doesn't get you to read it out in class. Okay?'

He smiled and nodded.

'Right, away down to the kitchen for your tea.'

When they had left, I wondered what Bunty was up to. Was she deliberately setting out to embarrass our family, as Roddy had suggested? I felt guilty about having these thoughts, as I liked her. We had become close friends after our talk that day Roderick had used his slipper to Roddy. She had also helped Donald by encouraging his friendship with Mary and sent Lachlan's journal to her father-in-law, so I was sure she wasn't doing anything to harm us. However, I would need to talk to her to protect Donald, but how could I do it without telling her the whole truth?

CHAPTER SEVENTEEN

When I saw Bunty at church on Sunday, I asked if I could have a word with her. There was always time for a chat after the service, so no-one would think it was odd that she and I stood chatting. Roderick was having a conversation with the minister and some of the other men while the children hung around trying not to play their usual boisterous games, as the Minister would frown upon it.

'Bunty, I hope you don't mind me asking, but I'm wondering why you've asked the children to do a family tree to share in the class.'

'I just thought it would be an enjoyable project for them to do. Is there a problem?'

'Yes. Donald's family tree isn't straight forward so Roddy told him to copy his. As I told you, his father was the Factor, Colin Donaldson. Donald's had a tough time over the last few years and he's worried that if you get him to read his family tree out in class, the children will tell you he's lying and bully him again.'

'I'm sorry. I didn't think it would be a problem. Doesn't Donald know his own family tree, then?'

What was I going to tell her? She seemed to have a knack for getting information out of me, information I didn't want to share.

'It's a long story, Bunty, but the short version is that Donald knows who his father and mother are, but not anything more than that, so it would be difficult for him to do his own family tree.'

I could see she was bursting to ask me more, so I relented and gave her what she wanted.

'Colin came to Canada and worked for us for a brief time when Roderick was ill and he took advantage of Heather, who lived with us. She was just sixteen when she had Donald and she died after his birth.'

I didn't realise I was crying until Bunty handed me a handkerchief.

'Here, take this, Chrissie. I'm sorry, I didn't mean to upset you. You must have been very fond of her.'

49

I blew my nose and nodded. I was quite overwhelmed talking about Heather again, and my rage at Colin surfaced unexpectedly.

'She would have been alive today if that man hadn't taken advantage of her. You don't know how much I hated him and how relieved I was when he died.'

Bunty looked shocked at my outburst, but she recovered quickly and gave me a hug. I became conscious that people were looking at us and pulled myself together.

'Please don't upset yourself. I'll only ask some children to read their paper out in class and I'll make sure Donald isn't one of them. Would that help?'

'Yes, it would, Bunty. Thank you. After Colin said Donald was his son, there was a lot of gossip. That's why Donald hasn't many friends and why he doesn't want it all dragged up again.'

'Yes, I can see that. You let him know I won't embarrass him.'

Just then, Mrs Macaulay came up to us and asked Bunty if she could have a word. I left them to it, but I was curious as I watched their earnest faces engaging in conversation. Just then Roderick called me, saying it was time to go. He seemed tense as we drove home in the buggy, but said nothing, and I knew better than to ask. He probably saw me getting upset when I was talking to Bunty and was embarrassed about it. But all became clear when we were talking later when the children were in bed.

'Roderick, is something bothering you? You've been tense since we left church this morning.'

'Yes, something is bothering me, Chrissie. You know I've been helping Bunty out with her Gaelic and either Calum or I have been picking up her weekly shopping for her?'

'Yes, I do. Although I don't know why she asked you to teach her Gaelic when I see much more of her than you do.'

'Well, that's what the Reverend Macaulay said to me. He asked me why I was giving her lessons. It was unseemly for a married man to be seeing a widow on her own so often. People were talking, he said.'

'Talking? What do you mean?'

I felt a slight flutter of anxiety in my chest. What were people saying?

'He said Bunty's been going around saying how good I am to her and how grateful she is.'

'Well, that's a good thing, isn't it?'

'You would think so, but apparently Mrs McIver and Mrs Campbell have told Mrs Macaulay that she seems all dreamy when she's talking about me, and they think she has a crush.'

I laughed.

'Och Roderick, you're old enough to be her father. Why would she have a crush on you?'

'Why indeed?' he snorted, but I could see my remark had hurt him. I got up and kneeled beside him.

'You're a handsome devil in a rugged way, so maybe I better watch out.'

He smiled and kissed me.

'You're the only woman for me, Chrissie Macdonald, so I don't want that schoolteacher getting the wrong idea. You better take over the Gaelic lessons from now on.'

Although he spoke lightly about the matter, I noticed he was never the same about Bunty after that and sometimes wondered if the Minister had said more than he had told me. That day, however, I was just relieved he hadn't noticed me losing control when I was talking to Bunty about Donald.

Donald was, of course, delighted when I told him he wouldn't need to read out his family tree in class, but when Roderick asked me the following week what had gone on between me and Bunty outside church, he was anything but delighted.

'That woman is nothing but trouble.'

'I don't know why you're saying that, Roderick. You liked her okay until the Minister spoke to you on Sunday. Did he say something that you haven't told me?'

'No, he said nothing else. It's just the way he said it. I felt like I had been acting inappropriately towards Bunty. It just made me feel uncomfortable and am wondering if she said something to him.'

'Och, why would she do that?'

'Why indeed? I'm sorry Chrissie. It's just made me unsure of her, especially now that Roddy is saying she doesn't like him. Why did she get the children to do a family tree, anyway? Roddy's right. She's just a nosey parker.'

'Och, I don't think so Roderick. She was very sympathetic when I told her about Heather and Colin.'

'I can imagine.'

'What do you mean?'

'Well, she got a lot more information out of you than you intended giving her. You know we need to be careful about what happened in Canada so that people don't discover Donald's heritage.'

'I know, I know. Please don't go on. Hopefully, what I've told Bunty will have satisfied her curiosity and she won't ask any more questions.'

I felt so disloyal talking about Bunty like this, and wished Roderick would be more tolerant. Instead of blaming Bunty, he should blame Mrs Campbell, Mrs McIver, and the Reverend Macaulay. It was they who were having bad thoughts and making assumptions about what had gone on between Roderick and Bunty. I had a good mind to speak to them, but I didn't want to make Roderick any angrier than he seemed to be about the whole thing.

CHAPTER EIGHTEEN

It was the first time Bunty had gone to church in North Uist. Her uncle was a Methodist, so it hadn't occurred to her to go to church when she came to the island. However, the Reverend Macaulay had other ideas about this new teacher and paid her a visit, so she felt compelled to go along.

To her surprise, she was quite overwhelmed with emotion as she sat with Mary, listening to the Reverend Macaulay. His sermon that morning was about family and how important they were in God's plan for us. He ranted and raved about the sinful girls who got themselves in the family way without having a ring on their finger and about the men who shirked their responsibilities. He even raised a titter when he mentioned the solicitor in his sermon.

'These girls inundate the Sheriff Court with their petitions for paternity and although it keeps Mr Abernethy in a job, it is the children who must pay for the sins of their fathers and mothers. The stigma of illegitimacy follows them their whole lives. So, you young men and women of this parish, think about what I've said today before you consider committing the sin of fornication out with wedlock.'

It made Bunty think of her mother and she tried to imagine how she must have felt when she realised she was pregnant after her father had left for Canada, but found it impossible. She could summon up no sympathy for her mother. But when the precentor sang the first psalm, and the congregation responded, the sound that rose out of these coarse people in their strange language was both beautiful and haunting as it swelled and dipped to fill the church. The hairs on the back of her neck stood up and she could hardly believe it when her throat contracted and tears filled her eyes. She wondered what was happening to her. She rarely felt such raw emotion unless it was anger.

When Chrissie asked to speak to her as they were leaving the church, she was still feeling emotional and wished she could just go home. However, when Chrissie asked about the family tree project, her ears pricked up. Hearing the story of Donald's parentage made Bunty realise that not just her family history was complicated. It had also surprised her to see Chrissie show such anger towards Donald's father, but she fully understood how she felt. Her feelings towards Roderick Macdonald were the same. When someone had caused a person you love to die, then you had a right to be angry with them and to take revenge. She was sure Chrissie would understand why she wanted to hurt her husband if she ever found out.

They had been interrupted by Mrs Macaulay, who had asked to speak to Bunty on her own. Bunty thought she knew what it would be about, and she was right. Mrs Macaulay had been very discreet, but basically she said people were talking about her and Roderick Macdonald, and it was best if she found someone else to deliver her shopping and teach her Gaelic. She protested at first that the gossips were wrong, but then confessed to Mrs Macaulay that she herself was becoming a little worried about how often Roderick was visiting her and she asked Mrs Macaulay to thank her husband for sorting things out. She smiled to herself when she got home. Her plan was taking shape.

CHAPTER NINETEEN

We went to the croft for the new year as usual and I wondered what 1921 would bring. Everyone in our settlement went round each other's houses first footing to bring good luck in the new year. The talk was all about the land that the Laird was releasing over Solas way and about the grants that were being given to build new white houses. The black houses were notoriously unhealthy according to the government and, in some ways, it was true. There was very little ventilation, and the conditions that people lived in caused the consumption. It was something we all dreaded, especially me, because of Roderick's history of it in Canada. Although he seemed healthy enough, it was always in the back of my mind that it could return one day.

Johnny, who was up from Glasgow without Janet, was enjoying a dram and when he and I were talking, he probably gave more away than he intended to. He had come home to Uist after the war, but he and Janet had become close, and as she didn't want to come back home, he had gone to Glasgow. He had got a job in Fairfield's Boat Yard, which paid well, but it was difficult finding somewhere to live, so they rented lodgings in a tenement in the Ibrox area of Glasgow. They had separate rooms though, as Johnny would never do anything to spoil Janet's reputation and yet they had still not married. And now here he was back home on his own, so I knew something must be wrong.

'No Janet?'

'No, we've been arguing a bit recently, and she said it would be good for us to have a break.'

'I thought you and Janet would have been married by now, Johnny. You've been engaged for nearly two years. She must be fed up waiting.'

'Och, I know, but I just can't settle in the city, and she still doesn't want to come back home. But listening to the conversations tonight, I think I might have more chance of getting

55

her to come home if *Athair* builds one of thon white houses. He would qualify for the grant.'

'But how would that help with you and Janet if she doesn't want to come back to Uist?'

'That's because she thinks there's no chance of getting a job as a nurse up here. But Morag Campbell told me they're looking for a district nurse to help the new doctor, so if *Athair* and I were to build a brand-new house, don't you think that would change her mind? We live in two miserable rooms in someone else's house, so coming home would be a big improvement. We would have our own room, a bathroom with running water and a range to cook on.'

'It sounds too good to be true. Would the grant you got run to all that luxury?'

'Yes. Haven't you seen Mr and Mrs McClelland's new house? It's very smart.'

'What do *Athair* and *Mathair* think about it? They're set in their ways and I'm sure would take some convincing to give up their black house.'

'Is that you going on about the white house again, Johnny?'

My father had heard our conversation.

'I've told you. My father and mother and my father's father lived in this house, and I won't be moving from it.'

Johnny was expansive because of the whisky and gave my father a bear hug.

'Come on auld yin. You'll need to move with the times. You can't live in the past forever.'

'Your *Mathair* and I are happy living in the past, as you call it,' he said, giving Johnny a friendly shove. 'It's served us well for the past fifty years.'

'But now, you wouldn't want to lose your only son to the wilds of Canada, would you, *Athair?* For that's what'll happen if Janet doesn't come back to North Uist and marry me. I'll take one of thon grants that the Canadian government is offering.'

'Your sister didn't like it,' he said, looking at me to be his ally.

56

'No, you're right *Athair*. I thought it was a godforsaken place. I much prefer our small island for all its shortcomings.'

Roderick then entered the conversation and threw the cat amongst the pigeons.

'So, is it Canada you're all talking about?'

'It is Roderick, it is. Are you sorry you had to leave?'

'Yes, I thought it was a land of great opportunity if you were willing to work hard. But getting sick put paid to that. Are you serious about going, Johnny?'

'Well, only if this old man won't build a white house so that I can bring Janet to live somewhere decent as my bride.'

'Where would you go?'

'I'm not sure. If I go, I might do something different from farming now that I've learned other skills in the shipyard. I learned about engines in the army and how to repair them as well, so I'm sure I could find work somewhere.'

'I hear tell there are lots of factories opening in Chicago in America. You might find work in one of those,' said Roderick.

'America!' my mother now joined the conversation. 'We need you back here, Johnny, so don't be getting big ideas. Your *Athair* will come round in time, won't you, Angus?'

And that was that. When I heard my mother backing Johnny's idea of building a white house, I knew it would happen. At the prospect of having my friend Janet back living close by, I became excited. I missed her. Although I liked Bunty, she could never replace Janet, who I had known since I started school.

CHAPTER TWENTY

Bunty was feeling quite satisfied with the way things were going. Although she had been here for over six months now, she was in no hurry. Wasn't there an adage from somewhere saying that revenge was a dish best served cold? She may have come up to this island in haste, but that didn't mean she had to be reckless when avenging her father's death.

Roderick no longer came to the house, and she smiled when she thought about his awkwardness when he explained why he wouldn't be coming any longer.

'I'm sorry I won't be able to help you with the Gaelic anymore, Bunty, but now that I've been in the job a few months, things have become so busy, I just don't have the time.'

'I shall miss you, Roderick. Mary and I have become used to you coming round, but I understand,' she had said, fluttering her eyes at him shyly. She was being mischievous to make him feel uncomfortable, but there was some truth in it. She could never be attracted physically to a man his age, but there was something nice about having an older man being kind to her and it made her long even more for the father she never had.

His cheeks were pink as he replied.

'So, I've asked Chrissie to take over from me and Callum will still collect your shopping and deliver some peat from time to time, so you don't need to worry about that.'

'That's so kind of you, Roderick. Thank you.'

She and Chrissie had become firm friends, and she knew this would yield more information when she needed it. There was obviously some kind of secret they wanted to keep about Donald's mother, but she was confident she would find out what it was when she needed to. She remembered seeing a photograph of a young girl with a baby in her arms on the mantlepiece in Chrissie's drawing room that day she had told her about Lachlan and his poetry. So perhaps that was her. She would need to look more closely at the photo the next time she was up at the big house.

In the meantime, she had decided to send a little letter to the Laird. When she was in the shop chatting to Mrs McIver, Mrs Nicolson had come in bleating on about what a wonderful person Roderick Macdonald was and how glad she was that he was the Factor.

'Why is that Annie?' asked Mrs McIver, who wasn't a supporter of the new Factor.

'Well, I was struggling to pay my rent this month, so when he visited me to talk about it and I said I was short, he suggested perhaps I could pay with a hen or black pudding, something that they could use up at the big house. I was very grateful.'

He would do anything to get the locals to accept him, but Bunty was sure the Laird would be far from pleased that crofters were getting away with paying their rent. Before writing the letter, she thought about how to cover up that it was she who had written it. She would need to make sure there were some mistakes in the English and perhaps throw in a word or two of Gaelic so that everyone would think it was someone local who had written it.

CHAPTER TWENTY-ONE

It was the first visit by the Laird and his guests of the spring season, and Roderick was out with them, doing some hunting and fishing. There were no wives with the men this time, but when there were, it was my job to keep them entertained. This was not a straightforward task as they were used to constantly socialising and meeting up with other people like themselves and North Uist was hardly a hub of sophistication. It was one of these women, Lady Ancaster, who had given me the idea of setting up a women's group.

'You're a smart woman, Mrs Macdonald. You should get involved in the island's politics. Although we women have the vote now, we can't rest on our laurels. There's still work to be done.'

I remembered Bunty saying something like that to me on the day I was upset about Roderick hitting Roddy. She was right, some women still couldn't vote because they weren't old enough and men did still hold all the power.

'What do you think I could do, Lady Ancaster? Men are the ones who have always run the parish council and stood for parliament. I can't see the locals welcoming a woman trying to take on that role.'

'You're probably right, but think about the problems facing the island just now? I know there are issues about the lack of land to allow the government to fulfil Lloyd George's promise of Britain becoming a land fit for heroes, but what other things are bothering the islanders and the women in particular?'

When she said this, I thought about Johnny. Although he had fought in the war and I considered him a hero, there was no prospect of him getting his own croft if he and Janet came back to North Uist. He was pinning all his hopes on the new white house my father was building to entice Janet to come back to the island. Work on the house was going well as all the men in our settlement helped one another just as they did at the time of the peat cutting, the sheepshearing and the cattle drives for the market. I also thought back to my time in Canada and the work of the Grain Growers Association and Homemakers. Perhaps I could set up something like that, not so much for political reasons, but for social reasons. Women were pivotal in the lives of crofters, shopkeepers, big houses such as ours where they worked as servants, even in the herring industry preparing and salting the fish for export, so we deserved some time out for ourselves. What was lacking here in North Uist was a place for women to meet and discuss issues that were important to them.

I pondered my own problems and what was important to me. As the Factor's wife, I had a relatively easy time of it as I didn't need to worry about scratching a living on a croft like most other people on the island, but what I had were young sons who were emotionally troubled. That made me think of the many women and children on the island who had lost loved ones in the war, and I wondered how they were coping with the loss of their fathers, husbands, sons, and brothers. No-one ever really talked about their feelings, but I knew how upset my family had been when Lachlan was killed.

I thought about how we women met up now and mostly it was when there was a wedding, a funeral, a peat cutting or at sheep shearing time. But our involvement revolved around our ability to supply food. Women on the island were sociable, and I was sure they would welcome the chance to meet up just for the fun of it. As if it was meant to be, the next issue of the People's Friend had an article about the Women's Institute or the Rural, as it was called in Scotland. From it I found out that a Mrs Blair had set up the Women's Institute in Scotland in 1917 in Longniddry, which was somewhere on the East Coast of Scotland. Mrs Blair was a farmer's wife, and she wanted to help the women of rural Scotland to not only be good housewives and mothers but to develop their role in other areas of life too.

This reminded me of Violet McNaughton, who I had heard talking at a meeting of the Grain Growers Association when I lived in Canada. It was through Violet's insistence that the committee recognise her as a delegate to the 1913 Grain Growers Association Convention that a women's section had been set up. She was an absolute inspiration and believed that men and women had to co-operate together to make a living, but they needed to live a life as well. So, it was important that women should have free time from their chores to discover their higher selves. It was then I decided I wanted to find my higher self and resolved to write to Mrs Blair asking her how I could go about setting up a Rural Association.

While Roderick was out with the Laird, I went through the mail. I had little to do in terms of household duties, as Mrs McAllister did most of it, so I helped Roderick with the administrative side of his job. I dealt with the mail, kept the rent ledgers, and sent out overdue notices for rent. I enjoyed the work most of the time, but it was always difficult sending letters to the crofters who couldn't pay their rent. Sometimes Roderick accepted payment in kind such as a chicken or eggs, which Mrs McAllister and I accounted for in the household budget as she wouldn't need to buy them, but he couldn't do that for everyone. If the Laird ever got word of it, he would be in trouble. But who was going to tell him? Certainly not the crofters who received help from his kindness. How wrong I was.

I opened the mail automatically, thinking more about what I would say to Mrs Blair, so didn't notice until it was too late that I had opened a letter addressed to the Laird. When I read the contents, I could hardly believe my eyes. It was an unsigned letter telling Sir Arthur that his Factor, Roderick Macdonald, was not doing his job properly. He was accepting chickens, meat, and other produce for rent. The writer thought the Laird would wish to know. I shivered as I thought about how to tell the Laird I had opened a letter addressed to him and about how he would deal with Roderick's misdemeanours. I had thought our troubles were over after Donald's nightmares had stopped, but it seemed we were never to have a simple life with no problems. The pleasure I had felt about starting the women's group left me.

CHAPTER TWENTY-TWO

Roderick was whistling happily when he came home from the hunting trip with the Laird, obviously feeling relieved that the visit with Sir Arthur was going well. They had bagged a deer, much to the delight of his guests, and the fishing had been good.

'Hello Chrissie, you're looking bonnie if you don't mind me saying. You have roses in your cheeks. The Laird has invited us to the hotel tonight for a meal.'

As he approached me to give me a kiss, I burst into tears.

'Oh Roderick, I've done something awful. I opened this letter and didn't notice until afterwards that whoever sent it had addressed it to the Laird.'

'Well, that's okay. I'm sure he'll understand. It's nothing confidential, is it?'

'It's about you.'

'Me?' he said, taking the letter from me.

He read it slowly, with a look of incomprehension growing on his face.

'Who would do such a thing, Chrissie? I've bent over backwards to be fair to everyone.'

'I know you have Roderick. You've been more than fair taking produce in place of rent.'

'It's so unlike our people. We all look out for each other, don't we?'

'Yes, we do Roderick. I know some folk resented you getting the job of Factor, but you would think they would be over it by now.'

'I don't want to lose this job, Chrissie. We've got Roddy and Donald to think about. They've been through enough without us having to uproot them again. If I find out who's done this, I'll, I'll...'

Obviously stuck for a suitable punishment of the culprit, he sat down and put his head in his hands. I went over and tried to offer sympathy.

'Leave me be, Chrissie. You can't pat me on the back and tell me everything will be okay.'

63

'What will we do Roderick? I was wondering whether to just throw the letter away without telling you about it, but I decided against it. I thought it was important that you knew someone was out to get us. But could we not just ignore it and not show it to the Laird? He would be none the wiser.'

Roderick looked at me with cold eyes and I felt myself flush with shame.

'That would be dishonest, Chrissie. I'm surprised you can even suggest that. There's nothing I can do but show Sir Arthur the letter.'

'But he and his guests are having such an enjoyable time. He'll be angry if he needs to cut their fun short by having to deal with something like this. He might take against you without doing a proper inquiry.'

'I know what you're saying, but I can't do that. I think he would turn against me even more if he knew we had received the letter and hadn't drawn it to his attention.'

In the end, we waited until the trip was over and his guests had left the island before giving the letter to Sir Arthur. But I used the time to go over the estate ledgers to make sure everything was in order in case the Laird wanted to look at them. Mrs McAllister helped me as she had household books to manage and the two needed to tie up. Flora, as I called her now that we worked amicably together to make sure things in the house ran smoothly, was on our side. Although the Trust employed her, she was a local woman and would never side with the Laird against us.

When we showed the letter to Sir Arthur, he didn't seem too bothered, but he asked to inspect the books. I hovered around while he looked them over, anxious in case he spotted anything untoward and wished to ask questions.

'Well Roderick, these books seem in order, so I'll accept your word that the letter is making a false accusation regarding the acceptance of produce for rent. Doing so is just not acceptable, no matter how sorry you feel for the crofters.'

64

His thin pale face looked sorrowful, no doubt worrying why crofters couldn't pay their rent and needed to offer produce in exchange.

'If you have done it, it's my opinion you're digging a hole for yourself. You can never do it for everyone and those same folk who you want to help will turn on you, mark my words. Future Factors won't be so accommodating, so you should not raise the crofters' expectations, as it will only cause trouble.'

I shivered. Was he threatening Roderick indirectly that he may not be the Factor for much longer?

'I understand Sir Arthur.'

'Good man, good man. So, who do you think sent the letter to me then? Anyone holding a grudge against you?'

'I know some people weren't happy that I got the job, but I didn't think they would go this far.'

'It's not a well-written letter, so I don't think anyone with any education could have written it. No offence to your kinsmen,' he spluttered, looking uncomfortable at criticising the English skills of the islanders. 'Here's hoping you haven't made an enemy, Roderick.'

'Here's hoping,' Sir Arthur.

CHAPTER TWENTY-THREE

It delighted Bunty when Chrissie came to pick up Donald, obviously in a state of agitation.

'Come in Chrissie. You look like you could do with a cup of tea.'

'Your cure for all ills, Bunty, but I think I need more than a cup of tea. I'm so angry.'

'What's happened? Didn't the Laird's visit go well?'

'Yes, it was a very successful visit. He and his guests had a wonderful time, but I opened an envelope addressed to the Laird and inside was a letter complaining about Roderick.'

'Oh no! What about?'

'Well, sometimes he takes foodstuff when people can't pay their rent.'

'And that's what the complaint was about?'

'Yes, but I think that's a good thing to do, don't you?'

'Yes, yes, of course. It was only a few weeks ago Mrs Nicolson was telling Shona McIver how grateful she was to him.'

'Annie Nicolson told Shona McIver. That means anyone could have written the letter to the Laird. Mrs McIver's not known for her discretion. She might even have written it herself.'

'My goodness, how awful for you! I know she wasn't happy about Roderick getting the Factor's job.'

'She told you?'

'Yes, on one of my first visits to her shop.'

'I've a good mind to go round and see that woman. I can't just let someone get away with sending a letter like that to the Laird.'

'Will it affect his job?'

'No, I don't think so, but it could have. Luckily, the Laird didn't seem to think the allegation was too serious, although he checked the books just to make sure all was as it should be. But I suppose if anything else happens, he might not be so understanding.'

'Well, I hope nothing else happens then.'

Bunty felt put out by the news that the Laird hadn't been too worried about this misdemeanor by his Factor, but she had obviously upset Roderick and Chrissie which was good. It was also good that Chrissie had decided to go visit Mrs McIver and confront her. Bunty wished she could be a fly on the wall at that conversation.

CHAPTER TWENTY-FOUR

Although I told Bunty I was going to see Mrs McIver, I didn't. Apart from it being too late, as the shop would be closed, I had Donald with me and wouldn't want to cause a fuss in front of him. But I couldn't just let this go. Someone had sent that letter and I would need to find out who. I thought about the best way to do it, as I couldn't just go in accusing people. They would just deny it anyway and it might encourage them to become even more vindictive towards Roderick. I would need to think of a way to be more subtle about it. I decided to have a chat with my mother as she knew most of the families in the community well and might know who would do such a thing.

When I went round to the croft the next day, mother and I sat and chatted for a while and I told her about the Rural and how I was thinking of writing to Mrs Blair. Although I still wanted to find out who had written the letter, I was feeling relieved that things had gone well with the Laird and there appeared to be no further consequences for us.

'At last,' she said, smiling at me, 'my daughter has let go of her silly notions that life is all about fashion and romance and is getting involved in matters that affect our real lives.'

I didn't tell her I still liked fashion and, in fact, besides the People's Friend magazine, I had ordered a regular copy of the Women's Life explicitly for the fashion. Although my mother scoffed at romance, she couldn't wait to sit down with a cup of tea and the People's Friend when I was finished with it.

When I told her about the letter, she was perplexed. She didn't think it could be Shona McIver or Morag Campbell, despite what Bunty had said.

'Shona McIver and Morag Campbell are more likely just to gossip about it or say something to your face, Chrissie. Writing a letter to the Laird shows a vindictive streak and I can't think of anyone like that, can you?'

I had to confess, I couldn't.

'You should raise it with the women when you talk to them about setting up the Rural. They might have some idea of who would do such a thing.'

So, I wrote to Mrs Blair straight away and decided I would arrange a meeting with the women as soon as I had some idea of what I should be doing. She responded within the week with enthusiasm and told me lots about how the women organised their meetings in her part of the country. When I read it, I felt I had enough experience from my time in Canada, so was confident I could do it in Scotland. The first thing I would need to do would be to make up a poster and put it up in prominent places in Lochmaddy. Lochmaddy would only be the beginning though, as I was sure women all over North Uist would appreciate meeting up.

I decided I better talk to Roderick before I did anything. I needed him on my side, but he was dead against it.

'How can you think about doing something like this when we've just got over the problems with the boys and we have someone sending anonymous letters to the Laird? Your role as their mother is more important now than it's ever been.'

'My role as a mother will always be important, Roderick, but I want more than that. I feel things have settled with the boys, don't you?'

'I'm not so sure. Although Donald seems happier and is talking more, I'm not sure about Roddy. He keeps complaining about school and I'm worried he's going to lose interest. He needs to do well if he's to get into the secondary at Portree.'

'But organising the Rural won't take up all my time so I can supervise Roddy and make sure he's alright. I can also ask Bunty to let me know if there are any problems.'

'Maybe she's the problem, Chrissie. Have you ever thought of that?'

'Och, now you're just being unreasonable. Bunty's been a good friend to me, so I won't hear you saying that about her. She was really helpful when I told her about the anonymous letter.'

'What do you mean, helpful?'

69

'Well, she told me she had heard Mrs Nicolson telling Shona McIver about you taking eggs and black pudding, so I knew that word would get out all over the place.'

'Do you think Mrs McIver could have written the letter?'

'No, I spoke to *Mathair* and, as she said, Shona McIver and Morag Campbell were more likely just to gossip about it than send a letter. She thinks it's someone with a vindictive streak, but she couldn't think of anyone. Can you?'

'From what Roddy says, Bunty sounds rather vindictive towards him.'

'There's no talking to you when you're like this. Well, I'm going ahead with it anyway and you can like it or lump it.'

The look of shock on his face made me want to laugh, but later when I calmed down I couldn't believe I had spoken to him like that. I had never done it before and wondered if it would change things between us. The way he had taken against Bunty annoyed me too and if I'm being honest, his negativity was having the opposite effect from the one he wanted. I was more committed to our friendship than ever.

CHAPTER TWENTY-FIVE

I enlisted Bunty's help to make up the poster, as I thought she might have some skills given that her father-in-law was a printer. She said she didn't, but I was quite pleased with the finished article. I wrote the words, and she drew some designs with coloured paints she had in the school, which I thought were eye-catching. I also made typewritten leaflets to hand out to women that we met in the street or in the shop. The poster and leaflets were only for information. I decided to wait until the sheepshearing to talk to the women about it. I would have a captive audience then. Bunty put the poster on the front door of the school so that parents could see it when they brought their children in. We then went to Mrs McIver's shop and then the Post Office to ask them to put one up for us and to take some leaflets.

To my surprise, Mrs McIver seemed interested in the project and asked me how it would work.

'Well, the way I see it, Shona, we would hold the meetings in my house or the schoolhouse each month. I would make up a list of topics which women would find interesting and, if possible, enlist some local people to talk to us. We're all experts in some things, aren't we? For example, I could talk about being a post mistress, Bunty could talk about being a teacher and Flora, if she agreed, could talk about being a housekeeper for the Factor.'

'And I could talk about running a shop.'

'Exactly. So, you'll put the poster up and take some of our leaflets?'

'Yes, you leave it with me. I'll spread the word.'

For once, her gossipy nature would come in handy.

It was a different story at the post office, though.

'What's this, Mrs Macdonald?' said Ian Fraser, the new postmaster, his little moustache twitching with curiosity. He was thin and balding for a man of his age, which he tried to cover up by pushing some hair he did have over the top of his head.

'It's a poster about a new group for women that I'm trying to set up.'

'A group for women. I've never heard of such a thing.'

'Well, you're hearing about it now, Mr Fraser,' said Bunty. 'Will you put the poster up for us or not?'

'I think not, Mrs Hepworth. I don't think it's suitable material to be putting on a public building.'

'But Roderick and I always put notices and posters up for the community.'

'Well, that was you, Mrs Macdonald. This is me and I'm not putting it up.'

'We shall write and complain to the post office, Mr Fraser, if you don't.'

'You may do your worst, Mrs Hepworth, but I'm not putting that poster up. Good day to you both.'

We gave up and left the post office, but it didn't put us off. We were sure we would get a sympathetic response from the local women.

When I took some leaflets over to the croft for my mother to hand out, my father was not in favour.

'You're making a mistake, Chrissie. Men won't like the idea of women meeting up on their own.'

'Why not? Men meet up together to have a drink or a smoke. Why shouldn't women?'

'I hope you don't mean to have a drink and a smoke?' he laughed, but then put on a serious face.

'You've had more freedom than most women on this island Chrissie, travelling to Canada and back and working in the post office. People have only just got over the fact that Colin Donaldson was Donald's father, so I think you should keep your head down and stick to being the Factor's wife and nothing else.'

'I know you have a point, *Athair*, but this is something I really want to do and perhaps if women join and get something from it, they will forget about the scandal and just accept us. That would be good for all our family, wouldn't it?'

72

'Well, knowing you, you'll do what you want, anyway. Good luck to you.'

I then dropped by the Minister's house, hoping to speak to Mrs Macaulay. Elizabeth had told me one day when we were chatting that she had been a university student during the suffrage years. Although not an active member of the movement, she told me she had supported their right to fight for the vote. I was sure she would be sympathetic to my plan to set up a women's group. So, disappointment swept over me when it was the Reverend Macaulay himself who answered the door. The Reverend McEwan had retired last year and Reverend Macaulay had taken his place. Although he was younger and didn't hold the same authority, the Reverend McEwan had commanded, he was still the Minister and had a lot of power.

'Hello Mrs Macdonald. It's lovely to see you. Come on through and have a cup of tea.'

'Well, it was Mrs Macaulay I wanted to see. I can come back another day.'

'Not at all. She's away visiting a family where the mother has just had a baby, so won't be back for some time. You can tell me, and I'll pass the message on to her.'

As I sipped my tea, the minister chatted away about the weather, asked me how Roderick and the boys were until finally he asked me what I wished to let his wife know. My stomach was full of butterflies as I began.

'Well, I've been thinking about this for quite a long time now. I saw an article in the People's Friend a wee while ago. Does Mrs Macaulay get the People's Friend?'

'No, she doesn't. I don't approve of the silly romantic stories they publish. But you mentioned an article, not a story.'

'Yes, it was about the Women's Institute or the Rural, as it's called in Scotland. Have you heard of it?'

'No, I can't say I have. What is it?'

I told him what I had read in the magazine and the information Mrs Blair had sent me.

'So, you want to set up a similar group here in North Uist, do you?'

I told him about the Homemakers in Canada and how helpful they had been when Roderick had the consumption. Forgetting who I was talking to, I got carried away and went on at length about Violet McNaughton and how much I wanted to have a more fulfilling life.

'A more fulfilling life, Mrs Macdonald? What could be more fulfilling than being a wife to that husband of yours and a mother to those two boys? I hear Donald has been having nightmares and Roddy has been getting into trouble at school.'

'How do you know that, Mr Macaulay?'

'We live on a small island, Mrs Macdonald, so there's not much gets past me or my wife.'

'Well, it's partly because of the problems I was having with the boys that I thought of setting up a women's group. A trouble shared is a trouble halved, isn't that a saying?'

'It might very well be, but tell me how would meeting up with other women make your life more fulfilling? A fulfilling life comes from loving God and doing what He wants you to do, not from following silly notions of freedom and independence like those suffragettes.'

I wondered how we had got from the Rural to the suffragettes.

'Well, they helped us women to get the vote, Mr Macaulay.'

'Indeed, they did, Mrs Macdonald, for all the good it will do the likes of you and the crofters' wives in the Hebrides. But I shall pass your message on to Mrs Macaulay when she gets back. Say hello to that husband of yours. I hear he had a visit from the Laird.'

I didn't bother asking him how he knew that. As he said, it was a small island, and nothing got past the Minister.

CHAPTER TWENTY-SIX

Bunty and Mary were now regular churchgoers as they looked forward to having something to do on a Sunday. It was a dry day otherwise, as no-one did anything on the Sabbath. But Bunty had to admit she looked forward to the Reverend Macaulay's sermons and to the singing. On this day he talked about what the bible said was the role of women and chose some passages from Timothy. As she listened, she became annoyed. Women had to be quiet, they couldn't teach or assume authority over a man and then basically he said women were responsible for the Fall because Eve was the first sinner. She almost laughed when he said women would be saved through childbearing. She remembered her own childbearing experience, the pain followed by a mental breakdown, a psychosis the doctor had called it. If she needed to be saved, then that experience would surely have done it.

She wondered where he was going with all this, and it then became clear. He was getting at Chrissie and her wish to set up the Rural. She looked over at Chrissie, who was sitting with Roderick and the boys. She was wringing her hands, obviously agitated by the minister's attack. But then she noticed Roderick looking at her with a smug look on his face, as if to say I told you so. That man was a bully. She knew it. Hitting Roddy with a slipper, even although he deserved it, and trying to force Chrissie to give up her dream. Well, he wouldn't get away with it.

But then Reverend Macaulay went off in another direction and it sounded to Bunty that he was criticising the men of the community who let their wives become involved in such a thing. That made her smile. Anything that would hurt Roderick's reputation in the community was a good thing, as far as she was concerned. It could also cause a further rift in Roderick and Chrissie's relationship. She had told Bunty about standing up to Roderick and telling him she was going ahead with her meeting, whether or not he liked it. That made her think of her own mother, who had never stood up to her stepfather. She was such a coward.

When they got outside, she joined Chrissie.

'What the minister said wasn't right, Chrissie. Don't you let him put you off.'

She looked at Bunty, her eyes full of doubt.

'Oh, I don't know, Bunty. I really want to do it, but the minister has a lot of influence and what he said today will have put many women off, I'm sure. I think there'll be plenty of arguments between husbands and wives tonight.'

Just then, Elizabeth Macaulay joined them.

'Good morning, ladies. Talking about my husband's sermon this morning?'

She smiled when they nodded but said nothing.

'I thought it was shameful and I want to let you know you have my support, Chrissie. When do you plan to talk to the women about setting up a group?'

'I was going to do it at the sheep shearing next week.'

'Right, I'll see you there.'

Just then Roderick came up, smiled coolly at Bunty, and took Chrissie's arm.

'Time to go home, Chrissie.'

'Okay, I'm coming Roderick. Goodbye, Bunty. Goodbye Elizabeth. I'll see you at the sheepshearing next week.'

Bunty could see them arguing as they made their way towards the buggy and smiled.

CHAPTER TWENTY-SEVEN

The sheep shearing was always a busy time and took about three days all in. Prayers for pleasant weather were said every time as wind and rain made the men's jobs more difficult. Although each crofter had their own sheep, they grazed the animals on common land and when it was time for the clipping, everyone joined in to round them up. Each crofter clipped his own sheep the following day, but if someone was too old or if it was a woman who owned the croft, then the others would help. Wool was an important part of the island economy as we used it for knitting and for making tweed.

The boys loved going along with my father and I always helped my mother, and the other women prepare the food for the men. I had chosen the sheep shearing as it would be an ideal place to put feelers out to the women to see if they might be interested in having a group like the Rural on the island. It was always better to speak to people face to face. The school term was now over, and the children were running around bare footed as they always did in the summer.

I was so pleased when Bunty told me she and Mary weren't going home to Manchester for the summer. I felt I needed her beside me if I was to get the Rural up and running as she was such a supporter of what I was trying to do. But I felt guilty when Donald told me Mary was disappointed. She told him she missed her Grandma and wished her mother would take her back to Manchester, even for a quick visit. I wondered briefly why Bunty didn't want to go home but put it to the back of my mind. It suited me for Bunty and Mary to be here for the summer, partly because of the Rural but also because Donald would have had no-one to play with. Although things between him and Roddy seemed okay, his favourite pastime was sitting in his room reading. I wondered what would become of him. Roddy was still full of bravado, so I wasn't sure the slippering Roderick had given him had done much good. But he was looking forward to working with my father on the croft over the summer and was especially looking forward to the sheep shearing.

At the end of the school term, Bunty did a test with the children. Donald passed with flying colours, but Roddy didn't do so well.

'It's not my fault, *Mathair*. I told you Mrs Hepworth doesn't like me, and she gave me lower marks than Archie Campbell, even although our answers were the same.'

'How were they the same? Did you copy him?'

He looked a wee bit scared as he shook his head.

'Well, he copied me. You know he has bother with the reading and writing so I help him when I can. You won't tell *Athair*, will you?'

Perhaps Roderick's beating had left more of a mark than I thought.

'No, but I think I should speak to Mrs Hepworth if she's marked you down. That's not very fair, is it?'

'I don't want to cause any trouble, *Mathair*. It doesn't matter this year anyway, but it will when I have to do my test for the high school. I don't want to fail that exam. It would mean I couldn't go to school in Portree, and I want to.'

'I'm glad to hear that. I was thinking you were enjoying the croft so much; you wouldn't want to spend more time at school.'

And leave home. Because of the lack of secondary schools here in Uist, the children had to go to Portree in Skye or Inverness for the secondary education.

'Oh, I love working with *Seanair*, but I want to do something with my life and the only way I can do that is to get away from this island.'

'Yes, I suppose it is.'

It was a sad fact that there were few opportunities for work here and that most of our young people were encouraged to leave the island to seek their fortune. I prayed he wouldn't want to go to Canada or Australia, but would settle for living in Scotland. At least then I could see him and if he got married and had children one day, then I could see them too. I knew I was getting ahead of myself as he was only ten, but the years passed so quickly sometimes they were gone before you knew it. But I decided I would speak to Bunty, anyway. Maybe Roddy needed extra help, and it was important he got it now so that he was ready for the exam in a couple of years' time.

The day of the sheep collection dawned bright and clear, so Roddy, Donald and I were a cheerful party as we made our way in the buggy over to the settlement. When we got there, the men were already assembling, and we women began dishing out cups of tea and sandwiches. The sheepdogs were excited too, barking and running around with their tails wagging. Molly, our dog, ran up to me, jumped up and then ran round, chasing her tail. The dogs were an important part of the sheep collection. They worked in harmony with the men, who blew whistles and shouted to them in the Gaelic where to go and where to bring the sheep to. I breathed in the fresh clean air and realised I was happy. Although Roderick was being a little offhand with me still for talking back to him, everything else in my life was going well for a change, and I was looking forward to talking to the women about setting up the Rural.

After the men and boys had left, Bunty, Mary and Elizabeth Macaulay arrived, so I put my idea to the women and the girls who were there. They just stared at me not saying anything, so I was pleased when Morag Campbell was the first to comment.

'I don't know why we have to set up a meeting. Sure, we meet all the time, don't we? There's always plenty going on where the men need fed.'

'But that's my point, Morag, we only ever meet when we have something to do for the men. Why don't we just meet up for ourselves?'

There was a slightly scandalised intake of breath.

'What about what the reverend said in his last sermon, Mrs Macaulay? He didn't seem to be much in favour of us women having a group,' said Shona McIver. 'I thought it was a good idea when Chrissie told me about it, as I could talk about what it's like running a shop, but I wouldn't want to get on the wrong side of the minister or of Alex.'

'Don't you worry about my husband, Shona. I don't.'

'And if we were to go to the meeting,' said Annie Nicolson, 'what would we do there?'

'Well, I've been in touch with Mrs Blair in Longniddry, who started the Rural and she says they have guest speakers to talk about interesting things.'

'Interesting to who Chrissie? What makes you think we'll be interested in talking about the things you want to talk about?' said Morag.

I knew that to be true, but of course it wasn't all about me, was it? Or was it? Was I being selfish, unrealistic?

'Well, it would be up to the women in the group to decide what they would like to talk about.'

They were all looking at me doubtfully.

'Well, for example, I used to work in the post office, and I thought you might find it interesting to know what was involved in that job and Shona has already said she would be happy to talk about running the shop. You Rhona, you were a herring girl once upon a time, so you might talk about that.'

She laughed. 'Och yes, I'm sure you all want to know what it's like standing in the freezing cold gutting fish.'

'But there's so much more to it than that. The girls used to earn more money than the men. You used to travel round the country chasing the fish. You must have lots of stories you could tell us.'

I felt myself becoming quite enthusiastic as I realised all jobs had so many stories and so much to teach us.

'I'd like to know what being a herring girl is like,' said Mairi, Morag Campbell's daughter. 'I would like to earn more money than the men.'

And that was it. They became more animated the more we talked about it, and we agreed to hold our first meeting after the harvest.

CHAPTER TWENTY-EIGHT

We held the meeting in my mother's house with just the women in our settlement to start with. On the day of the meeting, I was up early. Full of nervous energy, I went down to the kitchen to make sure Flora had made the scones that I would take to my mother's that afternoon. My mother, Bunty and Mrs Macaulay would definitely come, but hopefully more. I drove the buggy to the school, picked up the boys, Bunty, and Mary, and went to the croft. My mother had a pot of tea sitting on the new range she had got for the white house, which even supplied hot water for the washing and the bathroom. Modern living indeed. She and I buttered the scones, gave one to each of the children, then put the rest on the table together with the teacups. Afterwards, we sat and waited. I resisted the temptation to look out the window to see if anyone was coming. I wanted to look relaxed, not like a frightened rabbit at my first ever meeting.

My mother's wall clock tick tocked rhythmically as we waited. Normally I found the sound soothing, but today I just found it irritating. It was a full fifteen minutes before Morag Campbell arrived quickly followed by six of the other women in the settlement. I said a silent prayer of thanks and welcomed everyone. However, after they had drunk their tea and ate the scones, they got up and moved round the kitchen eyeing up my mother's new range and I wondered if they had just come to see the new kitchen rather than to talk about setting up an association.

But I needn't have worried. Morag, funnily enough, was the one who brought the meeting to order and by the end, they had agreed that they would like to have an association and that I should be the chairwoman and the first speaker. They thought I would have plenty to talk about seeing as I had been to Canada, had worked in the post office and was now the Factor's wife. When they put it like that, I thought I would have plenty to talk about and wondered if perhaps I was already on my way to finding my higher self.

I stopped in at Bunty's on the way home and we chatted about the meeting. I had never spoken to her about Roddy's test results, so this was the ideal opportunity.

'Bunty, before I go, can I ask how Roddy's getting on at school? His mark for his test at the end of last term wasn't very good. I meant to talk to you about it, but then it was holidays and I forgot.'

'Yes, he didn't do too well last term, but it might just have been because it was a tough year for him. Although Donald did okay, and he had a hard year too.'

Was there a hint of criticism in that remark? Did she favour Donald over Roddy as he had complained?

'It's just that this is an important year for him as he will need to do the test to get the bursary to allow him to get into the secondary school in Portree. He really wants to go, and I wondered if you could suggest what might help. Are there obvious areas of weakness that we could get him to concentrate on?'

'Roddy could do better if he put in the work. He prefers talking to his friends in the class rather than listening to me, so he misses things. If you like, I could give him extra homework, which might help.'

'Yes, I'd be happy if you did that, but I'm not sure Roddy will be,' I laughed.

Surprisingly, Roddy was happy when I told him.

'I'll do all the homework she gives me *Mathair* and then you'll see that it's not that I'm not working hard, it's that Mrs Hepworth just doesn't like me.'

How I wish I had paid more attention to what he was telling me, but I didn't.

CHAPTER TWENTY-NINE

Before I knew it, the harvest was over. It was nothing like our harvests in Canada, of course. Just potatoes, turnips, oats and other vegetables we could use to feed ourselves and the animals. The nights were drawing in as we headed towards the last part of the year, the lamps were being lit and the fires were burning cosily. We'd had two meetings of the Rural and they had accepted our application to be included in the Register. I was feeling quite pleased with the way things were going. But as usual, something came along to spoil my happiness.

Roddy had been doing well at his homework and Mrs Hepworth had told him she was pleased with his progress. Then one day he came back from school in a storming black mood, breenged through the door and threw his jacket and schoolbag on the floor before running up the stairs to his bedroom. When I followed him up and asked him what had happened, at first he said nothing, but then he blurted out what was bothering him.

'It's that, Mrs Hepworth. She hates me.'

'I'm sure she doesn't, Roddy.'

'How would you know? You're all pally with her because Mary's friends with Donald. He's all you care about.'

'That's not true, Roddy. I love you too. Come on. Tell me what Mrs Hepworth's been saying that's upset you so much.'

'She never asks me to go to tea with Mary and I'm the only boy in the class who isn't getting a place in a play we're doing for Christmas.'

'A play for Christmas? I've never heard of such a thing. Sure, doesn't she know we don't celebrate Christmas in North Uist?'

'I told her that, but she said I was being cheeky and as a punishment, I was to write out fifty lines saying *I will not be cheeky to my teacher.* Then she told me I wasn't getting a part in the play.'

He took a few gulps of breath and then carried on.

'But Donald and Mary are getting the star parts of Mary and Joseph. It's just not fair, *Mamaidh.*'

I smiled inwardly and felt relieved that it was nothing more serious. I remember being jealous of my sister Morag when she got a prize at Sunday school, and I didn't. It was only natural. But I thought I better speak to Bunty.

I made a point of taking the buggy into Lochmaddy to meet the boys from school the next day. The children were just coming out when I arrived, and Donald ran towards me for a hug. Bunty was standing at the door and waved to me.

'Hello Chrissie. Would you like to come up to the house for a cup of tea? I've got some biscuits.'

'Yes, that would be nice. Thanks Bunty.'

Donald was delighted and ran on in front with Mary, while Roddy scowled and walked to the schoolhouse beside me and Bunty with his head down. Once the children had gone out to play, the tea was poured, and we sat nibbling on the biscuits. I put my question to Bunty.

'How's Roddy getting on now? He seems to enjoy the extra homework you're giving him.'

'He's getting on fine. Why do you ask?'

'Well, it's just he seems really disappointed that you haven't included him in the school play you're organising for Christmas, something very unusual in these parts, by the way.'

'I know that now. Roddy told me plainly that it wasn't an island tradition.'

'I do hope he wasn't cheeky to you, Bunty.'

She smiled conspiratorially.

'I sorted that out by issuing him with some lines. I prefer that to the use of the belt.'

'You use the belt, then?'

'If I must. It's the only way to keep discipline sometimes. Your Roderick thinks so anyway, doesn't he?'

For a moment, she looked like another person. A flash of anger sparked in her eyes before she gathered herself together and was back to her normal smiley self. She was, of course, referring to Roderick hitting Roddy with his slipper, but I felt a sudden rush of

84

pity for her when I remembered what she had told me about her stepfather hitting her with a belt. My father used to threaten us with the belt, but he had never used it.

'Do you think you could give Roddy just a small part? I feel he's been working hard, and I want to encourage him to keep going. Although he likes to think he's a big boy now, he's still a child at heart.'

'Don't look so worried, Chrissie. I'm sure I'll be able to do that.'

'Thanks Bunty,'

I felt relieved that I had sorted things out for Roddy, but there was something about our conversation that left me quite unsettled.

CHAPTER THIRTY

When Chrissie called on her, whining that Roddy was upset at not having a part in the Christmas show, it took Bunty all her time not to laugh. It meant her tactics with Roddy were working. She wanted to upset the stability of that family and what better way to get to the parents than to upset or hurt their children? Bunty knew there was more Chrissie wasn't telling her about Donald's parentage, so when she stopped in after the Rural, she hoped they might talk again about who Donald's mother was but Chrissie was more interested in talking about Roddy than about Donald.

When Bunty told her she had given him lines instead of the belt for being cheeky, Chrissie had looked shocked that she would consider using use the belt. So she reminded her about Roderick using his slipper on Roddy, which shut her up. The discussion gave Bunty herself a shaky moment when she remembered her stepfather using his belt on her bare legs and the welts that her mother covered up with thick black stockings the next day so that she could go to school. She had needed to force herself to smile again or Chrissie might have seen a different Bunty to the one she thought she knew.

Agreeing to give Roddy a part in the play was a small price to pay if it convinced Chrissie that she was a genuine friend in whom she could confide. It was important to keep up the pretense if she was to get the information she wanted. All this talk of Christmas made her think it was time for another letter. No point in letting the Macdonalds have a happy yuletide celebration.

CHAPTER THIRTY-ONE

As the time for the Christmas play drew near, the children became increasingly excited. Mrs Hepworth got them to make paper chains and decorations and they made the costumes they would wear for the play.

'After the play, we will all get a treat and there will be cakes and lemonade to drink,' Donald told me, hopping round the room in excitement. Even Roddy seemed thrilled, as he and his brother joined hands and swung each other round in a kind of reel.

'You will come to see us, *Dadaidh?*' they asked Roderick.

'I'm afraid I won't be coming along. I don't approve of Christmas, as you two well know. It goes against our Presbyterian way of life and stinks of paganism.'

He was a confirmed Presbyterian and, like others on the island, was unhappy about the incomer introducing a Christmas celebration. It had not been a done thing in Scotland since the Reformation, so we celebrated the winter solstice at the end of the old year and the start of the new year instead.

Donald burst into tears.

'Please come *Dadaidh*. I've got a big part in it. You must come to see me.'

'I'm in it too, *Athair*. I would hate for you to miss it. Please come.'

Roderick looked at the two pleading faces and he softened.

'I'll come along, but don't ask me to enjoy it,' he said grumpily. 'Bloody woman,' he muttered under his breath.

I was looking forward to it, as were many of the mothers who had children at school. Winter was a lonely time for many women, as they rarely had an excuse to get out of the house. Although the Rural had helped a bit with that, the thought of having a diversion that would brighten the bleak mid-winter month of December and get us out of the house earned Bunty a lot of support.

In the few weeks leading up to Christmas, those of us who collected our children from school would stand at the gate

87

discussing the play and what we would wear. Crofting women wore rough sewn skirts which suited their working lifestyle, but they also had Sunday clothes they wore to church and which they either made themselves or bought from a catalogue from companies on the mainland. I loved my sewing machine and often thanked Mr Singer for allowing us women to buy these machines on hire purchase.

When the day of the play dawned, the boys were up and out with no coaxing from me or Mrs McAllister. They couldn't wait. When the boys left for school, I sat down to do my administration work. Most of the time I enjoyed it, but it was always difficult sending letters to the crofters who couldn't pay their rent. It made me think back to the letter that someone had sent to the Laird about Roderick accepting payment in kind and wondered again who it could have been. I thanked God they hadn't sent another one. As if I had the second sight, when I opened the last envelope it was a letter from the Laird himself saying he had received another anonymous letter. This time they were accusing Roderick of ignoring poaching and that was something he could not ignore. He proposed calling on us after the new year to discuss what was going on. The Christmas play became unimportant as I wondered how Roderick would react to this letter.

When he came in for his lunch, I showed him the letter.

'It must be the same person who wrote the last letter. This time, they're saying that you don't deal with poachers.'

He took the letter from me, scanned it quickly, then paced the room, running his hands through his now grey hair as he was prone to do when he became agitated. Protecting the Laird's land from poachers and ensuring there was sufficient game and fishing for his guests was, of course, one of Roderick's most important duties. The person who had taken against us must know the Laird would not treat such an allegation lightly. Roderick suddenly stopped pacing, and I saw the rage in his eyes. I think if he had found out there and then who had written that letter, he would have done them some damage.

'I'm going back to work.'

'Remember we have the Christmas play this afternoon?'

'Christmas play! I'll be damned if I'll go to that blasted pagan party. It wouldn't surprise me at all if it's that woman who's been writing the letters.'

'But you'll disappoint the children. They've been so looking forward to you watching them in the play.'

'Well, they'll just have to be disappointed,' he said, as he slammed out of the room

My heart was heavy when I drove down to the school. I knew how disappointed the boys would be. They had been so looking forward to showing off their talents to their father. But there was little I could do about it. I could understand why he was so angry, but it wasn't fair to take it out on his sons. It was almost as if he had transferred his anger from the person who had written the letter to Bunty, who he clearly saw as an incomer bringing English ways to the island. The notion that Bunty had written the letter was absurd. She had befriended our family and besides, it was clear someone with a poor education had written it.

Other parents crowded the room, and I felt the sting of being there on my own. How I dreaded the look of disappointment I was bound to see in my sons' eyes when they realised their father wasn't coming. The room grew quiet, and the play began. Mary, Joseph, and the baby Jesus were sitting on the floor with the glowing fire at their back. As Roddy said, Mary and Donald had the star parts. They sang a sweet song I didn't recognise before the other children joined them. They were dressed as shepherds, one of whom was Roddy. My heart swelled with love as I remembered how he had asked to borrow my father's *cromag*. Like all the other children, he looked towards the group of parents, eager to impress. I could see the look of puzzlement that his father wasn't there with me, but he smiled and waved enthusiastically, anyway.

Roderick was waiting for us when we went outside. There was snow on the ground and although it was nothing like the snow we had in Canada, he thought I might be nervous about coming home and had walked in to ride back with us in the buggy. How I loved that man.

'Why didn't you come to see us in the play, *Dadaidh*?' asked Roddy. 'We were looking for you.'

'I had some bad news and couldn't make it. I'm sorry. But you had a good time without me. I can tell by your smiles.'

'We did, we did. I was Joseph and Mary was Mary and Roddy was a shepherd, just like *Seanair*.'

'We sang a song and afterwards we had lemonade and look *Dadaidh,* we got a book,' Roddy said, holding up a copy of Pilgrim's Progress in English.

I was thankful it was a book Roderick would approve of even if it was in English, otherwise poor Bunty would have had even more scorn poured on her.

Roderick smiled. 'I'm glad you had such a good time, boys.'

CHAPTER THIRTY-TWO

The day of the party was one of those clear winter days that promised snow and, as Bunty walked to school with Mary, she felt her spirits lift. She loved snow. It even made Manchester look beautiful, covering its muck and poverty with a veneer of white beauty. She could feel Mary's excitement in the little skip of her walk and the occasional smiles they shared as they walked along the path. Her excitement wasn't so much about the party, but about how Roderick Macdonald would react to the letter she was hoping he had received by now from the Laird. She had timed her letter to Sir Arthur so that it would arrive before the school break. Nothing like a dressing down from your boss just before you were about to embark on festive celebrations. His family didn't deserve to spend a pleasant time with their father. She had never got to spend any kind of time with her father because of him.

At last, the school bell rang. All was ready. She looked round the schoolroom and felt pleased with the effect she had created. The coloured chains the children had made draped the room, the desks and chairs had been moved to create the stage where the children would perform, there was a bright peat fire burning in the grate and there was the smell of the spiced tea that she had made with cloves and cinnamon. A bundle of little parcels wrapped in newspaper sat at the side of the fire, ready to be distributed to the children after the play. All that was needed now were the parents.

She felt pleased when she saw Chrissie coming into the room on her own, as she knew this absence of their father would disappoint the boys. Donald had kept going on about his father coming to see him in the play.

'My daddy's coming along, Mrs Hepworth, even although he thinks it's a pagan thing,' he had said, totally unaware of what pagan meant or that he might offend her. Perhaps the Laird had written to Roderick, and he was too upset to come along. She did hope so.

91

After the play was over, she put on some gramophone records and there was dancing. The gramophone was one of the things she had transported up to North Uist when she moved here. She loved the latest dance tunes, and she and Mary would dance together in the evening. It had been so long since she had danced with a man, she enjoyed the attention of the fathers who had come to see their children. She noticed several of their wives frowning, no doubt jealous that their husbands were holding a young woman close. But who could blame them? The women here were all frumpy, not a bit of fashion between them.

She spoke to Chrissie for a short while during the party in between dances and was pleased to hear that Roderick had received unwelcome news, and that was why he hadn't come to see the play.

'It's very generous of you, Bunty, to put on this party and to give the children presents. I hope it hasn't left you out of pocket.'

'Well, perhaps a little, but it's Christmas and in England it's a time for giving presents.'

Money wasn't a problem for Bunty as she had her wages and her widow's pension, but she also received a generous allowance from her mother, who had inherited a good income from her husband's estate when he died. He would turn in his grave if he knew Bunty was benefiting from it.

'Are you going home to Manchester for Christmas, Bunty?'

'No. I'm afraid my family is going away for the holidays, so Mary and I will just stay here.'

'Why don't you and Mary come to us on New Year's Day? I hate to think of you spending all the holiday period on your own.'

'That's so kind of you, Chrissie. Thank you. Oh, it's snowing again. I just love the snow, don't you?'

'Not really. I had a terrible experience in Canada and I'm always nervous when I need to travel in the snow. I'm afraid I shall have to go now, before it gets too heavy.'

Bunty wondered what the terrible experience had been and why she still felt like that about snow. The weather was always wild on the island, especially in the winter, and she thought everyone would be used to navigating the roads in all weathers. She thought of her father again and the terrible experience he had suffered at the hands of Roderick Macdonald and was glad the letter from the Laird would fill his thoughts over the festive period.

CHAPTER THIRTY-THREE

The festive break passed quietly as Roderick was in no mood to celebrate anything with a visit from the Laird hanging over him in the new year. What a start to 1922 we were going to have. It annoyed him when I told him I had invited Bunty and Mary over for a meal on New Year's day.

'I wish you hadn't, Chrissie. You know how much I dislike that woman.'

'Unreasonably so, in my opinion, Roderick. Anyway, it's the least I can do when she put so much effort into the Christmas Party for the children. She can't go home as her family is away for the holiday so it would be heartless to let her spend the whole time on her own.'

I also invited my mother, father, and Johnny. He had arrived home from Glasgow unexpectedly on Hogmanay, telling us he and Janet had broken off their engagement.

'Janet refuses to even come and see the new house, so I told her I could see no future for us, and I handed in my notice at Fairfield's, so you've got me back.'

'I'm sorry Johnny,' I said.

'Ach, so am I, Chrissie, but what can you expect? She doesn't want to live on Uist even if it is in a white house, and that's all there is to it.'

'You two were so well suited.'

'We thought so, but perhaps it was just the war. Everything seemed so different when you knew the Boche could kill you at any moment.'

My mother and father were pleased, but I felt sorry for him. He looked miserable and got so drunk that night he could hardly stand. I wasn't sure he would come to ours, but in the end, it was only him who came. The festivities of Hogmanay were enough for my mother and father.

It was a cheery little party. Mrs McAllister had made us a feast of smoked trout and roast venison, a present from the Laird, potatoes, roast mutton, crowdie, white pudding and fruit dumpling. Bunty brought several packets of shop biscuits and a bottle of mulled wine instead of the mulled tea she had served at the school play. Johnny, of course, brought whisky. Despite his hangover, he was still in the mood for a drink. I worried about him sometimes.

'So, is that you back on North Uist for good, Johnny?' asked Roderick.

'I think so, but there's always Canada. You know there's talk of incentives to go to Canada.'

'Canada? But surely you wouldn't leave North Uist?' I said.

'Och, I wouldn't want to. But now that Janet and I have split up, I'm unsettled and not sure what I want to do. I only know I don't want to live in some big city like Glasgow. I hated it there.'

'I understand how you feel, Johnny,' said Bunty. 'I come from Manchester, which is a big industrial city like Glasgow. I can't tell you how much I love it on the island. The air is so much cleaner and healthier here.'

I could see Roderick looking at her. He was still unconvinced it wasn't her who had written the letters to the Laird.

After we had eaten, Johnny supped away on his pipe and told a story to the children about Giant MacAskill. My father used to tell us this story when we were small, and I sat to listen, almost feeling like a child myself with no responsibilities and no worries ahead of me in the new year.

'Do you know, Roddy, that you are related to a giant?'

'A giant?' asked Donald, his eyes wide with wonder.

'A giant indeed,' he said, taking a puff of his pipe and blowing out the smoke. I could see the boys and Roderick sniffing it up appreciatively. Poor Roderick still had to do without his pipe, as consumption was rife in the islands. I was thankful we had a proper fireplace to burn our peat, unlike in my parents' old house, where everything was dark and smoky. It was surprising none of them had developed TB.

'He was your great, great, great uncle Angus, and he lived on Berneray, but he had to leave Scotland because the owners of the

95

island cleared the crofters from their land. He ended up in Cape Breton in Nova Scotia.'

The children already knew about the Clearances from my father and mother, so they understood what Johnny was talking about.

'Is that where you might go, Uncle Johnny?' asked Roddy, who had been listening to the conversation earlier.

'It's possible, but if the Board of Agriculture sort more land out, then I might get a place of my own. Anyway, back to my story. When he left, Angus was just an ordinary boy like you two, but he grew into a giant.'

'Do you think Donald and Roddy will become giants?' asked Mary, all agog.

'You never know. But anyhow. He grew to be a giant. He was seven feet, nine inches tall. Do you have any idea how tall that is?'

They all shook their heads.

'Right, I'll show you.' And before Mary knew what was happening, he had picked her up and put her on his shoulders. I remember my father used to pick Morag up just like that when he was telling us the story. We all let out a gasp.

'No', said Bunty, becoming as absorbed in the story as the children and me. 'Nobody could be that tall.'

'Because he was so tall, he became a performer with Barnum's Circus and travelled all over the world. He and General Tom Thumb, who he worked with, were even introduced to Queen Victoria in Windsor Castle and she gave them a gold ring.'

'General Tom Thumb? Who was he? Was he a soldier?' asked Mary, who was now on the floor again.

'No, he was a performer like Angus, but he was as small as Angus was tall. Sure, Angus used to hold him in the palm of his hand. He was so small.'

The children accepted what he said, just as we had as children, not thinking about how small he would have to be for that to be possible.

'What happened to him?' asked Roddy.

96

'Och, he hurt himself when he was trying to lift a ship's anchor and he was never the same after that. So, he stopped working for the circus, bought a shop and settled down. When he died of the brain fever, the entire country mourned his passing.'

Tears slid from Mary's eyes, and Bunty lifted her onto her knee to give her a cuddle.

'Don't be sad, our Mary. He had a good life. Shall we play the Grand Old Duke of York?'

So, we all got up and began marching up and down and singing until Mary was laughing with glee. We adults were all becoming red in the face and sweating from the effort, so I suggested we ask Mrs McAllister for some cold lemonade. I took the children down to the kitchen and after Mrs McAllister had poured the lemonade into a jug, we took it back upstairs. All was quiet when we came into the room again. Bunty was holding the photograph of Heather that had been sitting on the mantlepiece above the fire.

'Who is this?' she asked.

Roderick and I looked at each other as she gazed at Heather's image.

'That's Heather, Donald's mother. Why do you ask?' Roderick replied.

'I'm sorry. It's just that she looks like my uncle. Same shape of nose and lips.'

'Your uncle?'

'Yes, my stepfather. Her colouring is darker than his, but if I didn't know better, I would think they were related.'

'No, that wouldn't be possible. As I told you before, Heather was born in Canada and is Roderick's daughter.'

'Oh, I didn't know you had been married before Roderick.'

He didn't answer.

'Silly me,' she said, putting the photograph back on the mantlepiece.

'I think it's time we got going, Mary. It's getting late.'

Mary looked as if she might cry again, so Johnny began carrying on with Roddy and before long, Mary and Donald had joined in, too. There were bursts of giggling as the children wrestled about on the floor with Johnny, who was like a big bairn himself, and it took us a while to get them disentangled and to get the message that Bunty and Mary needed to go home now.

'I'll walk you down to the schoolhouse, Mrs Hepworth.'

'Oh, call me Bunty, please.'

'Bunty, it is.'

I thought little about it at the time as I watched the three of them walking down the road, Mary's hands held firmly by Johnny on one side and Bunty on the other, but in hindsight I can see that was the beginning of the affair that would affect all our lives.

CHAPTER THIRTY-FOUR

Flora and I went over the books just to make sure everything was in order, in case Sir Arthur wanted to look at them again when he came over. He hadn't been too concerned the last time about taking produce for rent, but this allegation was more serious. Poaching was a criminal offence, and if he thought Roderick was guilty of letting the locals off with it, he would be in serious trouble this time. The Laird duly arrived in the middle of January and he didn't beat about the bush. He was livid.

'It's one thing to accept a few eggs or a chicken to help the crofters pay their rent, but it's another thing entirely to let them away with stealing from me. That I will not tolerate.'

'I can assure you, Sir Arthur, I have let no one away with poaching. Calum and I frequently inspect the land. We would know if there were poachers. This is a small island and word gets round.'

'So, you don't let them get away with stealing the odd hare or trout?'

Sir Arthur had apparently lost his anger and was now smiling conspiratorially, and I wondered if Roderick would fall for this obvious trap to get him to confess that yes, he did sometimes. I knew he did, as my mother occasionally praised the trout that my father had caught for tea, which made a grand change from the salt herring that they normally ate. I held my breath.

'Och no, Sir Arthur. I know my job depends on keeping the law around here and protecting your lands. That's something you don't need to worry about, sir.'

'Well, I'm warning you Macdonald. If I find out you've been lying to me, you won't be the Factor here for much longer. You might also find your guardianship of that boy Donald will be at an end, too.'

'What do you mean, Sir Arthur? Colin set the Trust up, and it made provision for our guardianship of Donald until it was time for him to go to a private school for his secondary education,' I said.

'Trusts can be challenged, Mrs Macdonald, if we find the guardian to be failing in their duty towards their ward.'

'What do you mean, failing in their duty?'

His face softened slightly when he saw tears starting in my eyes.

'I know you love that boy like your own Chrissie, but I've heard stories that all is not well between your son Roddy and Donald. I've heard that Roddy is cruel to him and that you, Roderick, had to take your slipper to him. That, coupled with you ignoring criminal acts on my land, I feel would be sufficient reason to look again at the Trust.'

'Who told you this, Sir Arthur? It's true the boys' relationship could be better, but Donald is not in any danger,' said Roderick, his face looking like thunder. 'Did you receive another anonymous letter?'

'No, I didn't. I heard it from the constable, who heard it from Mrs Campbell, who heard it from her son, Archie, who is friendly with your boy Roddy. When I visited the school recently, I heard from Mrs Hepworth that Donald's only friend is her daughter Mary. I'm just not sure that Donald is in the best place.'

'The reason Donald has no friends is because of Colin Donaldson, not us. That Mrs Hepworth is just trying to cause trouble. I bet it's her who's written the letters.'

'Don't be ridiculous, man. She's an educated woman and those letters are not from an educated person. I'm going to see the constable now and will ask him to be extra vigilant. You, Roderick, would do well to find out who this person is creating mischief for you because if I get another letter accusing you of something, you are out.'

When Sir Arthur left, I felt relieved that Roderick still had his job, so we still had a house and the boys would be secure for a while longer. But what he had said about challenging the Trust and having Donald removed terrified me. Who could have sent that letter? Who disliked us so much that they would do that?

'Why did you say to Sir Arthur that you thought Bunty had written that letter Roderick? He'll just think there's something in the rumours that went round last year about you and her are true.'

'What rumours? That she had a crush on me?'

'Well, it wasn't just that though, was it? There was a suggestion that you were a bit too interested in her; giving her lessons, picking up her shopping and so on.'

'For goodness' sake Chrissie. You sound like a jealous wife.'

'I just don't understand why you dislike Bunty so much. She's done her best to be friendly, yet you could hardly speak to her at New Year when she was over.'

'I don't know what it is, but there's something about her that makes me uncomfortable. What did you think of what she said about Heather?'

'I was surprised and, if I'm being honest, unsettled. I can't think why Heather would look like her uncle. He never lived in Canada, so far as I know, from what she said.'

'What about her father? Has she told you anything about him?'

'Only that he went away to find work, but she didn't say where.'

'What if her father went to Canada? He could be James Adams and that's why there's a family resemblance.'

We looked at each other, contemplating the implications.

'You mean Heather wouldn't be your daughter and Donald wouldn't be your grandson?'

He nodded, suddenly looking old and grey.

'Don't you think *now* it might be Bunty who's been sending the letters, if she's connected in some way with James Adams?'

'But she knows nothing about our connection with him. I still think it's someone local with a grudge and it leaves a sour taste in my mouth.'

A sour taste in my mouth was nothing to the freezing fear that Donald was not Roderick's grandson and, if that were the case, there would be no foundation for us being his guardian. I resolved to ask the women at the next Rural meeting if they had any ideas as my mother had suggested.

CHAPTER THIRTY-FIVE

It surprised Bunty how much she had enjoyed visiting the Macdonald family on New Year's Day. Although Roderick was reserved and it felt obvious to her he didn't like her, Chrissie and Johnny had more than made up for his lack of warmth. Roderick was part of the temperance movement, like her uncle, all tight and sober faced. He didn't even try her spiced wine, and she could feel his disapproval when she took some of the whisky Johnny had brought. Yet Chrissie had taken some of her wine and some of the whisky too and he hadn't seemed to disapprove of that. Wasn't it a Scottish tradition after all?

But it wasn't just the enjoyment of the evening that she thought about, it was what she had discovered when she took the chance to have a closer look at the girl in the photograph she had noticed when Chrissie had shown her Lachlan's photograph. When she picked it up, the last thing she was expecting was the face of someone who looked like her uncle. Although it was of a young woman, and her skin was quite dark, she had a look of him, the same shape of nose and mouth. When she had asked who the girl was, Chrissie and Roderick had looked positively uncomfortable. It turned out she was Donald's mother and Roderick's daughter. She noticed he hadn't answered her question about being married. At last, she had found out more about the family, but it didn't explain why the girl looked like her uncle.

She had accepted their explanation at the time, but the more she thought about it, the more she decided they were hiding something. But what was it? If the girl was related to her family, then the only explanation was that her father had married someone in Canada and had a child with her. She pushed down the feeling of betrayal that surfaced at the thought that he had abandoned her and her mother for some unknown woman in Canada and concentrated instead on her need for revenge. Rather than telling herself the girl's similarity was just a coincidence, she let her thoughts run wild and decided the girl must be her half-sister. But why was the girl living with Roderick and Chrissie, and why was Roderick saying that he was her father? She would need to look at her uncle's paperwork again to see if there were any clues, but that would mean telling her mother where she and Mary were. She had left the house in Manchester without telling her mother where she was going, but this was more important. She needed to find out the truth about this girl, Heather.

CHAPTER THIRTY-SIX

It was time for the rural meeting, and I was to be the speaker. I'd already talked about my life in Canada, so decided to talk about being the Factor's wife this time, as I thought it might allow me to bring up the subject of the letters to the Laird. I remembered what my mother had said: that the women might know who would be likely to send such letters. The rural had been meeting for about six months now and I was happy with how things were going. I also felt the women were more accepting of me now than they had been before, and I was so glad I hadn't run around accusing Shona McIver or Morag Campbell, as I had told Bunty I was going to do. My mother was right. Those two would be more likely to gossip about us than to write to the Laird.

The meeting was being held at my mother's house. Shona McIver had given Bunty a lift to our house, as Catriona, our housemaid, was looking after Mary and the boys while we were at the meeting. Flora had joined the Rural too, so she and I went with Bunty in Shona's buggy. It was a chilly afternoon, so it was a pleasure going into my mother's kitchen and feeling the heat from her new range. Mrs Macaulay and most of the other women who normally came were already there, so I didn't waste any time in getting started on my talk. When I'd finished and asked if anyone had questions, Morag Campbell was first as usual.

'Not so much a question, Chrissie. More an observation,' she said with a cheeky smile. 'It sounds to me like you have the life of Reilly now you're the Factor's wife. Poor old Flora here does it all.'

I laughed, as she was right so far as managing the house was concerned, so it warmed my heart when Flora stood up for me.

'Come on now, Morag. You know Chrissie helps Roderick with the letters, the rent collections, and the books.'

'Och, I was only teasing. I know Chrissie also needs to entertain all those snooty women who come along with their husbands for the shooting and fishing. I wouldn't want to do that.'

'Aye, it's not my favourite part of the job either, Morag.'

'Chrissie, why don't you ask the women about the letters the Laird has received?'

'What letters are thon?' asked Shona McIver, her ears pricking up.

'Well, they were telling the Laird that Roderick wasn't doing his job right.'

'Not doing his job right?'

'Aye, you know, taking a hen or eggs sometimes instead of rent and letting the men poach the odd trout or hare, that kind of thing,' said my mother.

'Sounds like he's doing his job right to me,' said Annie Nicolson. 'Why would any of us complain about that?'

'Well, that's what I said to Chrissie, but the Laird says the letters were poorly written, so he thinks it's someone local who's done it.'

'So can anyone think of someone who might write a letter like that?' I asked.

'Well, it wasn't me,' said Morag Campbell. 'I can hardly string two words together. My tongue is better than my writing.'

We all laughed.

'Does anyone hold a grudge against you or Roderick, Chrissie?' asked Bunty.

'I know it wasn't the most popular decision to give Roderick the factor's job, but I can't think of anyone particularly.'

'What about before he went to Canada? Did he leave a woman behind who might be out for revenge?' Bunty laughed as she said this, not realising that she was touching a nerve.

There was an uncomfortable silence as she waited for my answer, which was loudly interrupted when the door flew open and Johnny and my father came in, bringing in the cold air with them.

'Sorry to interrupt you ladies, but we're in dire need of a hot cup of tea. It's freezing out there on the moor,' said Johnny.

All at once the atmosphere in the room changed as it usually did when men came in and I could see Mairi Campbell's cheeks glowing pink as she looked at Johnny with puppy-dog eyes. Young love! Oh, to be seventeen again.

'You've come just at the right time. I was about to put out the tea,' said my mother, getting up off her chair.

'I'll help you, Mrs Macdonald,' said Mairi. 'How do you like your tea, Johnny?'

So, our discussion ended, as we all sat, drank our tea and chatted to the men. Nothing had become any clearer about the letters, but at least I was sure no-one here would have sent them. Roderick would be pleased to hear they were on his side.

I was doing the washing up when Morag Campbell came up to me.

'Chrissie, I've been thinking about the letters you were talking about and I'm just wondering if they could be connected with Canada?'

Why was she mentioning Canada? Did she know something?

'It's just when Bunty asked if Roderick had upset anyone before he went to Canada, it made me wonder if he had upset anyone when he lived in Canada.'

'Och, we've been back here for nearly eight years, Morag. I think if someone from Canada was out to get us, they would have done it by now, don't you?'

'Aye, you're probably right. Well, the only other suggestion I can make is to go to the post office and ask Ian Fraser if he knows who sent those letters because if someone local sent them, he would know.'

'Why didn't I think of that, Morag? You're a genius.'

'Aye, well you think you would've thought of that as you worked in the post office, Chrissie.'

'Aye, you would Morag.'

I would go and see Ian Fraser as she suggested, but as soon as she said his name, it made me wonder if it was he who had written the letters. He had been so unhelpful when Bunty and I had gone to ask him to put up a poster about the Rural. I would ask Roderick what he thought about it when I got home.

Soon it was time to leave, and we made our way outside. Johnny was busy stacking the peat into piles at the back of the house.

'That reminds me, Shona,' said Bunty. 'I'll need to buy some more peat from you. Could you get your husband to bring some round tomorrow?'

'No need for that, Bunty,' said Johnny. 'You can have some of this. We've got plenty. I'll drop it round later.'

'That's very kind. Thank you Johnny. I'll see you later then.'

CHAPTER THIRTY-SEVEN

Bunty had just got Mary to bed when she heard a knock at the door. As she thought, it was Johnny with the peat.

'Hello Bunty. I've stacked the peat at the back of the house for you. Just let me know when you need more.'

'Come in for a cuppa, Johnny. It's the least I can do.'

'Alright then. I never say no to a nice cup of tea.'

'Are you like me then and think it cures all ills?'

'Maybe not all,' he smiled sadly, his big brown eyes looking like a spaniel her mother used to have and she realised he must be talking about splitting up with his fiancé.

'I can see you're sad, Johnny. Is it because things didn't work out with Janet?'

'Yes. I thought she was the one. Although I'd known Janet most of my life as she was Chrissie's best friend, we met again one night at Chrissie's house when we were both home on leave during the war and that was it. We just clicked.'

'I know how that feels. My husband, Harry and I were like that. We didn't have long together though as he was killed in Ypres not long after the war started.'

'Aye, so many lives lost. Our brother, Lachlan, was killed in the war too.'

'Yes, Chrissie was telling me about his journals, so I've written to Harry's father, who's a printer, to see if he knows anyone who could publish them.'

'Is that so? You'll make my mother and father happy about that. And Chrissie. She's desperate to get them in print. His poems were published just after the war but she's keen to get his diaries published too as they tell so much about the horror of war. Anyway, how are you and Mary settling in? How long is it you've been here now?'

'That's us been here just over a year and we've settled in fine.'

'It's good you and Chrissie have become friends. I think it was hard for her coming back from Canada. Being away from a place for a while can change things.'

'Have you found that, Johnny? I mean, you were away in the war and then you went to live in Glasgow.'

'Yes, that's true, but no. My old friends are still here, and we enjoy going to the ceilidhs of a Friday night. Have you been to one yet?'

'No. I haven't.'

'Well, why don't you and Mary come along to the one that's on next month?'

'Oh, I would feel awkward going on my own. Isn't it all couples?'

'No. Everyone goes, old and young, couples and singles. I'll come and pick you up.'

'But I don't know how to do Scottish dances.'

'Right, well, I'll teach you and Mary a few steps before we go. Most of it's just twirling round, anyway. Well, I better be getting back. I'll be seeing you.'

He smiled and saluted. What a nice man he was, nothing like his grumpy old brother-in-law, she thought. That made her think back to the Rural meeting. Chrissie hadn't answered her question about Roderick. Had he been jilted she wondered? Maybe getting to know Johnny better would help her find out more about Chrissie and Roderick and about their life in Canada.

CHAPTER THIRTY-EIGHT

I went into the post office the next time I was in Lochmaddy. Ian Fraser was nowhere to be seen. It was his wife who was behind the counter.

'Hello Mrs Macdonald. Can I help you?'

'Yes, I was hoping I might get a chance to ask your husband something. Is he around just now?'

'Yes, I'll let him know you're here, but you may need to wait. He's just finishing his lunch, and he doesn't like to be interrupted when he's eating.'

'Yes, of course,' I said, imagining him carefully putting each tiny morsel into his mouth and chewing it slowly.

When Mrs Fraser came back, she looked a little flustered, so I made conversation.

'And how are you settling into the post office, Mrs Fraser?'

'Aye, we're settling in fine. We worked in a post office on the mainland, so we know what we're doing.'

'That's good. Mr Macdonald and I had never worked in a post office before we got the job here at the start of the war, so we had a lot to learn.'

'It must have been hard for you delivering all those telegrams. We had a young boy to do that for us.'

'Yes, it was one of the worst jobs. I hated it.'

There was an awkward silence as our conversation ran out, so I was relieved when Mrs Fraser spoke again.

'Maybe I could help you, Mrs Macdonald, and you wouldn't need to wait for my husband.'

'I wanted to talk to him about two letters that were sent to the Laird from here.'

'Oh, is it to do with estate business?'

'Yes, and no. What I wanted to ask is if Mr Fraser remembered the letters and if so, who it was that handed them in for posting.'

Just then, the door opened, and Mr Fraser came out, his face looking as pinched as usual.

'Hello Mrs Macdonald, sorry to have kept you waiting. How may I help you?'

'Mrs Macdonald was just asking if you remember two letters that were sent to the Laird from here.'

'Thank you, Sarah. I'll speak to Mrs Macdonald now. You can get on with your work.'

'Okay, Ian.'

That woman needed to join the Rural.

'I'm afraid that even if I could remember the letters Mrs Macdonald, I would never reveal who sent them. As you well know, that would be against the rules of the post office. I'm surprised you've even asked.'

'But it's important, Mr Fraser. They were anonymous letters, poison pen letters.'

'Poison pen letters sent to the Laird.'

I could see it scandalised him that anyone would send such letters to the Laird, but he had got the wrong end of the stick.

'They weren't aimed at the Laird, Mr Fraser. They were aimed at my husband.'

When I said this, his face changed as if he were losing interest in the subject, but I wondered if it was because it was him who had written the letters.

'If you think someone has committed a crime, I suggest you contact the constable.'

'I appreciate you need to obey the rules of the post office, Mr Fraser, but can you at least tell me if you remember the letters?'

'I'm afraid I can't, but even if I could remember, I wouldn't necessarily know who had posted them. If I were sending a poison pen letter, I wouldn't be coming into the post office to send it. I would put it in the postbox.'

'Yes, of course. Thanks Mr Fraser. By the way, Mrs Fraser, we'll be having a meeting of the Rural in the schoolhouse next month. Why don't you come along? I'll get Mrs Hepworth to let you know the details.'

I couldn't help smiling in triumph when I saw the look on Ian Fraser's face as I left the post office.

'What are you grinning at?' asked Morag Campbell, who was passing.

'Hello Morag. I've just been in checking if Mr Fraser remembered anything about the letters to the Laird, but he doesn't. He says whoever sent them would probably have posted them in a post box rather than take them into the post office, which makes sense.'

'Maybe ask Murdo. He might remember something. By the way, he told me that Bunty received a large parcel in the post.'

'Did she indeed? I'll maybe pop in on my way home.'

It occurred to me my growing association with Morag Campbell and Shona McIver was rubbing off, as I was curious to find out more. I was also growing more convinced that Ian Fraser could have something to do with those letters. He wasn't for helping and it was probably to cover up what he had done.

CHAPTER THIRTY-NINE

Murdo Mackenzie, the postman, stopped outside the schoolhouse just as Bunty and Mary were on their way out to school. The wind was blowing so fiercely, she had to hold her hat on her head with one hand while gripping Mary's hand with the other.

'Good morning Mrs Hepworth. I have a parcel here for you,' he shouted over the wind.

'Oh, thank you Murdo. I'll open the door and you can leave it inside if that's okay. Mary and I are just on our way to school.'

'Aye, that'll be no bother at all. I see they've sent it from Manchester.'

Bunty knew from experience that Murdo would be curious about who the parcel was from and what was inside. Normally she liked to pique his curiosity more by giving him little hints of what might be inside, but when he said Manchester she couldn't help the quiver of excitement she felt and took the parcel from him. Murdo was no fool and could see Bunty's eagerness by the way she scrutinised the parcel, so he was desperate to play their usual game, where he would offer suggestions about what might be inside the parcel, and she would agree or disagree.

'Och, is this something you've been expecting? You and Mary won't be able to wait until the end of the school day to find out what's inside.'

But Bunty wasn't playing today.

'Indeed, we won't Murdo. Thanks. Hope the rain stays off for the rest of your deliveries.'

And off she walked, leaving him with his mouth hanging open in disappointment.

Murdo had been right. She couldn't concentrate on the children and the lessons she had prepared for them today. All she could think about was the parcel and what information it would hold. She deliberated whether to go home at lunchtime but decided there would not be enough time to do the parcel justice and left it until the evening. She had prepared the usual sandwiches she made for her and Mary and as they sat together munching them and drinking tea, Mary asked her about the parcel.

'Who is the parcel from Mummy? You looked excited when Murdo said Manchester. Is it from Grandma?'

'Yes, I think it will be, Mary. I asked your grandma to send me some paperwork and I think that's what it will be.'

'Do you think she will have sent something for me too, Mummy?'

It annoyed Bunty that Mary was so desperate to hear from her mother and was short with her.

'I doubt it, Mary. She hasn't sent you anything since we came here, has she?'

This was a lie, of course. Her mother didn't know where she had taken Mary, so couldn't write to her.

When Bunty opened the box that had been wrapped inside the brown paper parcel Murdo had brought, she saw there was a letter for her and a letter for Mary on top of the papers. She quickly shut the box so that her daughter wouldn't see them. Her mother had a cheek writing to Mary. Mary was *her* daughter. Bunty could see it disappointed Mary the parcel didn't hold something for her, so although she was desperate to look through the paperwork, she spent time with Mary after school. They made some pancakes and ate them with butter and jam. She also lingered longer while reading her bedtime story, but at last she was on her own.

She opened the box and took out the two letters her mother had written and put them in the fire without reading them. Her mother would have said nothing she wanted to hear. She then took the pile of papers out of the box and stared at them, wondering what they would reveal. She noticed her hands were trembling when she picked up the first thing on top of the pile.

The first letter confirmed that her father had been married. It was dated 1909 and was from the Saskatchewan authorities to her uncle, telling him it appeared that his brother, James Adams, had been missing since approximately 1896 and was therefore presumed dead. This matter had come to their attention as James

Adams had not farmed the land that had been assigned to him by the government. It was therefore a requirement that his land either be transferred to a member of his family or be sold on the open market. The letter said that although James Adams was married, his wife had never claimed his estate, and it was therefore assumed that she too was missing, believed dead.

As she sat staring at the fire, she thought about her father. He must have gone to Canada with such high hopes. She wondered if he had ever received the letter her mother had sent him telling him she was pregnant. It was unlikely, or she was sure he would have sent for her. Perhaps he had replied, but her mother had already married her stepfather by then. Who could blame him for taking a wife? He must have been desperately lonely in a foreign country on his own. She must look more closely at the papers to see if they had had a child together.

She picked up the papers again and resumed reading. The next piece of paper on the bundle was a writ issued by the High Court in Manchester saying that as James Adams had been missing for thirteen years, he was now pronounced dead, and his brother was to be appointed as his executor. A letter from his uncle's solicitor to Saskatchewan State Council followed this, telling them to sell the land. A Bill of Sale to a man called Aleksander Bukowski followed this. It detailed all the measurements and the boundaries of the land and showed that it had belonged to James Adams. His executor, Frederick Adams, her uncle, had given consent to the sale.

She thought of Canada and wondered what it was like. One day, she would visit that place and see for herself. She also wondered if Chrissie and Roderick had lived near the town called Saltcoats that was mentioned in the Deed and if they knew the man who had bought her father's land. If they did, then Roderick would have been her father's neighbour. But how would she get this information out of Chrissie without arousing her suspicions? Deciding to think about it tomorrow, she put the box with the papers away. She was too tired to continue tonight.

CHAPTER FORTY

Murdo called up to the house with the morning mail and could tell me I had a letter from my sister. He seemed to know the handwriting of everyone who sent letters. Either that or he opened the letters and looked inside. I was pleased to see him and thought perhaps his nosiness would help with the anonymous letters.

'I see there's a letter from your sister, Morag. Hasn't been one of them for a while. I wonder how she's doing.'

'I'll let you know Murdo once I've read her letter. Now I have a question for you that I'm sure you'll be able to answer.'

He stood upright, put his post bag down, and straightened his hat.

'A question you say?'

'Yes. You collect the mail from the post boxes on the island, don't you?'

'Yes, I do.'

'Well, I want to ask you about letters that might have been put into one of the post boxes that you pick up from.'

'And why do you want to ask me about them, Chrissie?'

'You might have heard, Murdo, that the Laird has received two anonymous letters making accusations about Roderick.'

'Yes, I have Chrissie. Such a terrible thing.'

'Well, I just wondered, with you being so good at recognising the writing on the post you deliver, whether you noticed the letters to the Laird and were able to guess who had written them.'

He took his hat off and scratched his head.

'And when were the letters sent? There's a lot of mail goes through my hands Chrissie on the way to the post office in Lochmaddy.'

'Och, I know that Murdo. You're a very busy man. They sent the first letter last April and the second one just before Christmas.'

He put his hat back on his head and stood looking up at the sky. I held my breath. If he knew, what was I going to do about it?

'A cup of tea and one of Flora's soda scones might help me remember, Chrissie.'

The crafty so-and-so. He would do anything for a cup of tea, that man.

'Of course.'

As we walked through to the kitchen, I teased him about Bunty's parcel.

'I hear Bunty received a parcel in the post the other day. I bet you couldn't guess who had sent that.'

'Well, it was a bit difficult as she's never received a letter from Manchester before, so I couldn't recognise the writing.'

'Manchester, you say, and that's the first time she's had any mail from Manchester?'

'Yes, so far as I know.'

I wondered why that was. I would have thought Bunty's mother would have been in regular correspondence with her and Mary.

After Murdo had drank his tea and eaten his soda scone, I waited as he chatted with Flora but was becoming impatient to know if he remembered the letters. At last, he turned to me.

'I remember the letters Chrissie, as I wondered who would have cause to write to the Laird. Normally, Roderick deals with estate business.'

'And.'

'I didn't recognise the writing. Now that I know they were poison pen letters, I wish I'd paid more attention.'

'Is there anything you can tell me about the letters that would help?'

'Well, I think it was a woman, as when men write, the ink is much heavier and bold. The writing was light and scratchy.'

It disappointed me that he thought it was a woman rather than a man. But, of course, Ian could have disguised his handwriting to make it look like a woman's.

'Okay, thanks Murdo. You've been a great help.'

After Murdo left, the boys came home from school. Mary was with them as she sometimes came to tea with us now.

'Hello Mary. It's nice to see you.'

'Hello Auntie Chrissie. It's nice to see you too. Mummy and I are going to a ceilidh with Uncle Johnny on Friday.'

'Are you?'

I used to love going to the ceilidhs, but Roderick wasn't a dancer, so I hadn't been to very many.

'We might come along, too. Do you know how to dance then?'

'I didn't, but Uncle Johnny came round and showed Mummy and me a few dances. It was such fun.'

'I heard from Murdo that your mummy received a parcel from Manchester. Was it anything exciting?'

Her face fell.

'No. I thought my grandma might have sent me a letter or a present, but she didn't. There was just a lot of old paperwork inside the parcel.'

'Och, that's a shame. I can see you were disappointed.'

'I miss my grandma. It made me sad when Mummy took me away from Manchester and brought me here. I used to cry but I'm happy now because I have Donald as my best friend.'

Chrissie felt sorry for the wee girl, so tried to cheer her up.

'Och, maybe your mummy will take you home for a visit in the summer holidays.'

'No, she won't. She told me we would never leave this island and that Grandma would never visit us. I don't know what I've done to make my Grandma not want to see me again.'

Tears trickled down her cheeks.

'You won't have done anything, Mary. Don't you worry about that. Away down to the kitchen now. Flora's got soda scones waiting for you.'

I hadn't realised Bunty wasn't on good terms with her mother and wondered why she hadn't told me when she had told me so much about her father. I would hate it if my mother and I ever fell out.

CHAPTER FORTY-ONE

Bunty and Mary had a wonderful time at the Ceilidh. It was held in the village hall at a place called Carinish, and Johnny had called for her. He only had a cart, not a fancy buggy like Chrissie, but she and Mary didn't mind. Although it was April, it was still quite cold on the island, and Johnny wrapped a knitted woollen shawl around their legs to keep them warm. It took quite a while for them to get there, but that gave them an opportunity to see another part of the island that they hadn't yet visited. Some of it was just peat bogs, but in other places there were bright spring flowers peeking through on the side of the road. They saw lots of sheep grazing and some little horses, which Johnny told them were called Eriskay ponies.

When they got there, the hall was crowded with people she knew and people she didn't. Johnny was quickly in demand, and he left her and Mary on their own. She looked for Chrissie, who had told her she and the boys would be there too, and there she was chatting to her mother, so she went over.

'Hello Bunty, hello Mary. This is so exciting. I haven't been to a ceilidh in I don't know how long as Roderick doesn't dance.'

That didn't surprise her.

Mary ran off with Roddy, Donald, and some other children they knew, so she and Chrissie found a table and sat down and then the music began. There were four men with accordions, fiddles, and a bagpipe. She had bought a record of dance tunes for the lessons with Johnny, so she recognised the first tune that was played – a Dashing White Sergeant. Johnny came over immediately and the three of them were the first on the floor. And that was that. She was whirled round the floor all night and her feet flew through the jigs, reels, and strathspeys. Most of the dances were group dances, and it didn't seem to matter that she didn't have a partner of her own. Teenage boys and old men asked her to dance, and she enjoyed it with every one of them.

But her favourite dance of all was the slow one at the end when Johnny had come over, somewhat the worse for wear with the whisky he had been drinking and asked her to dance. His breath stank of the alcohol, but his arms were strong, and he held her close. It was so long since anyone had held her like that she didn't mind and was sorry when it ended. She was also sorry when Johnny told her that Chrissie would drop her and Mary home.

'I've had a little too much to drink,' he said, slurring a little, 'and I don't want to take the chance of hurting you and Mary if I fall off the cart. Chrissie would never forgive me.'

He kissed her lightly on the cheek and smiled kindly at her. She felt her heart miss a beat and thought again what a lovely man he was.

CHAPTER FORTY-TWO

I opened Morag's letter, wondering what her news would be. We hadn't heard from her for a few months. After we moved into the Factor's house, she left North Uist to work as a chambermaid in the Central Hotel where Katie had taken me that time I had visited her in Glasgow. She had done well in the job and gradually worked her way up from chambermaid to receptionist. I loved hearing about her life in Glasgow, which sounded way more exciting than North Uist. They had picture houses there where you could go to see moving pictures. In her last letter, she told me she had gone to see *The Sheikh* and had almost swooned when she saw Rudolph Valentino, he was so handsome.

The last thing I was expecting to hear was that she had moved from Glasgow, but that's what she was telling me. She had met and fallen in love with one of the senior managers of the hotel, and they were now married. They had wished to marry without a fuss as her new husband's father had just died, so it had been a quiet affair at her husband's local church. Although his father's death had been distressing, his legacy had allowed him to open his own hotel, which he had always wanted to do. His name was Michael Hamilton, so she was now Mrs Hamilton.

I am so happy Chrissie; I can't tell you. Michael is the loveliest man you could meet, and he and I are equally committed to this new venture. We have bought a small hotel in Helensburgh on the Firth of Clyde, which is not too far from Glasgow on the train. I've written to Father and Mother and asked if you would all come for a holiday so that you can meet Michael before we officially open the hotel. It won't be for a few months yet as we have a lot of work to do on it, so perhaps when the children stop for the school holidays you could come.

Morag's news amazed me. She had never even mentioned a boyfriend or being interested in anyone. It must have been a whirlwind romance, but I wished her well. It would disappoint

Father and Mother not to have seen their youngest daughter married but hopefully it would make them all the keener to visit her and meet her new husband. Although my father had been off the island, my mother hadn't, so it would be a big adventure for her. I hoped she would come with me.

When I told Roderick, he was less than enthusiastic about going on a trip to see my sister.

'I can't go gallivanting off while we have the Laird's threat to dissolve the Trust hanging over our heads.'

He began coughing, and I noticed he looked thinner. TB was never far from my mind and I hoped it wouldn't start again. All this worry about the boys, the letters and the Laird's threat were taking their toll on him.

'I know. It's a worry. I couldn't bear it if they took Donald away from us, and what effect would it have on him? He's been through so much already.'

'I think we need to check out if he could do anything legally, don't you?'

'Yes, just to set our minds at rest. So should we ask Mr Abernethy?'

'Why don't you stop off in Glasgow on your way to visit Morag and contact Maude? She was very helpful before when we were fighting Colin and now that she can legally practice as a solicitor, she could act for us rather than just advise us.'

'It won't be till summer as they're working on the hotel. Do you think we can wait until then?'

'We'll just have to hope nothing else happens between now and then.'

'Well, at least we know it's not been someone we are friends or acquaintances of. Everyone was so supportive of you being the Factor at the Rural.'

'That's good to know, but someone is up to no good.'

'Well, I've got an idea who it might be, Roderick.'

He looked at me with hope in his eyes. If we could find out who it was, we could tackle them and get all this to stop.

'I think it's Ian Fraser in the post office.'

His face fell.

'Ian Fraser? He hardly knows us. Why would he have it in for us?'

'I don't know Roderick. I only know he's been very unhelpful. When I asked him to put up a poster for the Rural, he refused and then when I asked if he remembered seeing the letters to the Laird, I thought he looked shifty.'

'You and your imagination,' he smiled at me. 'But I might ask Archie Morrison to have a word just in case you're right.'

What a relief it would be if it turned out to be Ian Fraser. Roderick began coughing again.

'Will you be alright with me going away? You seem peaky.'

'I'll be fine Chrissie.'

'Maybe I could fit in a visit to Janet as well while I'm there. I'd like to know why she's so adamant about not coming back to North Uist. I'm worried about Johnny and the amount he's drinking. He was quite drunk at the ceilidh and I saw him kiss Bunty on the cheek at the end. It wouldn't be fair of him to lead her on if he still has feelings for Janet and I think he does.'

'Drinking is a curse; I've always told you that. If Johnny's looking for a replacement for Janet, he could do far better than that schoolteacher. There are plenty of local lassies looking for a husband.'

I didn't bother arguing with him. He didn't like Bunty, and that was that. I just had to accept it.

CHAPTER FORTY-THREE

At a loose end and feeling rather restless, Bunty looked at the papers her mother had sent her again. She picked up where she had left off the last time she had looked at them. What she read was still shocking, even although she had read it before. It was a letter from the Canadian Mounted Police, telling her uncle that the new owner had found a skeleton on his brother's land, and they presumed it was his brother. He had been shot, and they were making inquiries about his disappearance. However, as it was over ten years ago since he had gone missing, there would likely be very little evidence. They sent their condolences on his loss.

Bunty let her tears fall silently. Her poor father, shot and then buried without a proper funeral. It was shameful. What kind of person could do that? She already knew what kind of person. Someone like Roderick Macdonald. She knew because the next letter from the mounted police told her so. He was a wolf in sheep's clothing. Pretending he was a nice man with his nice family. But she knew better and soon she would find a way of letting the entire island know as well.

She picked up the second letter from the Mounties and looked at it more carefully this time. It said that an unnamed witness had seen Roderick Macdonald going into the Golden Sheaf Hotel in Saltcoats around the time her father went missing and they had paid him a visit to see if he knew anything. The report noted that "although Mr Macdonald had confirmed that he went into the Golden Sheaf Hotel from time to time, he had no recollection of meeting James Adams."

It was then she noticed another reason the Mountie had visited Roderick was because he had an Indian woman living with him. They thought it was worth investigating, as there was evidence that James Adams had married a Cree squaw named Lily Norwest who had never been found, and they wondered if she had gone to live with Roderick Macdonald. But it turned out the Cree woman who had lived with him was called Waskatamwi and had a child and there was no record of James Adams and his wife having a child. Bunty's blood ran cold. Her father had married a squaw rather than her mother. What kind of man was he? The thought of him choosing a savage over her mother disgusted her, and she put the papers away. She had read enough.

Feeling agitated by what she had read, she took a cup of the mulled wine she had made at Christmas. She found it comforting and let her thoughts drift and they drifted to Johnny and the night of the ceilidh. She remembered that soft kiss on her cheek and how her heart had missed a beat, and that made her think of Harry. When they met, they were very young, and it was their first sexual awakening. They were both only sixteen at the time and their desire for each other had been intense. She could hardly concentrate on her studies and was always being told off for daydreaming. He was constantly on her mind and her body ached for him. They met in his father's printing shop at night when no-one was there, which made it even more exciting because they might be caught at any moment. She had been pregnant before they got married, but it wasn't a problem because Harry was a true gentleman. He would never have abandoned her. It was only because of the war that she was on her own.

Johnny was like Harry; a true gentleman and she wondered if that kiss had meant something. She had liked Johnny as soon as she met him, but love wasn't on her mind, only revenge. But that kiss was making her think more about him. She liked his sense of humour, and his kindness, and Mary was quite taken with him too. Was it possible that they could have a relationship? But what about this Janet he had been engaged to? Chrissie had told her they had been courting since before the war ended, but nothing had come of it and now they had split up. That woman couldn't love him very much if she wasn't willing to give up her life in Glasgow to come back to the island. As far as Bunty was concerned, living in North Uist permanently with a husband to look after her and Mary would be a dream come true. She wouldn't ever need to go back to Manchester.

She decided she was going to get to know Johnny better. He seemed a kind and capable man and she was sure she could find minor jobs around the house that he could help a widow on her own with. She smiled to herself. The future looked bright for the first time in a long time. It didn't occur to her that if Johnny found out she had taken revenge on Chrissie's husband, there would be no relationship.

CHAPTER FORTY-FOUR

Johnny was now back working on the croft and when I was over visiting one day we got chatting.

'How are things, Johnny? Are you feeling any better about splitting up with Janet?'

'Not really, but I am enjoying being back here. This island is my home and it just feels right working on the croft with *Athair*. I would love to get my own place, but I'll just have to wait and see what happens with the Board of Agriculture.'

'I hear you've been helping Bunty out with some odd jobs she needed doing round the schoolhouse.'

'Yes. She must be clever, otherwise she wouldn't be a teacher, but she's hopeless with things around the house. I don't know how she's managed without a man to help her.'

His remark surprised me. Bunty had always seemed quite competent to me and had managed just fine since she arrived on the island. Men could be blind to a woman's wiles, but then I remembered that kiss Johnny had given her at the ceilidh and wondered if he needed much manipulation.

'So, you're her knight in shining armour, are you?' I laughed.

He looked abashed and laughed too. He knew how much work women had done during the war and he was a supporter of a woman's right to vote on the same basis as men.

'She's invited me round for tea with her and Mary to thank me for helping her. It will be alright for me to go, won't it? It won't set the tongues wagging?'

'Och Johnny, you know better than that. The tongues will always wag and probably already are. Look at when Roderick was helping her by collecting her shopping and taking her peat when she first arrived here. He got warned off by the minister.'

'No!'

'But you're a single man and I don't think the minister will be as disapproving. So, if you want to go, then go.'

When I told Roderick that I thought Bunty was interested in Johnny, he was anything but pleased.

'I hope your brother is smart enough to know he's being manipulated by that woman.'

'But it would be good for Johnny to find someone to love if he and Janet are definitely over.'

'Well Chrissie, there are plenty of Uist born young women for him to choose from. He doesn't need to go with an incomer like her.'

I was fed up with Roderick being negative about Bunty, so chose to ignore him and changed the subject.

'Did you speak to Archie about Ian Fraser?'

'I did, and he said he would have a quiet word and see if he could find out anything. But we must be careful we don't accuse someone unfairly, so don't go telling anyone, especially that Bunty.'

We were back to Bunty again, so I sat down and read my magazine. It was more enjoyable than hearing Roderick going on about her.

CHAPTER FORTY-FIVE

When Chrissie told Bunty she was going to visit her sister, she wondered if she would visit Johnny's ex-fiancé while she was there. A knot formed in her stomach at the thought of them discussing Johnny. He was nothing to do with that woman now. She had had her chance, and now it was hers. Things with Johnny had been going well. She had found plenty of jobs for him to do around the schoolhouse and although she disliked pretending to be a poor little widow who couldn't fend for herself, she judged he was the type of man who wouldn't be able to resist saving her and she had been right. Mary was delighted to see him when he came to the house and he always made a point of playing a game with her. He was ideal husband and father material.

Of course, since word had got out that he was single again, the gossip was that he was very popular with the many young women on the island looking for a suitable husband. She had witnessed this now that she and Mary were regulars at the local ceilidhs. There were about six women for every man and the men dutifully danced with them all, including her. The war had meant many women would never find a husband because of the losses the islands had carried, but she was determined not to be one of them. An invitation to tea was next on her agenda.

'As a thank you, Johnny, for everything you've done for Mary and me over the last few months,' and he had readily accepted.

'That would be just grand, Bunty. Thank you.'

It had been a very pleasant evening. She had made him a hotpot, which he had wolfed down, and afterwards they had listened to her gramophone records. It turned out they shared a similar taste in music. Harry Lauder, of course, was always a favourite, and he sang *I Love a Lassie* to Mary and swung her round the room, much to her delight. Bunty wished it was her who was being swung in his arms and thought he looked at her more than he should as he sang the song. Did he feel like she did, but didn't want to tell her in case he was wrong?

129

After that night, he came round for his tea often and she looked forward more than she should have to his visits. She had even taken to going out walking with Mary on a Saturday afternoon hoping she might bump into him if he was in for a drink at the Lochmaddy Hotel. She daydreamed about him like a love-sick teenager and imagined him taking her in his arms one night after they had put Mary to bed and making love to her. The thought of his lips on hers and the touch of his coarse working fingers stroking her body awakened a longing in her she hadn't felt since Harry.

She had thought little about Roderick Macdonald as Johnny was filling the void that had created her need for revenge. But, when she heard from Chrissie that she was trying to find out who had sent the poison pens letters, she decided it was time to look at the papers again. If they found out she had written the letters, at least she would have the evidence to back up her reason for trying to discredit Roderick, and she was sure Johnny would support her if he knew the truth about his brother-in-law.

As she read the letter about why the Mounties had visited Roderick, she thought about Heather. Was Heather the squaw's daughter?. Had Roderick Macdonald married a savage too, or had he killed her father so that he could steal his wife? She looked again at the letter from the Mounties. They had discounted Roderick as a suspect because of the child, as there was no record of James Adams and the squaw having a child, but what if this Lily was pregnant when Roderick killed her father?

According to the paperwork, he disappeared in the winter of 1896. She looked at the dates again and tried to work out what age Heather would have been if she were her father's daughter. Chrissie had told her Heather had just turned sixteen when she had Donald in December 1913, which meant she would have been born around 1897, which could mean this Lily Norwest could have been pregnant when Roderick killed her father. If she could somehow prove this, she felt she would have sufficient evidence to discredit Roderick and have him charged with murder. She would need to think of a way to prove it and then she could act.

130

CHAPTER FORTY-SIX

A letter arrived from Morag just as the summer holidays were about to begin, telling us she was now ready for our visit. So my mother, Roddy, Donald and I set off to see Morag and her new husband. We were all very excited at going on this adventure, and I wished Roderick were coming with us. He came to wave us off, and we shared a quiet moment together before we boarded.

'I want you to have a good time, Chrissie. It'll be a treat for you and your mother to see Morag again and to meet her new husband. But I don't want you to forget about speaking to Maude. We need to know if the Laird can dissolve the Trust.'

'I won't forget Roderick. Our family is the most precious thing in the world to me, as you know. I shall miss you. I'm wondering if you should go to the doctor just to get him to check you out. You're not yourself.'

'I'm fine Chrissie.'

The ferry blasted its horn. It was time to go.

'You have a good time, my pet lamb.'

I smiled. It had been a while since he had called me that.

We were all tired by the time we arrived at Glasgow Central Station, but it was a happy tiredness. My mother had loved just sitting looking out of the window at scenery she had never seen in her life before, while the boys played, *I Spy* and read their comics. Our bags felt heavy as I lifted them down from the rack above, but with the boys' help, we all managed to make our way off the train. The platform was bustling with people like us trying to make their way out of the station and others trying to make their way towards the trains.

The last time I had been here, it had been busy with men in uniform heading back to the front or heading home to their loved ones. I briefly thought of Lachlan and wondered how he must have felt when he made his journey back to France. Did he know he was going to die? Was that why he had left his journals and poems with me? It was then I remembered Bunty hadn't got back to me about whether her father-in-law could help with publishing his diaries.

Amidst the hissing and belching smoke from the trains, I spotted Katie waving to us and we made our way towards her. We hugged, and she called a porter over who took our bags and followed us out to Gordon Street where a row of taxis, both horse-drawn and motorised, were waiting. The stench of petrol and horse manure prickled my nostrils, but it gave me a heady feeling of excitement rather than revulsion. I was on holiday with my family for the first time in my life and I was going to enjoy every minute. Once, of course, I had spoken to Maude about our position as Donald's guardians and what the Trust could do to have us removed.

'Can we go in a motorised taxi, *Mamaidh*?' pleaded the boys.

'Will it be able to take us all, Katie?'

'Probably not, but I'll go in one with the boys, my treat, and you and Marion can take a horse-drawn one. Is that okay?'

I agreed but wished I could go in the motorised one too.

The boys jumped up and down with excitement as the driver turned round and opened the doors to let them get in. The porter put some of our bags beside the driver and some in a horse-drawn cab that my mother and I would go in. Katie gave him some coppers. My mother held my hand the whole way to Walmer Crescent in Cessnock, where Maude and Katie shared a house now. I wasn't sure if it was with excitement or fear. When the taxi cabs drew up in front of an elegant, curved terrace, I was impressed. Katie had come up in the world.

Maude was waiting for us.

'Welcome to Walmer Crescent, everyone. Come in. Let me help you with your bags.'

She had changed little since the last time I had seen her except she had her hair cut in the modern style and she wore what looked like sporting casual clothes, like she had been playing tennis. I knew from my magazine that this was the trend for well-off people. All the clothes nowadays were much looser and more casual than they were before the war.

'Hang your coat up there,' she said, pointing to an elegant dark wood coat stand, 'and I'll take you to your room. The bathroom is right next door, so you can freshen up and then come and have some tea and muffins before you go to bed.'

When the boys had gone to bed, I asked Maude if we could talk about the Trust so we went to her study, leaving my mother and Katie to chat.

Maude's study was not unlike her room in the last house she stayed in. There had been lots of suffragette posters and paperwork, but this time it was the Women's Co-operative Movement. I envied Maude and Katie's involvement in these women's groups and thought again about the Rural, which in its small way was going well.

'Do you mind if I smoke?' Maude asked.

'No, not at all.'

I watched as she fitted the cigarette into a holder and then lit it. I thought she looked so sophisticated.

'Would you like to try one?' she asked, obviously noticing my fascination.

I would have liked to try one, but the sensible me said no. I could imagine the gossip back home if I came back from Glasgow smoking the cigarettes.

'So tell me, what's worrying you about Donald's Trust? I thought Colin had arranged for you to look after Donald until it was time for him to go to boarding school.'

'He did, but the problem is the Laird is a Trustee and we've been having problems lately that are making the Laird think we may not be suitable to be Donald's guardians any longer.'

'Can you explain what's been happening then, just so that I'm clear before I give you my opinion?'

'Well, our problem is that someone has been sending anonymous letters to the Laird complaining that Roderick isn't doing his job properly.'

133

'That's not so good. Is there any foundation for their allegations?'

'Yes, and no. He does sometimes take produce for rent. But we use the money we would have spent on food for the house and put that in the books so the Laird doesn't lose any rent money.'

'That doesn't sound too bad.'

'They've also accused him of ignoring local poachers.'

'Hmm, that sounds a little more serious.'

'I suppose it is, but the locals have always taken the odd fish or rabbit and the Laird knows that.'

'So, what does this have to do with the Trust?'

'The Laird told Roderick that if there are any more anonymous letters and accusations, he would sack him and would also look at dissolving the Trust.'

'Is Roderick's job tied up with the Trust?'

'Not legally, no. Colin made us guardians, as you know, because Roderick is Donald's grandfather and I'm the only mother he's known. So, the Laird gave Roderick the Factor's job because he thought it would be good for Donald to live in the Factor's house as he too might become Factor one day, like his father.'

'I see.'

'He was also concerned about Donald's welfare. He told us he had heard stories that Roddy was bullying Donald and he was concerned that Donald had very few friends and spent a lot of time in his room.'

'And is there any truth in what he's saying?'

'Yes. It's been a tough time for our boys. Imagine how you would feel if you found out your parents were not your parents and that your brother was not your brother. So there's been tension between the boys, but it seems to have settled now. Donald lost all his friends when Colin began taking him around the island, showing off, so he's become less sociable. But he's a close friend of the teacher's daughter Mary and visits her regularly.'

'And you want to know whether the Laird could dissolve the Trust for the reasons he's given you?'

134

'Yes.'

I felt a headache starting. Talking about all this was so stressful.

'Well, I would obviously need to read the terms of the Trust Deed, but in any normal trust set up for a minor, if the guardians appointed turn out to be disreputable, dishonest or in any other way unsuitable to look after a minor, then yes, I'm afraid the trustees could remove them. I think Donald's welfare, however, is a graver concern than any misdemeanors Roderick has committed in his role as Factor.'

She gave me some time to digest this, then continued.

'The Laird would, of course, require to prove his case and if you contested it, there would need to be a court hearing to decide Donald's future.'

'What do you think we should do? Is it worthwhile appointing you as our solicitor so that you can get a copy of the Trust Deed just now?'

'I suppose it depends on this unknown person who is sending the letters. Do you have any idea who they are or why they are sending the letters?'

'I think it may be the local postmaster who took over from us when Roderick became the Factor, but I've no evidence. The constable is going to make some discreet inquiries and I think if we can put a stop to him sending the letters, we won't need to worry about that side of things.'

'But if it's not the postmaster and the letters continue to be sent, is there anything other than a bit of poaching and taking eggs in place of rent that they could accuse Roderick of?'

I shook my head.

'No.'

Although Maude had helped us deal with Colin and had seen the evidence the private investigators had come up with, she knew nothing about James Adams and Roderick's involvement in his death. If anyone got to know about those secrets from Roderick's time in Canada, who knew what they might accuse him of? But foolishly I decided not to share that with Maude.

'In that case, I think you should sit tight. If the worse comes to the worst, then I will get a hold of the Trust Deed quickly and we can see whether defending your right to be Donald's guardian would be the proper thing to do.'

'I don't know how to thank you, Maude. I feel lighter already. Please don't let me keep you from your bed any longer.'

CHAPTER FORTY-SEVEN

I shared a bed with my mother while the two boys shared the other bed and we all woke up the next morning feeling refreshed and went down for breakfast. We had porridge and toast, not so different from back home but also orange juice and crumpets with butter and jam. We ate in the kitchen, which was in the basement and not as bright as the other rooms, while the maid went about her duties. I had arranged a quick visit with Janet before we headed off to catch the train to Helensburgh, so asked Katie for directions to Whitefield Road where Janet lived.

She lived in a sandstone tenement, but it wasn't as grand as the place where Katie lived. She had a small room that had a bed, a wardrobe, a dressing table and a washstand with a basin, jug and soap dish sitting on top with a towel hanging over a rail on the side. I wondered why Janet preferred to live here rather than in North Uist with Johnny, even if she had to share with my mother and father.

'Hello Janet. Give me a big hug.'

She willingly gave me a hug and both our eyes were shining with happiness as we looked at one another.

'It's so lovely to see you, Chrissie. How are Roderick and the boys and your mother and father?'

'Och, we've had a challenging time of it, to be honest, Janet, that I'll tell you about, but I feel things are settling down now. I hope so anyway. We're really looking forward to this holiday and to seeing Morag and her new husband. What do you think of her getting married like that without telling us?'

'I think if I ever get married, I would like a proper wedding,' she smiled, then asked. 'How's Johnny?'

'Johnny is fine. I know he misses you, but he's been doing a lot of work for the new schoolteacher, so I think that's taking his mind off things.'

'New schoolteacher?'

'Yes. Her name's Bunty Hepworth. She comes from Manchester. She's a widow - her husband was killed in the war - and has a young daughter about the same age as Donald called Mary.'

'Is she pretty?'

I laughed.

'You're not jealous, are you? I thought you might have had a new boyfriend yourself by this time.'

'I wish I could find someone else, Chrissie, but none of the men I've gone out with are a patch on Johnny. He makes me laugh, and he's so kind. He'll be a real catch for some woman.'

'Then why let him go? Why don't you come back to North Uist? I would love to have you close by. Although Bunty and I have become friends, it's different from having you there.'

'I can't come back. I love my job here and I'm ambitious. I'm now a Ward Sister and one day I want to become a Matron. If I'd come back to do the District Nurse's job Johnny told me about, I would have been stuck in that job all my life.'

'Don't you want children, Janet?'

'Not now, no. They're the last thing I want. I have this restlessness in me. I want to find out about life and all it can offer.'

It surprised me that Janet was so ambitious. We were both just servants less than ten years ago, but she had been through the horrors of war and we all knew how that could change a person. She obviously wanted more out of life and who was I to try to stop her from doing that just because I wanted her to marry my brother?

She made tea, and while we drank it, and ate digestives, I told her all about what was happening in the family, about the boys, about the letters, the Rural, everything. It was such a relief to talk to someone I could fully trust about all my hopes and fears. Suddenly, the clock struck the hour and I let out a screech.

'I better get going or I'll be late. It was lovely to see you, Janet. Take care of yourself. I hope you find what you're looking for.'

When I got back to Walmer Crescent, everyone was ready and waiting for me. This time we took the subway into the city to get to

138

Queen Street station, where we would get the train for Helensburgh. At last, we and our bags were all on the train and we set off for the next part of our adventure. Morag, and who I assumed was her new husband, Michael, were waiting on the platform for us when we arrived. After introductions and hugs, they took us to their motorcar, which they had bought to carry hotel guests to and from the station. There wasn't enough room for us all, so my mother and the boys went with Michael, while Morag and I walked along the front to the hotel.

What a lovely seaside town it was, with a long promenade, a bandstand, and a bowling green. I also spotted one of the new picture houses I had read about in my magazine and hoped we could go along to that one day. The hotel was beautiful. It had been converted from a house that a wealthy family had lived in previously and there was separate accommodation on the grounds for Morag and Michael to live in. They hoped to accommodate up to ten guests at a time and thought it would be a success as Helensburgh was becoming not only the place for the wealthy to visit but also middle-class people looking for a seaside holiday. As I've said before, God works in mysterious ways, and my sister marrying a hotelier was to be very beneficial for what I eventually had to do.

CHAPTER FORTY-EIGHT

When we arrived back in North Uist, we were all exhausted but elated at the same time. Roderick was waiting for us with the cart and we dropped my mother at the croft before making our way home to the Factor's house. The boys were chattering ten to the dozen; they were so full of what they had done while we were on holiday.

'We went to a picture house, *Athair*,' said Roddy, 'to see Rob Roy MacGregor. It was so exciting seeing all the men fighting with each other.'

'And it was rather beautiful too, Roderick.' I added. 'All the ushers were so elegant, carpets so plush and the seats so comfortable. I wonder if we'll ever get a picture house here one day.'

'I doubt it,' he said, smiling at the notion of such a thing coming to our small island.

'And Roddy and I won a sandcastle competition, *Dadaidh*. It was great fun. I hope you'll come with us the next time we go.'

'We also went to a concert in the bandstand on the front. There was a full orchestra and the music was lovely,' added my mother.

'The hotel is splendid, Roderick. I think it would do you the power of good to come along with us when we next visit. Most of the rooms look out over the Firth of Clyde and I believe you can go fishing for mackerel and the like.'

'I think we have enough fish in our own waters, Chrissie. I don't need to go on a long journey to Helensburgh to do the fishing.'

'Och, don't be such an old grump,' I laughed.

Once the boys went to bed, Roderick and I settled down by the fire, which was unlit at this time of year. He brushed my hair, and I felt a sense of contentment as we sat companionably. Morag had tempted me to have my hair cut into a bob, but I was glad I hadn't now. However, she had shown me how instead of wearing a bun at the nape of my neck, I could wind my hair into two braids and twist them round at either side of my ears and it would give the illusion that I had a bob. I would speak to Bunty and maybe we could try doing it together.

'I can see you've enjoyed your holiday, Chrissie, but I wonder if you have news for me from Maude.'

'Of course, I have, silly.'

'I thought perhaps all that high living had turned your head.'

He kissed the top of my head as he brushed my hair slowly and gently so I turned my face up to his and pressed my lips against his eagerly. How I had missed him.

'You must go on holiday more often, my pet,' he said, his voice husky with desire. 'Now hurry and tell me what Maude said and then we can go to bed.'

I tingled with anticipation and was glad that the news I was sharing was not so bad that it would spoil the moment and, in my excitement, I forgot to ask if there was any news from the constable on Ian Fraser.

CHAPTER FORTY-NINE

The opportunity for Bunty to find out more about when Heather was born came along when Mary's birthday was approaching. She was making Mary and Donald their tea when they came in from school on their usual Wednesday arrangement. She had learned now to bake a little and had made them little sponge cakes. While they were eating, Bunty asked Mary if she would like to have a special tea for her birthday.

'It won't be long now, only another two weeks. If you want to have a birthday tea, we could invite some of your other friends from school, as well as Auntie Chrissie and Roddy. Would you like that?'

'I would love that, Mummy. Will you bake me a cake?'

'Well, I don't know if my baking has improved that much, but I could ask Auntie Chrissie to help me. I'm sure she would know.'

'I didn't have a birthday party last year.' said Donald.

'Why not chook?'

'Well, my proper mother died when I was born, and it made me feel sad.'

Bunty saw her opportunity. She wondered if he knew any more about his mother than he had when she had asked the class to do their family tree.

'I think you and Mary should have a joint party, then. We could also celebrate your mother's birthday if you like. Do you know when her birthday is and what age she would be now if she had lived?'

'Well, when we did the family tree, my mummy told me a little more about Heather, so I know she was born in August, but I can't remember what date. She was sixteen when she had me and I'm going to be ten in December, so she would have been,' he screwed his face up and looked at his fingers, 'twenty-six this year.'

'You're good at your sums, Donald. Well done.'

As far as Bunty was concerned, this was evidence that Heather was her father's daughter as he went missing in the winter of 1896 and a child was born 8 months later. She could not be Roderick's child, so it meant Donald was living with a family who was not his kin. She had more claim on him as his aunt than Roderick Macdonald did. For Bunty, a blood relationship was more important than who had fed, clothed, and nurtured you, perhaps because the man who brought her up had never nurtured her.

She relaxed a little about the letters as she was enjoying what she thought of as her courtship with Johnny. She was sure he liked her more than a friend, although he had said nothing directly. But Chrissie had told her she had spoken to Janet when she had visited her sister and she was sure she wouldn't be returning to North Uist. She had ambitions that couldn't be fulfilled on this island. Bunty felt sure all she had to do was wait and things would work out for them. She just needed to be patient.

CHAPTER FIFTY

Not long after the harvest, there were articles in the paper about Mr Lloyd George accusing him of taking money from newspaper owners for peerages, and Roderick thought he would probably need to resign, which would mean a general election. He was right, but it wasn't the peerages that caused the problem. It was the news that an American publisher was paying him a lot of money for the book he had written about his war experiences. The public were more upset about that than about peerages, and despite Mr Lloyd George's assurances that he would use the money he earned from the book for good causes, the Conservatives forced him to resign.

The result was that a general election was called for 15 November, only a month away. I was thrilled. This would be my first time using my vote, and I wondered if other women felt the same. But who to vote for? We had Mr Donald Murray, the Liberal who the people of the Western Isles had voted for in 1918, but there were bound to be other candidates. I thought it might be a good idea to invite the women who could now vote to come along to a meeting to talk about this exciting event. Perhaps they weren't sure who to vote for either, so it would be good to hear their thoughts. At the next Rural meeting I put my idea to the members. They were in favour and thought it might be a way of getting other women to join our group, so we agreed to put up posters all over the island, not just in Lochmaddy. Bunty and I volunteered to go round with them.

Our first stop was Lochmaddy post office and, as we expected, Mr Fraser was no more supportive of this proposal than he had been of the Rural. I suspected it was partly to do with the conversation Archie had had with him. Although he hadn't told Ian Fraser that it was me who suspected him of sending the letters, I'm sure he must have guessed. Archie had told Roderick there was nothing to support my suspicions, but that didn't make them go away. I just didn't like the man.

144

'What's this, Mrs Macdonald?' he said. 'It's bad enough you women getting the vote, but it's a step too far organising a meeting to discuss the candidates. What do any of you know about politics?'

'Well Mr Fraser, it's true we know little about politics, but if we are to vote for the government of this country, then we need to learn, don't you agree?'

He harrumphed but said nothing else. He had never forgiven me for encouraging his wife Sarah to join us, although the poor woman never had. I hoped when she saw the poster that she would stand up to him and come to vote with us. Katie had sent me an anti-suffragette poster from the last election, which made women out to be ignorant and not fit to have the vote, so I was determined to find out as much as I could. It would be a disaster if they took away the vote from us because we didn't show enough interest in politics. Women had fought so hard for us to have this right; I was determined not to let them down.

I talked to Roderick and read the papers to find out about the candidates and learned that two men were standing. The present MP, Mr Donald Murray, and a National Liberal called Sir William Cotts, who was, according to Roderick, a friend of Lord Leverhulme who was proposing to set up a model village and a fishing business to supply employment in Stornoway on the island of Lewis.

'But it's the land that's important to us here on the islands, Roderick. So, the candidates should concentrate on that. Poor Johnny still hasn't received an offer of land from the Board of Agriculture.'

'I know Chrissie, but the election is about a lot more than just our islands, so you should try to understand national politics as well.'

He was right, of course, so I did more reading and tried to understand the difference between the Conservatives, the National Liberals, and the Liberals. I also found out there were to be Labour, Nationalist and Communist candidates standing in

145

other areas of Scotland, England, and Northern Ireland. It was quite overwhelming trying to fathom out what all these different parties stood for and who else I might vote for if there had been any of these other candidates standing for the Western Isles.

Roddy was interested in what I was reading, and he and I had some discussions about the various parties. I was pleased he was taking an interest in the election, as it showed he was maturing and would be ready to go to the high school next year. Fortunately, he had passed the bursary exam, so we didn't need to worry about finding the money to send him to Portree. He said it was Bunty's fault he hadn't done well in last year's test, but I suspected he had to blame someone else in case Roderick took the slipper to him again.

At last, it was time for the meeting. We had agreed to hold it over in Carinish Hall where we had all gone to the ceilidh earlier this year as it might encourage women from different parts of the island to come along. There were more settlements on that side of the island than there were near Lochmaddy. I stood biting my lip, wondering if anyone would turn up while Bunty made sure the fire was stoked with peat. The wind had whipped up, and it was bitter outside, so it delighted me when a good number of women that I didn't know and who weren't part of the Rural came to the meeting.

'So, if I might call the meeting to order,' I said. 'I know not all women can vote yet, but it's a historic time for women like me who can vote for the first time. How many of you could vote in the last election?'

Only a couple of hands went up, although I could tell from their ages that more of the women would have been eligible to vote.

'I didn't bother voting,' said Morag. 'I couldn't see what difference it would make to our lives here.'

'But if everyone thought like that, no-one would bother voting and the rich and powerful could do whatever they like. Although we only have two candidates standing here, in other parts of Scotland and the rest of Britain, there are Socialists, Communists

146

and even Scottish Nationalists, so there could be a major change in government by the end of the year.'

'Och, I know you're right, Chrissie. So, I'll vote this time.'

There were some cheers from the other women. At the end of the meeting, we agreed that all women who could vote would meet at the schoolhouse and go into the polling station together. Bunty agreed to watch the children if any women couldn't get their child looked after, as she was still too young to vote.

The night before the election, I couldn't sleep. I was excited about casting my vote for the first time but also a little anxious that there might be some angry scenes when we women tried to vote. It turned out not everyone was happy about women having the vote still, and someone had defaced our posters and replaced them with horrible anti-suffrage posters like the one Katie had sent me. I thought Roderick might have been unhappy that I wasn't going to the polling booth with him, but he told me he was proud of what I was doing and that in fact he might even join our group to show his support.

The boys were off school as the voting was taking place there, so it was closed for the day. They were happy to have a holiday and indeed there was a festive feeling in the air. Roderick brought round the buggy and Roddy, Donald, and I climbed in. When we got to the school, there was bunting fluttering on the fence and there were men handing out leaflets about the two candidates. Mr McIver had set up a sweetie stall and there were lots of children gathered round. My two asked for pennies to buy some, but I told them they could get them later as I needed to get along to the schoolhouse so that I could join the other women.

To my delight there was a large group of women already gathered and I eagerly joined them. Someone shouted to me to go to the front.

'We need a leader, Chrissie, so you better get up to the front,' shouted Shona McIver.

I can't tell you what that meant to me, but I can tell you my heart swelled with gratitude and pride that the women had such confidence in me.

It was a short march to the polling station, but we had spontaneously begun singing a traditional waulking song that women would sing when they were on the last stage of tweed making. I sang the verses and the women behind me joined in to sing the chorus. However, as we approached the school building, a group of men stood in a line holding up anti-suffrage posters and shouting insults towards us. We stopped marching and fell silent. Ian Fraser was raising his fist and shouting the loudest. He scared me, I can't deny it, but no-one was going to stop us from voting that day. So, I began to march and sing again, and the women joined in behind me. I don't know where I got the courage from, but it made those men move. Then Roderick joined me, and Alex McIver, the Reverend Macaulay and many other husbands of the women in the Rural and we all walked proudly together into the polling station. I felt I had at last reached my higher self.

They had set the school room out with a table at the door, where voters registered. I held my breath in case my name wasn't there, but it only took a minute for the man to hand me a voting slip with the names of the two candidates and which party they represented. On the other side of the room, were two timber booths set up with a table inside and a pen and ink for us to mark our X on the voting paper. It was a secret vote, so I didn't need to vote for the same candidate as Roderick. I would, but not because he was forcing me to, but because we had discussed the two candidates and had both agreed that Mr Donald Murray would stand for the interests of the crofters better than Sir William Cotts. I'll never forget the thrill as I dipped my pen in the ink and wrote my X. Nothing would ever replace the special feeling of that day, even although I voted in every election in the future.

Unfortunately, voting for Mr Murray made no difference as Sir William, a National Liberal and a supporter of Mr Lloyd George, won the election in the Western Isles by a majority of just over a thousand. There was quite a low turnout of voters and an even lower turnout of women. It surprised me, as I had hoped the little group of women who had marched together that day would have some influence, but it was not to be. The Conservatives won that election, closely followed by the Labour Party and Mr Lloyd George never held office again.

CHAPTER FIFTY-ONE

Bunty decided it was time to move things forward with Johnny. He had been helping her with minor jobs round the house and had been for his tea almost every week for the last few months. She and Mary had been to several ceilidhs with him, Chrissie, and the boys. Boring old Roderick never went along to anything that was fun. Janet seemed to be out of the picture completely, as Johnny never mentioned her now and he looked less sad than when Bunty had first got to know him.

Tonight, was the night. She had asked Chrissie if Mary could stay over as she sometimes did nowadays. When she had told Mary that Johnny was coming over and they were going to have some time together, she had said she wished Johnny was her daddy. Bunty felt a lump in her throat. She wished that too, and if things worked out tonight, then he would be.

'It would be nice, wouldn't it? But I'm not sure Uncle Johnny likes me like that.'

'Why not, Mummy? You are a very bonnie woman. That's what I heard Mr McIver in the shop say one day.'

She smiled at the Scottish lilt her daughter was gaining in her speech and hoped that all would go well. She winked at Mary and said, 'Well, who knows what will happen tonight. Maybe you'll get a new daddy.'

It was December and close to Christmas, so she had asked Johnny to bring her an extra creel of peat. She relied on him now and liked the feeling of being cared for. He always made a fuss of Mary when he came and the jobs he did round the house made her life easier. After dressing carefully, she brushed her hair till it shone. Hotpot was on the menu, his favourite meal, and there was some of her mulled wine, which he liked to drink with it.

The minutes on the clock ticked by slowly and she wished it would speed up. She hoped what she planned tonight would be the right time and he would be ready to take the next step. If only it was, she would be happy and would consider giving up this desire for revenge against Roderick. If she got found out, she now realised, her relationship with Johnny would surely end, no matter what happened tonight.

At 6.30 pm on the dot, Johnny arrived. He didn't need to knock as her door was open, as most of the islanders' doors were. She couldn't help comparing it to Manchester, where everyone locked their doors for fear of robbers. That was something she didn't have to fear in Uist. She felt the locals were accepting her and Mary and although Donald was still Mary's closest friend; she was popular in school and had made other friends that she played with.

'Hello Bunty, it's a cold one tonight,' said Johnny, blowing into his hands as he removed his coat, scarf, and cap.

'Where are your gloves, man? You'll get frostbite on a night like this.'

'I know, I know. Is that hotpot I smell?'

'It is,' she smiled. 'Sit at the table and I'll dish up. Mary's staying with Donald tonight, so we have the house to ourselves.'

'Aye, we never got to stay with any of our pals. There was hardly enough room for us all in our house without having a visitor over. You and Chrissie are lucky you've got space.'

For Bunty, the little schoolhouse was much smaller than what she had been used to in Manchester, but she didn't tell Johnny that. She wanted him to think she felt lucky to live here. When they had eaten, they sat at the fire. The peat was burning brightly with a sweet fragrance in the hearth. The copper tongs and shovel were gleaming in the light from the flames and Bunty felt a cosy, safe feeling she rarely felt. Johnny coughed and smiled at her. He looked uncomfortable, she thought. He must sense something different tonight and was wondering how to handle it.

'It feels funny, Mary not being here tonight,' he said, smiling over at her.

'Yes, it does. She loves you; you know. Only today she said she wished you were her daddy.'

151

Johnny coughed and took out his pipe. It was his way of buying time; she understood that. She had seen him doing it before. When he had filled his pipe and had it going, he turned to her.

'I know Mary is fond of me, Bunty, and I am fond of her too, but I could never be her daddy.'

'Why not, Johnny? You seem less sad about breaking up with Janet now than when I first met you and you're not the kind of man who would want to be alone all his life, are you?'

He didn't answer, just looked at her in that dumb way he had sometimes, not knowing how to respond.

'North Uist is home to me now, Johnny. You know how much I love it here, so you wouldn't need to worry that I would want to up and leave.'

'I know how much you love it here, and I'm glad you've settled. It's nice for Chrissie and Donald to have friends they can rely on. After what happened with Colin, things have been difficult for them both.'

The conversation was moving away from where Bunty wanted it to go, so she rose to put more peat on the fire and tripped. Right onto Johnny's lap. He caught her in his arms, and she could smell the mellow aroma of pipe tobacco on his breath. He was so close, her stomach contracted with desire. As she looked into his eyes, she wished he would look at her the way Harry used to, so full of love and longing for her. But there was only surprise. Had she misjudged what would happen?

Then their lips touched, and surprise turned to desire. His lips caressed hers like a whisper, and Bunty felt her breasts swell with passion as he pressed his body close to hers. She could feel his arousal pushing against her, so gently slipped from his lap onto the rug in front of the fire and drew him down towards her. She kissed him, still gently, not wishing to scare him off, and touched his hardness. He sighed, and she knew she had him. His tongue searched for hers and his hands stroked her neck then moved to her breasts. Not wishing to lose the momentum, she drew up her skirt, but he pulled back from her momentarily and she thought all was lost.

'Is this really what you want, Bunty?' he asked, his voice hoarse with desire.

'Yes, Johnny, yes,' she moaned.

And then he was inside her. He was hers.

When it was over, she leaned into him, expecting him to lie with her in the warmth of their love, cuddling and caressing each other the way she and Harry had always done, but he pulled away from her. He stood up abruptly and quickly pulled on his trousers and tucked in his shirt. She had no choice but to stand up too and to pull her skirt down. She felt abandoned.

'We can't do this, Bunty.'

'We already have. Didn't you enjoy it?' she said, taking a step towards him and looking up at him with dewy eyes. He stepped back.

'Please forgive me, Bunty. We're two lonely people taking comfort in one another, but the truth is I'm still in love with Janet. It wouldn't be fair to you or Mary to let you think something might come from tonight. The wee one would become confused. I'm so sorry.'

Bunty felt as if he had stabbed her in the heart with a knife; the pain she felt was so physical. Why had he led her on, made love to her? He had let her think she was attractive to him when she clearly wasn't. He had used her for his physical desires and was now tossing her aside like an old rag.

'There's no need to be sorry, Johnny. I understand. Your heart lies elsewhere. You can't help it. I expect you'll want to go now that I've satisfied your sexual needs.'

He came close and took her face in his hands.

'Och Bunty. I didn't mean to take advantage, and I thought you wanted it too.'

Tears plopped onto her cheeks, and he wiped them away gently with his fingers. She shivered, still craving his touch.

'I hope this doesn't mean we can't be friends anymore. Over the last year, I've become fond of you and Mary. I would hate if this spoiled our friendship.'

'I'm an adult, Johnny. I can handle rejection. I've lived with it all my life.'

'Don't say that,' he said, taking her hands. 'It's not that I'm rejecting you. It's just not the right time. I don't want to hurt you or Mary when I'm still so mixed up in my mind about Janet. Say you understand.'

So, he was trying to let her down gently by saying it wasn't the end. It was just the wrong time. What a coward? Her sadness turned to anger, but she played along with his game.

'I understand Johnny. Sorry if I was a little upset. I do like you very much and I'll wait until you're ready. There's no rush. I would rather I was the one you wanted truly in your heart and not a second-hand substitute.'

'Thanks Bunty. I'll see you and Mary at the Hogmanay Ceilidh, won't I?'

'Yes, of course.'

But it was over as far as Bunty was concerned. Her and Mary could manage without Johnny MacIntosh. It was time to get back to what she had come to North Uist for.

CHAPTER FIFTY-TWO

I was sitting at my desk doing my paperwork the day the constable arrived. It was Mrs McAllister who let him in and came to tell me.

'The Constable's at the door, Chrissie. He wants to see Roderick. Shall I show him in?'

'Yes, of course. Will you bring some tea and a scone? It's cold outside and I'm sure he'll welcome a hot drink.'

When he came in, however, I could see something was bothering him and he might need more than a cup of tea.

'Hello Archie, it's good to see you. How are you? Are you looking forward to the Hogmanay celebrations?'

We were on first-name terms after the sensitive way he had dealt with Lachlan when he had deserted from the army. I would always be grateful for his kindness. He didn't answer my questions but got to the point of his visit.

'I need to speak to Roderick urgently, Chrissie. Do you know when he'll be home?'

'Soon. He'll be back for his lunch. He's out checking the grounds and calling on people about unpaid rent.'

'Is it alright if I wait? I've something to show him.'

'Yes, of course. Would you like a wee whisky while you're waiting?'

'I would love one, but better not while I'm on duty.'

'I'll get you a cup of tea then and one of Mrs McAllister's scones.'

Although I put on a bright face, my stomach was skittering with nerves. Whatever he wanted to talk to Roderick about looked serious. Although I had asked Flora to bring up the tea, I went to collect it so that I could warn Roderick when he came in. I had just reached the kitchen when the back door opened and he arrived, stamping his boots, and blowing on his hands.

'It's freezing outside. I hope you've got some of my favourite broth, Flora.'

'I do Roderick, I do. But the constable's here to see you. Do you want to wait until you've spoken to him?'

'I can take him a cup of tea if you want Roderick, while Flora gets your soup. I'll keep him talking for five minutes.'

'If you don't mind, Chrissie. I'm starving. You look worried. Do you think it's something serious? It's not really a time for poachers, so it can't be that.'

'I don't know, Roderick, but I just have a bad feeling. Sup your soup as quickly as you can, and we'll find out.'

Archie and I made small talk while he drank his tea and ate his scone, but I was relieved when Roderick came into the room. Archie immediately put down his tea and wiped the crumbs from off his uniform.

'Hello Roderick,' he said, holding his hand out to shake Roderick's.

'Hello Archie. What brings you here today? Not poachers, I take it.'

'No. It's more serious than that. I've received this letter,' he said, handing over an envelope.

My heart missed a beat. Was it another anonymous letter from our secret enemy?

Roderick sat down and took the letter out of the envelope. He scanned it, then read it slowly and with each word, his face grew paler and more drawn. His health hadn't been good for several months. He had a persistent cough and was often tired, but despite my pleas to see Dr McInnes, he refused, batting away all my arguments about why he should go.

'What is it Roderick?'

'Someone is accusing me of murder,' he said, handing the letter over to me.

My hands trembled as I read the thin scratchy writing.

The Mounties in Canada questioned Roderick Macdonald about the murt of a man called James Adams, and he ran back to Scotland to stop them from putting him in priosan. He's not a fit person to be the Factor and I've written to the Laird about him. You

156

need to do something about that man and get your bosses to open the case again.

My God, did someone know what happened back in Canada? But how? My mother and father were the only people who knew, and they wouldn't have written such a letter. Why was this happening? Who hated us so much they wanted to destroy us? My thoughts went to Ian Fraser. But how would he know anything about what happened to us in Canada? So far as I knew, he had always lived in Scotland.

'I'm going to ignore it, Roderick. We don't deal with anonymous accusations, but I'm afraid word will get out. You know what this place is like. Nothing gets past Murdo the postie. The envelope wasn't completely stuck down when I received it and I'm afraid my housekeeper, Mary McIntyre, might have read it as it was lying on my desk when she was dusting.'

I was grateful that Archie was not going to act on the letter, but I knew someone who would. The Laird had warned Roderick that if there were any further allegations of misconduct, he would be out of a job. We needed to find out who was writing these letters before it was too late.

'What can we do about this, Archie? This is the third anonymous letter telling lies about Roderick. They sent the other two to the Laird.'

'Do you have any idea who could have written the letters?'

'At first we thought it might have been an islander who was unhappy about Roderick getting the job as Factor, but he's been doing the job for three years now, so I don't think it can be. I've asked the women in the Rural, but they can't think of anyone who would be so vindictive.'

'Perhaps it's not an islander. Although there are some Gaelic words in the letter, very few of us write in the Gaelic because we only learned to read and write in the English. I'll have a think and maybe have a quiet word with one or two people. I don't think you'll be able to keep this quiet, so it won't make any difference if I mention it discretely.'

157

'Thanks Archie,' said Roderick, coughing. 'Can I ask you something while you're here?'

'Yes, of course,'

'If you showed the letter to your bosses, would they contact the Canadian authorities if they believed the accusation?'

'I'm not sure Roderick. I doubt it, but if the Canadian authorities contacted them, that might be a different story. But don't you be worrying. I'll not be showing the letter to my bosses. In fact, here, put it on the fire. The fewer people who see the letter, the better.'

The three of us watched silently as the letter crackled and crumpled in the flames, but its destruction changed nothing.

CHAPTER FIFTY-THREE

The constable was right. Word got out, as I discovered when my mother visited me unexpectedly a few days after new year. Mother was always uncomfortable when she came to the house. Although she and Flora were friends and would visit each other from time to time, she was used to sitting in the kitchen. Coming upstairs to the sitting room was a different story, and she paced the room nervously.

'Sit down *Mathair*, you're making me nervous.'

'You should be nervous,' she said, as she sat in Roderick's chair at the fire. I hoped he wouldn't come back before she left. He didn't like anyone sitting in his chair.

'What do you mean?' I asked, although I already knew, but I wanted to know what people were saying.

'Everyone's saying your husband is a murderer, Chrissie, that's what I mean. Mary, who works for the constable, told Morag Campbell, who told me that Murdo had delivered a letter to Archie, accusing Roderick of being a murderer.'

'It's true *Mathair*. Archie brought the letter to let us see it. But because it's anonymous, he's not taking any action. In fact, he threw it in the fire.'

'Throwing it in the fire won't make all this go away. Who knows about what happened in Canada?'

'No-one. Only you and *Athair*. And remember, Roderick is not a murderer.'

'No, but he got rid of a body and took the man's wife to live with him. If the story got out, there would be a terrible scandal, not just for you, but for Donald. Someone has *an droch-shuil* on the pair of you.'

The evil eye. I thought back to when I had first met Bunty. Surely it couldn't be her? We were close friends. She knew a little about our history, but not about James Adams. No, I refused to believe it. Our friendship felt so strong and it wouldn't, would it, if she had put the evil eye on us.

'Don't be so superstitious *Mathair.*'

I tried to shrug off the sense of dread I was feeling when I went to collect the boys from school. Although the other mothers nodded and smiled at me as usual, I sensed a coolness but chided myself that it was just me. However, when the boys came out of school, they ran straight for me.

'*Mamaidh,* Flora McIntyre said my *dadaidh*'s a murderer. It's not true, is it?' cried Donald.

'Of course, it's not true, is it *Mathair*? My *Athair* would never do a thing like that.'

It pleased me that Roddy wasn't taking the allegations as the truth.

'But why did she say it then? People don't tell lies.'

'Don't be so stupid, Donald. People tell lies all the time.'

'Right boys, hush now. Let's buy you a sweetie and then get you home. We'll talk about it there.'

When we went into the shop, Mrs McIver was chatting with some of the other mothers who had collected their children from school, but when they saw it was us, they stopped. I smiled at them.

'Don't stop on my account. I like a good gossip as much as anyone.'

'Och no, Chrissie, it's not the gossip we're having. We're just talking about the weather. What can I get you then?'

'Just some sweets for the boys, Shona. Thank you.'

While the boys picked the sweets they wanted, no-one spoke. They just stared at us, no doubt wondering if they were in the company of a murderer's wife.

CHAPTER FIFTY-FOUR

While the boys were having their tea in the kitchen, I spoke to Roderick about what happened.

'We're going to have to tell Roddy and Donald about the letter. Word has obviously got out, as Archie said it would. Flora McIntyre has already told Donald that you're a murderer, and the women were all gossiping about us when I went into the shop. I think I need to tell Bunty about the letter too, as I want her to protect the boys from being bullied.'

'Be careful what you tell that woman. I still think it could be her who's sending the letters. Remember when she said Heather looked like her stepfather, we thought there was a possibility she might be James Adams' daughter.'

I did remember but we hadn't spoken of it again, so I had put it to the back of my mind. I still couldn't believe Bunty was behind the letters and prayed that she wasn't. Our friendship would have been one big lie and it didn't feel like that to me.

'What shall we tell the boys and Bunty then?'

'We'll tell them the truth. That someone murdered a man way back when I first went to Canada, but his body was only discovered a few years ago. The Mounties asked me if I knew anything, but I didn't. I was never a suspect, only a potential witness.'

How I wished it was the whole truth. There was so much more to what happened with James Adams than this story we were going to tell the boys. I hated lying, but there was nothing else for it. We had to protect Roderick and our family. No-one must find out the truth for all our sakes.

I was relieved when the boys accepted our explanation, and we discussed what they should say if the other children said anything to them. I also spoke to Bunty the following day after school.

'Hello Bunty, could I have a word? It's about the gossip that's going around about Roderick.'

'What gossip? No-one has said anything to me.'

'Didn't you hear Flora McIntyre telling Donald that his father was a murderer yesterday?'

'A murderer? No, I didn't. I heard them squabbling, but I didn't hear what they were arguing about.'

'Look, can we go to your house, and I'll tell you all about it?'

I told her about the letter the constable received and what it had accused Roderick of. I also told her that Archie had thrown the letter in the fire as the police did not act on anonymous letters.

'But the truth of it is Bunty, Roderick was never a suspect. A Mountie simply questioned him because he used to go to the Golden Sheaf Hotel sometimes. Someone had suggested to the Mounties that he might have seen something as the hotel was the last place anyone saw this James Adams.'

'So, he didn't know James Adams or his wife?'

I hesitated. Why was Bunty asking about his wife? I hadn't mentioned his wife.

'I don't know if he had a wife, Bunty. Why do you ask?'

Her cheeks flushed pink, and she laughed.

'Sorry, I just assumed he had a wife. I heard they used to marry mail-order brides way back as they needed women to keep house while they worked on the farms. So, did Roderick know James Adams?'

'No, he didn't. Poor man. We only heard about him the day I arrived in Canada. It was Bill Preston, the owner of the Golden Sheaf who told us about his skeleton being found by our neighbour, Aleksander Bukowski.'

'What a terrible way to end up. Buried in unconsecrated ground without your family and friends around you.'

'Is that tears I see in your eyes, Bunty? You're a right soft wee thing, aren't you?' I said, giving her a hug.

'Don't be silly, Chrissie,' she said, pulling out her handkerchief, 'I just have a bit of dust in my eye. You get away home now. I'll keep an eye out for any bullying and tell them that Roderick was just a witness. Is that okay?'

'Yes, thanks, Bunty. I appreciate your help once again with my boys. How are things going with you and Johnny? I know how much you like him.'

'Yes, I do like him, Chrissie. He's a good friend to me and Mary. But we will never be more than friends. I think he's still carrying a torch for Janet.'

'Do you? I thought that was over and to be honest, I was hoping maybe you and him might have got together. It would have been lovely to have you as my sister-in-law.'

'I would have liked that too.'

Her lip trembled as she said this, so I gave her a hug again.

CHAPTER FIFTY-FIVE

A letter arrived from the Laird in the new year, telling us he had received another anonymous letter and would visit us in February to discuss the contents. Roderick was distraught even although we were expecting it after Archie's visit.

'What am I going to do, Chrissie? I'll lose my job and although I told you I was okay; I know my health's getting worse. What kind of job am I going to be fit for and who would want to employ a suspected murderer, anyway?'

'You're not a murderer, Roderick. You need to hold on to that fact.'

'But I covered up a man's murder and buried him without a proper funeral.'

'Yes, but you also looked after his widow and possibly his daughter and gave them a better life than they would have had with that ruffian.'

What Roderick said was true. I couldn't deny it. But it was all so long ago. Who could have found out, and why did it matter to them? Although Mr Abernethy had represented Colin in his claim for the custody of Donald, nothing about what happened with James Adams had come out from the private investigators. Indeed, Colin had made sure that Heather's death certificate was changed to hide her Cree heritage.

Thinking about Colin and his use of private investigators made me wonder if it would be worth our while hiring one. Morag had asked me all those months ago if it could be someone from Canada who was sending the letters and I had thought it a ridiculous notion. But now I remembered back to when I arrived in Canada and had heard the story of the skeleton from Bill. He said the Canadian government had traced a relative of James Adams and it was they who had given consent to the sale of his land to Mr Bukowski.

'What do you think, Roderick? We could ask Mr Abernethy to hire a private investigator for us.'

'But why Chrissie? I don't understand.'

'Well, the only person, other than my mother and father, who would know anything about James Adams and how he died, would be a relative of his. Remember when Bill Preston told us about the skeleton? He also said there was a surviving relative.'

'Yes, I see. So, if we can find this relative, we can find out if it's them who are sending the letters and put a stop to it. Hiring a private investigator will be expensive, Chrissie, and if I'm to lose my job, we need to save what money we have.'

I thought about what would convince him to go for my idea and, of course, it was obvious. Bunty. If hiring private detectives would lead to us finding out she was involved, then he would hire them. They would hopefully prove her innocence if my instinct was right, but in doing so we might find the real culprit.

'Roderick, you can't worry about money now. You think Bunty's behind the letters, so the private investigators will find out if you're right. Surely that's worth spending the money on.'

We made an appointment to see Mr Abernethy and put the question to him about hiring a private detective. He supped on his pipe while we were talking, never having asked us if we minded if he smoked. It annoyed me as I noticed Roderick was finding it hard to catch his breath.

'We know you have experience of doing this, Mr Abernethy, because of the work you did for Colin. Can you do the same for us?'

'Well, yes, but it does cost quite a lot of money and there are no guarantees that they will find out what you want. Why don't you tell me what it is you want to find out and then I will be better able to advise you?'

His grey eyes peered at us over his spectacles, obviously keen to hear why we wanted to hire him and no doubt knowing it was something to do with the rumours that were going around about Roderick.

'Well, Mr Abernethy, there have been several anonymous letters sent to the Laird about Roderick over the last couple of years. The latest letter is accusing him of being a murderer.'

'I see. And what is it you want to find out?'

'Well,' continued Roderick. 'We can't think of anyone from North Uist who would know about a murder committed in Canada and can only think that the person sending these letters is a relative of the man who was murdered, James Adams.'

'And were you involved in an investigation into his murder?'

'A Mountie questioned me, but he dismissed me from his inquiries.'

'Did you know this, James Adams? Do you have any information that you could share with the private investigators about him?'

'I didn't know him. All I know is what Bill Preston, the landlord of the Golden Sheaf Hotel, told us when Chrissie and I arrived in Canada.'

'And what did he tell you?'

'That as a man, who the Canadian Government had given land to, had not developed it as per his contract, they had investigated and found the man had been missing since 1896. They had traced a relative in England who had told them to sell the land. That was when Aleksander Bukowski had bought it. It was when he was tilling the soil that he found a skeleton which the Mounties believed to be James Adams.'

'And why did the Mounties question you?'

'I don't see how that's relative, Mr Abernethy,' I butted in, worried that Roderick would mention Lily and Heather.

'It's alright Chrissie. Apparently, someone saw James Adams going into the Golden Sheaf Hotel close to the time he disappeared, and they told the Mountie they had seen me in that hotel. They merely questioned me to find out if I had seen anything, but I couldn't help them.'

'Okay. So, from what you've told me, there should be a birth certificate for this James Adams if he was born in England and

166

from that, we should be able to find out if he has any relatives. I don't think the private detectives will need to contact the Canadian authorities unless they don't find a birth certificate for James Adams. Do you want me to use the same company who did the work for Colin, or would you prefer someone else?'

Roderick and I looked at each other. We hadn't discussed this.

'What is your opinion, Mr Abernethy?'

'Well, Colin gained enough evidence to claim Donald as his son through the work of those detectives, so you have evidence they can do their job.'

He couldn't help but smirk when he said this, but what he said was true.

'Okay. We'll go with them.'

'Right, I'll come back to you when I receive any information on this James Adams and his family, and then you can decide what you wish to do about it.'

CHAPTER FIFTY-SIX

'You're going to Canada? I can't believe it, Johnny. You've held on all this time waiting for Janet to come back to North Uist. Why would you want to leave?'

I was sitting in my mother's kitchen enjoying a cup of tea and some of her baking. Johnny's announcement surprised me so much, I almost spilt my tea.

'I know it's a bit sudden, but when I went to the meeting with the Canadian Government Agent and he explained the incentives they were offering to those of us who moved to Canada, it just seemed too good an opportunity to miss.'

'Where will you go?'

'Well, it looks like it will be Nova Scotia but I'm not sure yet.'

His news shocked me, as it was so unexpected. I wondered what would become of the croft, as my father wasn't getting any younger. It had been in my father's family for such a long time and it would be sad to lose it.

'Have you told Bunty? She has a soft spot for you.'

He looked shamefaced and glanced round to make sure my mother couldn't hear what we were talking about.

'Yes, I told her because she's my friend and I thought she should know that I wouldn't be able to bring her peat and help with odd jobs. But I wasn't prepared for her reaction.'

'What do you mean?'

'I was so shocked. But when I think about it, I can see why she would react that way. I did a terrible thing.'

'What kind of terrible thing?'

'At the end of last year, Bunty invited me round and in the heat of the moment, we …' He looked at me and then looked down. 'We had sex, made love, whatever you want to call it.'

'You and Bunty made love?'

He shushed me as my voice had risen.

'I can't believe she would do that. Was Mary there?'

'No, she was at your place. I didn't realise Bunty saw me as more than a friend until that night. It was she who led me on Chrissie, believe me.'

'You must be blind as well as stupid. Anyone could see she had fallen for you. What were you thinking, Johnny?'

'I know, I know, but I think it was finding out I was going to marry Janet and take her to Canada with me that hurt her even more.'

'You and Janet are getting married?' My voice was almost a screech again. 'When was all this decided?'

'Och, we've been writing to each other and when Janet said she felt like an adventure before settling down to married life, I thought Canada would offer that adventure.'

'Well, I hope you have a happier adventure than Roderick and I had in Canada. I shudder every time I think of it. But tell me how Bunty reacted.'

'Och, it was just awful. She went mad and began hitting me on the chest with her fists. It didn't hurt me as she's such a little thing, but I felt so bad. I never meant to hurt her so much. I just hope she'll be okay.'

'I better call on her and see how she is. You're such a fool, Johnny.'

'I know. I know.'

His eyes misted up.

'I shall miss you, Chrissie, but I've got to do this. Nothing will change here and in some ways, that's a good thing. It's our traditional way of life, but it's not what I want any more. I want to know what other lives are like.'

'When do you leave?'

'April. The Canadian authorities have commissioned a ship, the SS Marloch. It will leave from Lochboisdale. Janet and I will be married just before we leave. She's handing in her notice at the hospital and coming back to stay with her family until then.'

My mother came into the room, carrying some washing that had been on the line outside. It was stiff with frost, and she set it up in front of the fire to finish the drying.

'So, he's told you his news, has he?'

'Yes, *Mathair*. What do you and *Athair* think of it all?'

'Well, we'll miss him, of course, but it seems to be the way of life on this island that all the young men leave.'

'How will you manage the croft? *Athair* isn't getting any younger.'

'Don't let him hear you say that. He's only 55. Plenty of life in him yet. Besides, your Roddy is a great help. Don't be trying to make your brother feel guilty about leaving us.'

I thought of my father, who was a couple of years older than Roderick, yet to look at the two, you would think Roderick was the older. His health had deteriorated over the last few years, and I feared the worst. TB left people weak, and it could also return.

'I know Roddy loves helping *Athair*, but he will go to school in Portree this year and will probably go on to University after that.'

'Let's not worry about that now. God makes his plans for us and what will be will be.'

CHAPTER FIFTY-SEVEN

Johnny had sent Bunty a note saying he wanted to come and speak to her without Mary being there and when would be convenient. She wondered why. They were still friends, and he still brought her peat and collected her shopping, so it was rather formal sending a note to her. Perhaps he was coming to tell her that now was the right time for them to start a relationship, that he had got over Janet at long last. But it brought her no joy. Her heart had turned to stone that night in December when he had used her so cruelly. But for Mary's sake, if he wanted to marry her, she would agree.

It was February and still freezing, so she had asked Johnny to bring her a creel of peat. She made the usual hotpot for him, but there was no pleasure in it the way there used to be. As she cut up the meat and vegetables, she noticed how sharp the knife was and wondered what it would be like to stab it into Johnny's stony heart. Would she have enough strength to push it far enough into that broad chest of his? He had made her come to rely on him and she had liked the feeling of being cared for and the fuss he made of Mary. But it had all been a lie. He had just used her and Mary.

'Hello Bunty, it's a cold one tonight,' said Johnny, blowing into his hands as he removed his coat, scarf, and cap. 'Is that hotpot I smell?'

'It is,' she smiled. 'Sit at the table and I'll dish up. Mary's staying with Donald tonight, so we have the house to ourselves as you asked.'

There was little chat during the meal, and Bunty wondered again what he wanted to speak to her about.

'So, Johnny, what is it you want to talk to me about?'

'I've got some exciting news. I'm going to Canada.'

Bunty was speechless. This wasn't what she had been expecting.

'Did you hear me, Bunty? I'm going to Canada. I'm never going to get a place of my own here in North Uist, so I went to a meeting

171

in January with the Canadian government agent and the incentives they are offering are too good to refuse. There's nothing for me here.'

'But I thought you loved it here.'

'Och I do, but I want more than this island can offer me. And the good news is Janet is going to join me.'

'Janet?'

'Yes. She's been writing to me and wants to give our relationship another chance. We are going to be married next month and we'll be sailing to Canada in April.'

Bunty thought about the sharp knife lying in the kitchen sink waiting to be washed.

'What about Mary and me?' she whispered.

The eager expression on his face changed as he heard the anguish in her voice.

'Oh Bunty, you're not still holding a torch for me, are you? I thought you felt like me. That we were good friends but that we could be nothing else.'

'I don't know why you thought that. You knew I cared for you, and I thought you cared for me. Two months ago, you made love to me. You made me believe it was only a matter of time until you would be sure of your feelings. You've been so kind and attentive to me and Mary over the last two months, I thought you were coming to propose to me tonight.'

'Och Bunty, I've been kind to you and Mary because I felt so bad about what happened between us. It wasn't right, but I couldn't help it. You made it difficult for me to stop.'

She looked at him, but it was her uncle she saw. That's what he always said.

'I made it difficult for you to stop! You took advantage of a vulnerable woman on her own. I've a good mind to go to the constable and report you.'

A red mist rose in her head, and she began pummelling his chest with her fists. How dare he say it was she who had made it difficult for him to stop? She suddenly realised he was grasping hold of her wrists.

'Stop, Bunty, please stop. I don't know what to say. I'm so sorry. I've been a bloody fool for not realising the strength of your feelings for me.'

Although she had known in her heart how Johnny really felt about her, being told to her face that he was back with Janet and they were going off to make a new life together, left her feeling bereft. When her uncle had told her she didn't belong to him, she had felt the same way. She was another man's daughter, so how could he love her? Johnny belonged to another woman, so how could he love her? She was unlovable.

'Please leave Johnny.'

'I'm sorry, Bunty.'

She gathered his things and pushed them into his hands.

'Now!'

He shrugged on his coat, twisted his scarf round his neck and pushed his cap onto his head before walking towards the door which she was holding open, allowing the cold winter air to break up the warmth in her home and in her heart.

When he left, she picked up the knife lying in the sink, lifted the sleeve on her blouse and cut into the soft skin on her already scarred arm. The red blood trickling from the wound brought some relief, but she was determined to have her revenge. Not just on Roderick, but on Johnny as well.

CHAPTER FIFTY-EIGHT

As soon as I got home, I told Roderick and the boys Johnny's news.

'Oh, I don't want Uncle Johnny to leave Uist. He's great fun and I enjoy working with him on the croft,' said Roddy.

'Mary will be disappointed,' said Donald.

'Why will she be disappointed?' asked Roddy. 'He's not her uncle.'

'No, I know, but I think she was hoping he might become her daddy. But if he's marrying Auntie Janet, then that won't happen.'

Roderick glanced over at me. He didn't know what Johnny told me had happened between him and Bunty, but it surprised me she had spoken to Mary about Johnny in that way. Had Johnny led her on, encouraged Bunty and Mary to see him as more than a friend? But when Janet told him she wanted an adventure, he had turned his back on them. It didn't seem like my brother, but what other explanation could there be? Why would Mary think he might become her daddy?

'Her daddy!' exclaimed Roddy.

'Yes. She said her Uncle Johnny, that's what she calls him, was coming over to see her *mamaidh*, and that was why she was staying with us to give them time on their own. She hoped that after he spoke to her *mamaidh*, he would become her daddy and she and her *mamaidh* would move up to the croft. It was the night she stayed here with us last week that she told me.'

Last week. I cast my mind back, but I couldn't remember having seen Bunty. I had dropped the children off at school the morning after Mary had stayed with us, but Bunty hadn't come out to greet us. I thought nothing of it, as she was always busy at that time in the morning and besides, it was freezing cold. I decided I better talk to her sooner rather than later. I didn't like to think of her being upset and having no-one to talk to about her feelings, but when I got there, she seemed quite composed. She assured me that Johnny had got the wrong end of the stick.

174

'I'm fond of Johnny. Who wouldn't be? He's a lovely man, but his heart lies elsewhere, and I've always known that. It was nice to have him as a friend and to have the help around the house.'

'But what about Mary? Why would she tell Donald she hoped he was going to be her daddy?'

'I don't know why Mary said that. She has grown fond of him as he's been around the house quite a lot and children make up stories, don't they? She obviously misses having a father, so has dreamed that Johnny might become her daddy one day. As I told you, I used to dream that my daddy would come back and rescue me from my uncle, but he never did.'

She laughed, but I thought I saw tears glistening in her eyes. If what Johnny said was true about her hitting him, then she wasn't telling me the truth about how she felt. She wouldn't have done that if she had no feelings for him, especially when they had been intimate, but I didn't pursue it. I didn't want her to know Johnny had shared that information with me. She must miss her husband terribly and I could understand why she would want to find comfort in someone like my brother, so I didn't blame her. But if word ever got out, it would cause such a scandal, she might even lose her job. The community would frown on a widow with loose morals teaching their children. And poor wee Mary must miss having a daddy. No wonder she had hoped Johnny might marry her mummy.

But there was little I could do. Johnny and Janet had made the arrangements for their marriage and were sailing to Canada, and that was that. But, of course, it wasn't.

CHAPTER FIFTY-NINE

The Laird arrived after we heard about Johnny leaving. He was in the taxi the Lochmaddy Hotel had bought to transport their guests around the island. The noise of the engine spluttering and the sound of the tyres crunching on the gravel made us all look out the window.

'*Mamaidh*, can we look at the motorcar?' asked Donald, his face bright with excitement. It was easy for a child. They lived in each moment and didn't need to worry about the future. I wondered what our future would be after the Laird had spoken to us. Perhaps it would be Roderick and me who would work the croft when Johnny left and my father passed, as I doubted Roderick would be the Factor for much longer.

'Yes, let's all go. But the Laird wants to discuss business with *Dadaidh* and me, so you boys play outside or go to the kitchen and sit with Mrs McAllister.'

The car was dark green and had a canopy over the top to supply shelter from the elements. It had two enormous wheels at the front and one at the back and a lamp sitting on its bonnet. Its burnished chrome mirrors and door handles glinted in the sun. I thought it was rather handsome. After Sir Arthur came out, the driver let the boys jump in and sit in the back, then he let them take turns of sitting in the driver's seat. The child in me wanted to do the same, but the adult in me knew she would need to face the Laird and whatever his decision was going to be about our future.

Once we had settled in the drawing room, exchanged pleasantries, and drank tea, he began.

'I've received another letter, Roderick.'

He passed the letter to Roderick, who then passed it to me. There were no surprises. It was almost word for word what the letter to Archie had said.

'So, what have you got to say? Were you involved in a murder investigation while you were in Canada, and did you come home because you were guilty?'

Roderick stood up and turned away from Sir Arthur, and I wondered if he was going to answer. He paced up and down the room while Sir Arthur looked at him expectantly.

'Will you believe me if I deny what the letter says, Sir Arthur? You're giving more weight to this person, who you don't even know, than you're giving to me, your employee of three years.'

Roderick surprised me. I didn't expect him to come out fighting, but I was proud of him. He was right to stand up for himself. The Laird looked a little taken aback and coughed.

'I know what you're saying, Roderick, but I need to investigate these things. Please, just answer my question. There must be some basis in truth to the letter, even if the allegation is a tissue of lies.'

'The truth, Sir Arthur, is that a Mountie came to my house and asked me if I had seen James Adams in the local hotel near the time that he disappeared. He accepted when I told him I had not. I was never a suspect. My health was the reason I came home from Canada, not because I was running away from anything.'

His face was flushed, and he was wheezing slightly. I was relieved when he sat down again.

The Laird took out a cigarette and asked if we minded. I would have preferred that he didn't because of Roderick, but when Roderick shook his head, he lit up and inhaled deeply. For a moment, I felt like asking him for one as it seemed to relax him, and I could do with something to relax me. My nails were digging into my hands as I sat and listened to their conversation.

'How is your health, Roderick? You don't seem yourself, if you don't mind me saying. I think you've lost weight.'

'I'm okay. This business of the letters is getting me down, that's all. I'm still fit for the job you pay me to do, if that's what you're worried about.'

'Don't talk to me like that. I'm your employer and don't you forget it.'

Roderick mumbled a sorry, and the Laird continued.

'I can understand that the business of the letters is getting you down, Roderick. Have you made any progress in finding out who's been sending them?'

'We've instructed Mr Abernethy to hire a private investigator. Chrissie thinks the only person who would send such letters must be a relative of James Adams.'

'Yes, you're probably right, Chrissie.'

I could contain myself no longer.

'So where does that leave us, Sir Arthur? You implied the last time you were here that if you received another letter, you would fire Roderick. Is that still your intention?'

'I like straight talking, Chrissie, so I'll tell you straight what I'm thinking. Looking at Roderick, I'm not sure he's well.'

'I am here Sir Arthur; you can talk to me.'

'Yes, sorry, old chap. I would like you to be examined by Dr McInnes. You said you came home from Canada because of ill health, so I don't think it's unreasonable of me to ask you to get checked over.'

'And then what?'

'We'll see what he says and then decide.'

'What about the Trust and our role as guardians?' I asked.

'I'll not take any decisions until Roderick's seen the doctor and it would be beneficial if you could clear up this mess of the letters. None of this is good for Donald and when I spoke to Mrs Hepworth on my way here, she told me your boys have been getting bullied at school because of the rumours that their father is a murderer.'

I burst into tears, but it made no difference to Sir Arthur.

'Right, I better get on. I've a ferry to catch. Let me know what the doctor says and what you find out from the private investigators.'

CHAPTER SIXTY

Roderick went to see Dr McInnes, who did some tests. He told him he didn't think he had the consumption again, but there seemed to be something causing him to lose weight and making him cough. He would need to send him for an x-ray to get his lungs checked. This would mean a trip to Stornoway, to the hospital there. We were both relieved that the consumption hadn't returned. That would have been the end of Roderick's working life and would probably have killed him within a couple of months.

The spectre of being a widow loomed large. What would my boys and I do without him? He was the only man I had ever loved and being without him was unthinkable. Bunty then came into my mind, and I resolved to have courage. She was younger than me, but had managed, so why wouldn't I if God decided it was Roderick's time? I didn't tell him what I was thinking, but I suspected he was having similar thoughts.

As if we didn't have enough to worry about, the stories about Roderick being a murderer didn't go away and the boys continued to complain when they came in from school that the other children were calling them names.

'I don't care what they say, *Mathair.* I don't believe them, and I threaten to punch them if they say another word.'

'Roddy's always getting into trouble with Mrs Hepworth for fighting.'

'Shut up Donald. You should stand up for *Athair* instead of snivelling every time someone says something.'

It surprised me when Donald said this. Bunty had promised me she would make sure the bullying stopped. Perhaps I would need to speak to her again and remind her.

But then the stories took on another dimension, and I wondered about Bunty and the role she was playing in our harassment. Donald came in from school one day crying.

'*Mamaidh,* why do I have black hair and Roddy has light brown hair like yours?'

'Where is all this coming from?' I asked. 'You have blue eyes, just the same as Roddy does. Why does it matter that your hair is a different colour?'

'Mary told me that my mother was a red Indian and that I'm one as well. What's a red Indian?'

Luckily Roddy answered him, as I was struck dumb.

'A red Indian is a person who was born in Canada and lived there before the British and French discovered it.'

'How do you know?'

'I read it in *the Boys' Own*, Donald. I'll show you, if you like.'

Donald went up to the mantlepiece and took down Heather's photograph.

'She doesn't look red to me.'

Roddy went over and looked at the picture with his brother.

'The photograph isn't in colour Donald, so I don't know how you can tell. All I can see is that her skin is darker than ours, but her eyes look light like ours. Come on and I'll show you what it says in my comic.'

When I told Roderick about the conversation, he grew even more pale than he already was.

'We are done for Chrissie. If someone knows about Heather being a native Canadian, they must know the rest of the story.'

CHAPTER SIXTY-ONE

Before I could do anything about speaking to Bunty, we received a message from Mr Abernethy telling us he had the report from the private investigators and to call into his office the following day. I wondered what the report would tell us. Was it someone on the island that we knew who had sent the letters or was it a stranger? Was it Bunty? My stomach was in knots as Roderick and I made our way into his office.

'Good morning Chrissie, good morning Roderick,' said Catherine, the receptionist. 'I'll let Mr Abernethy know you are here.'

We neither of us said anything while we waited, and I was conscious of Roderick's laboured breathing. I hoped he wouldn't need to wait too long for his x-ray. It surprised me when he took my hand and squeezed it. Was he trying to reassure me or himself? I squeezed his hand back and then Mr Abernethy was there, inviting us in to reveal what the private detectives had uncovered.

'Well,' he said, waving a folder with paperwork inside. 'You're going to be surprised at what Field and Fox have found.'

'Is it someone we know, Mr Abernethy?' I asked.

'For goodness' sake, man. Just tell us what they've found. This isn't a guessing game; it's affecting our lives and the lives of our boys.'

'Yes, sorry. I won't say any more. Read through the paperwork and see for yourselves. I'll get Catherine to make us some tea.'

He passed the folder over to us, and we read the contents eagerly. Basically, it told us that James Adams had a brother called Frederick Adams, and it was he who the authorities had contacted about his brother's land in Canada and about a skeleton being found on that land. He was now deceased, however, so he could not be responsible for the letters. He had left behind a widow and two children, who were now adults. The private investigators had spoken to the widow Grace Adams, but she told them she did not know who would send such letters. They thought she was evasive when they were talking to her and did more digging. Through talking to some of the household servants, they found out that Grace Chalmers had been pregnant when she married Frederick Adams and that the father of her child was his brother, James Adams. Frederick had married Grace to prevent the stigma of illegitimacy involving the family. That child, a daughter, was now a widow with a little girl and she had moved to Scotland to take up a teaching job. They had traced her to North Uist, where she was employed as a teacher in Lochmaddy.

We were sitting in stunned silence when Mr Abernethy returned carrying a tray with tea for us.

'Ah, I see you've read the paperwork.'

Roderick stood up and threw the folder back on Mr Abernethy's desk, almost knocking over a teacup.

'Well, I was right all along. I knew there was something about that woman.'

His eyes were gleaming with triumph but also with rage and I wasn't sure if it was at me or at Bunty.

'How could you have been so stupid, Chrissie? Trusting that woman the way you have. Letting her into our lives and the lives of our children.'

'Drink your tea, Roderick,' said Mr Abernethy, looking uncomfortable. 'The only person at fault here is Bunty Hepworth.'

Roderick looked shamefaced and sat down before bursting into a fit of coughing.

'You need to see the doctor, Roderick. That cough doesn't sound too healthy.'

'You're here to give me legal advice, Mr Abernethy, nothing else. Now tell us what we can do about that damned woman.'

CHAPTER SIXTY-TWO

Bunty was ready for Chrissie when she came calling. Normally, she didn't open letters from her mother, but luckily Mary had got the letter from Murdo, so she had no choice but to read it and she was glad she did. Her mother had written telling her that a private detective had been making inquiries about James Adams. So Bunty realised that Chrissie and Roderick must have worked out that the letters were coming from someone related to James Adams and were trying to find out who. Well, she was ready to face whatever the consequences were going to be. She believed she now had sufficient evidence to prove that Roderick was a murderer and had killed her father so that he could steal his wife.

When Chrissie arrived, she didn't beat about the bush.

'I know about you, Bunty Hepworth. I know it's you who's been sending these horrible letters to the Laird. How could you do that and why? We've done nothing to harm you. We've welcomed you into our house and our family. Your daughter is even our son's best friend. I don't understand.'

Mary was standing looking at Chrissie with her mouth hanging open. She had never seen her so angry and upset.

'Mary, pet, go through to your room and play. I need to speak to Auntie Chrissie.'

When Mary had left the room, Bunty turned to Chrissie.

'What don't you understand, Chrissie? Why I would want to take revenge on the man who killed my father? When you spoke about Colin Donaldson, murder was in your heart then, so I think you understand.'

She was right. After Heather died, Chrissie would have cheerfully stuck a knife in Colin Donaldson's heart. Anyone would do the same. But Bunty had never met James Adams. As far as Chrissie was concerned, he was her father in blood only and if she knew what a vicious drunk he was, she would surely see how wrong her actions had been.

'But Roderick didn't murder your father. He hardly knew the man.'

'So, he knew him then?'

Bunty noticed Chrissie's hesitation as the cogs of her mind tried to work out what Bunty already knew. She obviously had things to hide.

'I don't know if he knew him or not. Your father went missing before I arrived in Canada, and it was after I arrived they found a skeleton. I know a Mountie came to question Roderick, but he was never a suspect. What makes you think he killed your father?'

'I didn't know for sure when I first arrived, but he was the only suspect the Mounties told my uncle about and as I've got to know more about your family history, I have no doubts. Your husband killed my father so that he could steal his wife.'

The look on Chrissie's face made Bunty laugh out loud.

'Don't look so shocked, Chrissie. It didn't take me long to work out that Heather was my father's daughter. Donald was very helpful in that respect. He told me when her birthday was, and I did my sums. She was born eight months after my father went missing.'

'But you don't know for sure when your father went missing. You're making assumptions.'

'Am I? Why does Heather look like my father then? I must admit it disappointed me when I found out he had married a savage and had a daughter to her, but he was my father and his murder prevented him from coming back and saving me from my uncle.'

The look of anguish on Chrissie's face only enraged Bunty more.

'I don't need your pity, Chrissie, so you needn't look so upset.'

'But I am upset, Bunty. I've grown fond of you. You and Mary are part of our family.'

'I don't want to be part of your family, Chrissie. Don't you understand? I want to destroy your family.'

CHAPTER SIXTY-THREE

I could only stare at Bunty in astonishment when she told me she wanted to destroy my family. I had never seen the real Bunty until now. Everything I thought I'd known of her was just a front, a cover for who she truly was. Well, I would not let her do it. Despite what Roderick had done in the past, we knew the difference between right and wrong and Bunty was in the wrong. Mr Abernethy had told us what Bunty had done was not a criminal offence but a common law one. We could take her to court for compensation, but we didn't want compensated, we just wanted her to stop causing trouble with the Laird and leave us alone. Her next words made me realise she had no intention of leaving us alone.

'I plan to take legal advice about Donald. The evidence points to Heather being my half-sister, which means Donald is my nephew, and I would say that gives me more right to be his guardian than you and Roderick, who have no relationship to him.'

When the Laird had threatened to end our guardianship of Donald if there were any more complaints, I had been devastated, but this. This was different. It would mean more publicity and would cause Donald's heritage to become known, but worse than that was the thought that Donald could end up with a scheming, manipulative woman like Bunty was horrendous. I needed to stop her, but how?

'How can you reveal the truth about Donald without revealing his heritage? You sounded ashamed that your father had married a native woman.'

'Not so much ashamed, as angry that he would choose a woman like that over my mother and me. But it makes no difference to me what stock Donald came from.'

'But you will hurt Donald, too. He doesn't know about his heritage.'

'Don't think I want to become Donald's guardian because I love him. No, I want to do it because I want to hurt you and Roderick and if that means hurting him as well, so be it.'

'You're a monster.'

She cackled like a witch at me.

'You're such a hypocrite. Your husband shot my father, buried his body, and stole his wife. He didn't have the decency to give him a proper burial and you Chrissie Macdonald must have known about it and accepted it. So don't talk to me about being a monster.'

She was right. What Roderick had done was wrong, but he had done it for the right reasons. Revenge motivated Bunty so she was not thinking rationally. I wondered if the threat of taking an action for compensation against her would make any difference.

'We've already taken legal advice about your conduct and Mr Abernethy tells us we can sue you for compensation.'

'Only if you can prove that what I said was a lie, and I think I can prove most of what I've accused Roderick of. Besides, I'm a wealthy woman, Chrissie. As my husband was an only child, his family have bequeathed their estate to Mary and me. In addition, my uncle set up a trust for me from the money that was paid for my father's holding in Canada, and my mother pays me an annual allowance from the estate she inherited from my uncle when he died. The paltry sum you could claim would be nothing to me.'

The door creaked open and in walked Mary.

'Why are you and Auntie Chrissie shouting at each other? I'm frightened.'

She turned to Mary angrily. I'd never seen her be anything but kind to that child.

'I told you to wait in the other room, Mary. Now do what I tell you.'

Poor Mary looked even more frightened and left the room.

'You better go now, Chrissie. You've a lot to think about.'

I still had my coat on, and she ushered me out the door before I could say anything else. I was shivering even although it was a pleasant evening for the time of year. Our lives were about to be turned upside down yet again.

186

CHAPTER SIXTY-FOUR

It was a beautiful spring day when Johnny and Janet were married, but all the rumours flying around, Bunty's threat to apply to the Trust for guardianship of Donald and Roderick's deteriorating health, marred it for me. I had told no one about my conversation with Bunty. I wanted to wait until Roderick had been for his x-ray and I didn't want to spoil Johnny and Janet's wedding. But I wondered if Bunty would do anything to sabotage it as I now thought she might be capable of anything.

Janet's mother came from Knockline, so it was in the church there that they were married. As was the tradition, the wedding party and their guests tied white ribbons outside their houses. It was a delight to see them fluttering in the spring breeze and they gave a festive feel to the island. Although it was supposed to be a quiet affair, as often happens on the island, it turned into a large party. Janet looked lovely dressed in a navy-blue rayon dress, with a matching coat and cloche hat sitting on her short, bobbed hair. I had sent for a similar dress and hat from the catalogue, but in a dove grey. Johnny looked a little uncomfortable in his suit, shirt, and tie, as he was so used to wearing casual working clothes. In the end, Roderick stayed home as he felt too unwell to go along.

As I looked at them, both with happiness shining out of their eyes, I thought back to my wedding day and Roderick. There was no love shining out of our eyes. We hardly knew each other back then and although I naively hoped for love, it took quite a long time for it to develop into this love that we now shared. It had its passion back in the beginning, but the trials and tribulations of life had taken their toll. Ours was probably more of a loving friendship than a passionate love match, but we were still intimate, and he still brushed my hair most nights. It was one reason I had never had my hair cut in the modern style. This long-standing ritual was something I still treasured.

Because I hadn't told Johnny that it was Bunty who had sent the letters, he had invited Bunty and Mary to the wedding. So instead, I told him I thought he was being insensitive given that she had harboured hopes of them getting together.

'It will look strange if I don't invite them, Chrissie. Everyone knows you and Bunty are friends, that Donald and Mary are best friends and that I've been helping her with jobs round the house. I don't want anyone making any remarks about her absence to Janet.'

'I suppose you're right Johnny, but I can't help feeling you might rub salt in the wounds of her disappointment.'

When Johnny received a telegram from Bunty, hand delivered by Mr Fraser, on the day of the wedding, he was surprised.

'She's asking me to visit her before the wedding, as she has something important to tell me.'

'I don't know what she's up to, Johnny, but I don't think you should go. What kind of news could she have that's so urgent you have to see her on your wedding day?'

'I don't have time anyway, Chrissie. I'll see her at the wedding later and she can tell me then.'

But, as it turned out, Bunty and Mary didn't come to the wedding and Johnny was so happy to be marrying Janet that he forgot all about her. I was relieved that she hadn't come, but it was clear she was trying to cause trouble for the happy couple, and I hoped she had no other plans in mind to spoil their happiness, but, of course, she did.

CHAPTER SIXTY-FIVE

Bunty woke up feeling sick again, but this time she didn't need to vomit into the pot that sat under her bed. She had been feeling this way on and off for a few weeks and wondered what was wrong. It was the day of Johnny's wedding and although she hated the thought of watching him marry another woman, she hadn't yet met Janet and wanted to see this person that Johnny loved more than her. She might have a quiet word with her and let her know what her husband was really like and, who knew, perhaps she would leave him at the altar. Also, she didn't want to disappoint Mary. She was so excited to be going to a wedding as she had never been to one before. Bunty had sent to Glasgow for a dress, hat, and shoes for her. The dress was yellow with white polka dots on it and the straw hat had a yellow ribbon to match the dress. The shoes were white leather, totally unsuitable for North Uist, but Bunty wanted to spoil her.

As Mary sat waiting for her, Bunty pulled the dress she was proposing to wear from the wardrobe. She hadn't worn it since she and James had married. It was a calf length cream woollen dress which was not quite the fashion nowadays, but she had always liked the way she looked in it. Today, however, it wasn't sitting right. She looked bloated round her middle, and the dress was puckering. It was then she realised why she was being sick.

She was having a baby. One night with Johnny and she had fallen pregnant. She smiled as she slowly caressed the swell of her tummy and hugged this knowledge to her. He would need to call off the wedding and marry her now. Not that she loved him anymore, but the thought of spoiling his wedding day excited her. What a scandal it would cause and poor Janet. She would be affronted being left at the altar. She laughed as she imagined the scenario.

'What are you laughing at Mummy?' Mary said, coming into the room looking beautiful in her new outfit. Bunty hadn't even realised she was laughing out loud.

189

'You're looking very pretty Mary, but I'm afraid we won't be able to go to the wedding today.'

Mary looked as if she might cry.

'Why not Mummy? I really want to see Uncle Johnny and ask him if he likes my dress.'

'I know, chook, but I really don't feel well. I'm going to ask him to call round before the wedding, so he'll be able to see you then. How's that?'

'Okay mummy,' she said, but her little lips were quivering.

'Now run down to the post office and give this note to Mr Fraser to send Johnny a telegram.'

When she received no response and no visit by the time the wedding was due to take place, she knew it was over with Johnny. He didn't want her; didn't even want to hear her news. She sat staring into the fire for a long time and it was only when Mary told her she was hungry that she realised she was still in her nightclothes and hadn't given Mary any lunch or tea.

After Mary had gone to bed, she got out the mulled wine, poured a glass and thought of all the happy times she, Johnny and Mary had spent dancing together to the records on the gramophone. She picked some of them up and then slowly smashed them one by one until none of the records she had played with Johnny remained. When she thought about it, she no longer wished to marry him, anyway. He had made his choice, and it wasn't her. Men always let her down and he was no different from her father, her uncle and even Harry, who hadn't stayed alive and come back to her. She and Mary had had a lucky escape. But he wouldn't.

CHAPTER SIXTY-SIX

Although the weather was unusually mild, there was a chill hanging over the throng of people emigrating and the people waiting to wave them off at Lochboisdale. Sir Arthur had come to wave off the men and women who were emigrating, which I thought was insensitive given that he was partly to blame for them leaving their homeland. Word was that between Barra, the Uists, Harris and Lewis, there were 600 people, mostly young folk, leaving from Lochboisdale and Stornoway to go to Canada. It was too many people for us to lose and it would leave behind too many sad families who would never see their loved ones again.

The government was to blame as they promoted immigration instead of land settlement and encouraged the tour made by the Canadian emigration agents to the islands, who offered incentives for people to go. Those incentives and Janet's need for adventure had sucked Johnny in. Women were in great demand as wives and servants, so many of our women, who were finding it difficult to find a husband because of the loss of young men in the war, were going on that ship. It made me think of when I went to Canada with Roderick and how I had felt like little more than a mail-order bride in the beginning.

The dancing had gone on until the early hours and there were still some sore heads that morning. There had been a feverishness at the wedding, almost like the time the boys went off to war in 1914. The difference was these people would not be fighting and possibly losing their lives. They were going to a new life, in a new land, to seek their fortune. But for those left behind, it felt like they were going to their death, as they knew they were never likely to see them again. As the gulls circled and called above them, the murmur of voices stopped and there was silence as a ship came into view on the horizon. The SS Marloch had arrived.

I was standing holding Roddy and Donald's hand when I heard Mary's voice calling, 'Uncle Johnny, Uncle Johnny.' I turned and saw Bunty and Mary walking towards us. Johnny and Janet were hugging their respective families, so Johnny didn't hear her. I tapped him on the shoulder, and he turned to look at me.

'Bunty and Mary are here, Johnny.'

His face paled, and he glanced at Janet.

'You say goodbye to them, and I'll keep Janet out of the way.'

He smiled his thanks and hurried over to them, obviously not wishing to give Bunty the opportunity of speaking to Janet. I couldn't hear what was being said, but I could see Mary dancing excitedly in front of Johnny, showing off her dress, which Bunty had obviously bought her for the wedding. I wondered what Bunty was up to, coming to Lochboisdale like this. I hoped she wouldn't do anything rash. My thoughts were interrupted when Janet came up to me.

'Who's that Johnny's with?'

'Och, it's that schoolteacher I told you about that Johnny did some work for and her wee girl. They couldn't come to the wedding yesterday, so they've come to say goodbye.'

'Maybe I should go over and meet her.'

'There's not time, Janet. Come on, give me a hug. I'm going to miss you.'

As I looked over Janet's shoulder, I could see Bunty pointing over to where Donald and Roddy were standing, and Mary then ran over to them. She obviously wished to speak to Johnny without Mary hearing their conversation. I was curious and wished I was standing closer. Mary then ran over to me.

'Auntie Chrissie, Auntie Chrissie, do you like my dress? Mummy got me it for Uncle Johnny's wedding, but she was feeling sick, and we couldn't come.'

'That's a shame, Mary, because you look so pretty.'

'Who is this lady, Auntie Chrissie?'

'This is Janet. She's Uncle Johnny's new wife.'

'I'm pleased to meet you, Mary,' said Janet, crouching down and shaking Mary's hand.

Mary stared at her and was about to say something when there was a loud cry and we all turned. Johnny was grasping Bunty's arms, and she was trying to get away from him. When he realised everyone was looking, he let her go and Bunty called to Mary, who then ran back to her mother. Johnny picked up Mary, gave her a hug, set her down again, and then joined Janet and me.

'Are you alright Johnny?' she asked. 'You're crying. What was happening then? Why did that woman cry out?'

He looked upset, and I knew it must be something Bunty had said to him. I looked round to see if Bunty and Mary were still there, but they had gone.

'She twisted her ankle, and I grabbed her to stop her from falling.'

'But why are you crying?'

'Och, it's just that leaving my home for the last time is a reality and I just want to weep. Oh Janet, tell me we're doing the right thing.'

He was sobbing now.

'Come here, you soft lump,' she said, pulling him into her arms. 'Of course, we're doing the right thing. We'll be together and we'll make a go of it, don't you worry. And one day when we've made our fortune, we'll come back and visit.'

Suddenly, there was a loud blast from the ship's horn. The SS Marloch was now berthed and ready for its passengers. A quiet descended as the departing passengers said their last goodbyes to their loved ones again and made their way onto the ship. A lone piper played a lament as the ship left to make its way to Canada. We all stood and waved until the smoke belching from its funnel disappeared over the horizon.

CHAPTER SIXTY-SEVEN

Bunty was happy with the way things worked out with Johnny. His face, when he turned and saw her and Mary, was a picture. She knew he was wondering why she had come and was worried she was going to say something to Janet. But, of course, she knew what she was going to do, and it didn't involve Janet. She no longer wanted him for herself, but he didn't deserve to go on this journey with his new wife to a new land full of happiness. Knowing the sort of man he was, she knew telling him about the child would spoil everything.

'Hello Mary,' he said. 'You're looking awfie bonnie in that dress.'

'I got it for your wedding, Uncle Johnny, but mummy was sick yesterday so we couldn't come.'

He looked at Bunty.

'I'm sorry to hear that. I hope you are well today.'

'Mary, run over and show Donald and Roddy your new dress, while I talk to Uncle Johnny.'

'Okay Mummy.'

'I'm fine, Johnny. I now know why I've been sick.'

He looked puzzled at first, but when she put her hand on her belly, she could see he knew.

'You're having a baby!'

'Yes. You're going to be a father.'

'My God Bunty. How can you tell me this when I'm on my way to another country with my new wife? It's insane. You're insane.'

'You didn't use to think that, and you certainly didn't think it when you took advantage of me in December, Johnny.'

'Why didn't you tell me before?'

'I only realised myself yesterday, and I sent you a telegram to give you a chance to make things right before you married Janet, but you didn't take it.'

'If only I'd known.'

'What would you have done? Left Janet at the altar?'

I laughed, then moved my face up close to his and snarled at him.

'You've ruined me. I'll lose my job, my home, and my reputation. And God only knows what will happen to this baby. I couldn't let it live with the stigma of illegitimacy, so it will have to be adopted.'

She was enjoying the anguish on his face with each word she uttered and was unsurprised when tears began sliding down his cheeks.

'I'll tell Janet. She and I will look after the baby. We don't need to go today; we can go another time. They'll always be looking for people to emigrate.'

He was clearly desperate, but she didn't want him changing his plans.

'You're forgetting one thing, Johnny. I would need to tell people you are the father before you would have any right to take any part in its life and I don't propose to do that. People might suspect the father is you, but you won't be able to prove it. So, you might as well get on that ship and make the best of it.'

She was unprepared when he gripped her arms and cried out in pain as he pressed into the tender area where she had cut herself.

'Let me go, Johnny. You're hurting me. People are looking. You don't want them finding out your secret, do you?'

He let her go and looked towards Chrissie and his wife. He clearly did not know what he should do. The ship's horn blew, signalling it was time for departure, and he moved away from her. His head was bowed, and tears were running down his cheeks. Bunty wondered what lies he would tell his wife and Chrissie, who were looking over at them. She called to Mary, and they left without a backward glance. Her work for the day was done.

CHAPTER SIXTY-EIGHT

I had still not told Roderick about my conversation with Bunty, when the appointment for his x-ray came through. He had to go to Stornoway, and I went with him. The crossing was rough, which made us both sick, so he was weak by the time we got there. I had never been inside a hospital. Although the poor house in Lochmaddy was now a hospital, it was still mostly for poor people or for those who had lost their minds. I had never been inside and hoped with all my heart that I would never need to be. I still remembered that period of depression I had suffered in Canada and could see no benefit of being put into somewhere like that when a person already felt so low.

There was a strong smell of carbolic as we went into the reception area, which was devoid of warmth or character. Sterile white tiles covered the walls and dark green linoleum covered the floor. There were posters on the wall about TB and Scarlet Fever, the two big killers in the Western Isles. We approached the reception desk, and they quickly took Roderick through a green door while I was told to take a seat. I said a silent prayer to God that the x-ray would not reveal that Roderick had TB again. As usual, He answered my prayer, but not in the way I wished.

After about half an hour, the nurse at the desk called to me.

'Mrs Macdonald, the doctor would like to have a word with you. If you go through the green door, he will meet you there.'

I picked up my bag, pushed the door open and went through. A young man in a white coat and a stethoscope round his neck was waiting for me. I smiled, but he didn't smile back, merely took my arm and guided me toward a room off the corridor where Roderick was sitting. He didn't look at me as I came in, and I stupidly wondered why.

'Please take a seat Mrs Macdonald.'

I sat beside Roderick and took his hand, but he continued to gaze down at the floor, so I looked at the doctor.

'I'm afraid I have bad news for you Mrs Macdonald. I believe your husband has a cancer growth in his lungs.'

'A growth?'

'Yes, and one we can do nothing about. I'm sorry to tell you that your husband is dying.'

'Dying?'

Roderick stood up and folded my hands in his. It was then I noticed his eyes were red and moist from crying.

'I'm sorry Chrissie. You've not had an easy life with me and here you are going to be left a widow with two young boys. I'm so sorry to have let you down.'

I couldn't speak. He hadn't let me down, but the words I wanted to tell him wouldn't come. All I could think about were the boys and how I would tell them their *dadaidh* was dying. I heard a scream that screeched and reverberated around the room, and only when Roderick took me in his arms and held me to him did I realise it was coming from me.

CHAPTER SIXTY-NINE

The next few weeks went by in a blur. We told Roderick's family and my parents, but not the boys. We agreed to wait until the time was right, but I couldn't think when that might be. How do you tell your sons that their father is going to die? We also contacted the Laird and told him Roderick's news. He wrote back and said it did not surprise him as he had suspected something of the sort. He was sympathetic, of course, and said he would give Roderick a financial settlement so he wouldn't need to work his notice. We could also continue to live in the Factor's house until he could find someone to replace Roderick. In the meantime, Calum could look after the land and the stock, and I could look after the administration side of Roderick's job. It therefore surprised me when the Laird wrote to say that he planned to visit the island as he wished to talk to me on my own and asked me to meet him in the Lochmaddy Hotel.

Roderick didn't ask me where I was going as he was used to me coming and going for my Rural meetings and I was grateful. I couldn't think what Sir Arthur wanted to talk to me about, but it couldn't be good news if he didn't want to tell Roderick. When I arrived at the hotel, the receptionist told me Sir Arthur was waiting for me in the dining room.

'It's empty just now, so you'll have some privacy to talk.'

Rhona McLeod smiled pleasantly at me, but she would be full of curiosity about why it was me the Laird wanted to see and not Roderick. Word of Roderick's illness was not common knowledge yet, but people would suspect something was wrong before too long. We needed to tell the boys before that happened.

The dining room was still smelling of breakfast kippers when I went through, and I thought I was going to be sick. It made me wonder if something was wrong with me too, as I had been queasy often recently, but I couldn't think about that now. The Laird had something to tell me, and I doubted it was good news.

'Good morning Chrissie. I'm sorry to tell you I've had a letter that affects you and Roderick but as he is so ill, I thought it better to go over it with you first.'

'Not another anonymous letter, Sir Arthur? We know who's been sending the letters now.'

'I know. Mrs Hepworth admits she wrote the earlier letters to me.'

'And what is she accusing Roderick of this time?'

'Well, nothing, but she claims Donald is her nephew. She feels I should appoint her as his guardian, as we only gave you and Roderick the job of looking after him because we thought he was Donald's grandfather. She says that's not true.'

I burst into tears. This was all too much. I was going to lose Roderick and now Donald.

He offered me his handkerchief and sat, not saying anything while I sobbed quietly. When I calmed down, he continued.

'She also wrote that Donald is a half-breed and that his grandmother, who she claims was the wife of her father, was an Indian squaw. She says Roderick murdered her father and stole his wife.'

I looked at the Laird and wondered how much I could confide in him. I so longed to get all this out in the open. The burden of keeping these secrets locked inside was too much. Roderick was dying, so there wasn't much point in worrying about his reputation or the consequences of him being reported to the police. But I still needed to protect Donald and Roddy, so I said nothing.

'My problem is Chrissie, that now Roderick is dying, the link between you and Donald is less secure.'

'But I'm the only mother Donald's ever known, Sir Arthur, and I promised his mother on her deathbed that I would take care of him. You can't take him away from me. It would be too cruel.'

He nodded his head up and down, but I went on before he could say anything.

'And how could you consider making Bunty Hepworth his guardian? She has shown herself to be a vindictive woman who's

199

only out for revenge. She told me to my face that she didn't care about Donald, she only wanted to hurt Roderick and me. You can't let her have him, you can't.'

'Calm down Chrissie. She won't get him. The way Colin set the Trust up, Donald was to remain with you and Roderick until he was twelve and then he was to be sent to a private school in Glasgow.'

'Yes, I knew that. So, are you saying I can keep him until he's twelve, then?'

'No. I'm suggesting he goes early to get him away from all this. I've written to Victoria, and she's agreed he can stay with her until it's time for him to go to boarding school. She's investigating which local school would be best for him in the meantime.'

'But he's only nine. It would break his heart if he lost Roderick and me.'

'He's going to lose Roderick anyway, Chrissie, and you, my dear, are going to have to fashion a new life for yourself. It might be easier for you to do that if you only have your own boy. You will, of course, still have visitation rights and I'm sure you and Victoria will come to an amicable arrangement.'

Tears of rage, the likes of which I hadn't experienced since Heather died, streamed down my cheeks. I would not let Bunty Hepworth get away with this. I would make her suffer the way she had made us suffer these last two years.

CHAPTER SEVENTY

The next time Chrissie came to visit Bunty, she was unprepared and somewhat frightened. Although she knew they would know about the letter she had sent to the Laird, she was unprepared for the raw anger that Chrissie displayed. She sent Mary out to play, as she didn't want her listening to Chrissie's tirade of abuse.

'You are an evil, scheming person, Bunty Hepworth. Hurting our family for a man who wasn't fit to lick my Roderick's boots. You want to know the truth about your father? He was a drunk and a cruel bully. It was he who tried to kill Roderick. He would have shot him in the back without a second thought, and it was only the quick action of Harold Winter that saved Roderick. So, Roderick did not kill your father in cold blood and steal his wife, as your wicked mind had invented. You were wrong.'

Bunty felt herself grow cold. Had she got it wrong? The description Chrissie had given of her father sounded very like how she would have described her uncle. Perhaps cruelty ran through their genes.

'You'll be glad to know that Roderick is dying, but you won't be getting Donald. He's being sent to school in Glasgow, and his Aunt Victoria will become his guardian. The Laird would never consider giving him to a person such as you. You are wicked. I feel sorry for Mary having a mother like you.'

Bunty was stunned when Chrissie told her Roderick was dying and wondered what he was dying of, but at the mention of Mary, she felt her anger rising again.

'What you say may be true, but you can't deny that he buried my father in that terrible place to cover up his murder and took his wife and possessions.'

'Can't you see? He was doing it for the best of reasons. Way back then, Canada was a wild, unlawful place, and he wasn't sure what would happen to Harold Winter or to Lily. He thought he was doing the right thing and in the end he cared for her and Heather in a much kinder way than James Adams would ever have done. You got a lucky escape when he ran away and left your mother.'

All Bunty's pain and shame about the way her uncle had treated her rushed into her mind and she screeched.

'A lucky escape! My uncle made my life a misery and if it hadn't been for your husband, my father could have come back and saved me.'

'Don't you understand Bunty, he would never have come back to save you even if he had lived. He abandoned your mother, and he abandoned you. He was a bad, selfish man, just as you are a bad, selfish woman.'

With that, Chrissie stormed out of the house. Bunty found her legs were shaking and had to sit down in the armchair. If Roderick was dying, then there was nothing left that she could do to harm him. She cared nothing that Colin's sister would receive guardianship over Donald. She was going to have enough on her hands looking after her own daughter and this baby. She put her hand over her growing stomach and decided she would need to get rid of it. It was going to ruin her and Mary's life.

CHAPTER SEVENTY-ONE

I went to visit my mother after visiting Bunty. I was so livid I needed to talk to someone who would listen and understand. When I reached the croft, she had just come in from churning the butter and I could see from the look she gave me she knew there was something bothering me.

'Come away in Chrissie. The kettle's on. Let me make you a cup of tea. Have you eaten anything?'

'No. I've been feeling queasy all the time and can't face eating. I think it's because of all that's happening with Roderick and that Bunty Hepworth. I'm so angry at her *Mathair,* I could kill her.'

'That's a terrible way for you to feel, Chrissie. What has she done now?'

'She's written to the Laird and told him she wants to become Donald's guardian. I've just had a meeting with Sir Arthur, who luckily is ignoring her request. But he's transferring guardianship of Donald to Victoria because of all the trouble Bunty's caused. It means he'll go to Glasgow this year instead of when he's twelve. Oh *Mathair*, I'm going to lose Roderick and my two boys. I can't bear it.'

I burst into tears, and she cradled me in her arms, just letting me release all my fears and sadness. When I had calmed down, she made the tea. As I supped the comforting liquid, I spoke again.

'And the boys still don't know their *dadaidh* is dying. Will you come with me when I tell them?'

'Yes, of course, *mo graidh*. Let me know when you want me to come. You're not alone in all of this. *Athair* and I will support you every step of the way and the Lord is there to walk with you too if you'll let Him.'

I smiled at her and nodded. My mother's faith was so strong, it comforted me somehow.

'And I think He may already be working to help you through this time, Chrissie.'

'What do you mean, *Mathair*?'

'You say you've been feeling sick and off your food?'

'Yes, I have. But what's that to do with God?'

'I think maybe He is going to bless you with a baby.'

I looked at her as if she were mad. A baby? But it would explain why I had been off my food. A sensation of utter joy initially warmed me, and I thanked God for his goodness. Roderick and I had always hoped to have another child, but it had never happened. He would be so pleased. My mind began racing forward wondering what the future would be for this new life I was carrying. Images of Roderick and me smiling down on our new baby filled my imagination, until I remembered. Roderick wouldn't be here.

Why was God blessing us with a child now when Roderick wouldn't be able to share in that joy? Maybe He would let him live long enough to see the child born. I would do anything God wanted if He would only grant me that one thing. I fell to my knees, clasped my hands, and prayed in loud gulping sobs begging God to show mercy. I only stopped when my mother gathered me in her arms, shushing and patting me like a child.

When Dr McInnes next called round to attend to Roderick, I told him what my mother had said and asked him if he could check me over. He smiled sadly as he confirmed I was indeed carrying a child.

'You are around three months pregnant, Chrissie. Will you tell Roderick?'

'Yes, of course, we always wanted another child. It might bring him comfort in his last days.'

CHAPTER SEVENTY-TWO

Life became difficult for Bunty when news got out that it was she who had sent the letters to the Laird. Overnight she went from being a respected member of the Lochmaddy community to an incomer, a stranger who had brought trouble to one of their own. People shunned her and Mary in the street, the shop and the post office. Someone threw a stone through the schoolhouse window and spread dog faeces on the handle of her front door. She now locked her door at night. Several people sent letters of complaint to the education department; she was called in for an interview, sacked and told she had one month to find alternative accommodation.

Normally, Bunty was a good organiser, a person who could think things through and make plans, even if they were cruel and manipulative. But now, she had no focus. Hearing that Roderick was dying had confused her. She should have been happy that his life was ending, but a worm of doubt slithered in her stomach along with Johnny's baby. She should have been making plans to leave the island and find somewhere to live for her and Mary, but all she could focus on was getting rid of the baby. She had taken to having scalding hot baths every night, hoping that might work, but it didn't. Soon everyone would know and her and Mary's lives would be ruined. She couldn't see that she had already destroyed their lives on North Uist.

She continued to go to school every day and give out lessons to the children, but she took no interest in what they were doing. Chrissie was still sending the boys to school, and she wondered why, as the other children continued to rib them about their father being a murderer and Donald being a red Indian. Roddy was always getting into fights, but she didn't have the energy or the inclination to do anything about it. Donald had been angry with Mary when the news got out about Bunty sending the poison pen letters, but when she had told him they were cousins, it seemed to make a difference and they were still friends. But, of course, Chrissie didn't allow Donald to come for his tea anymore.

One day Roddy came into school, flung his bag on the floor, and approached her desk. He was almost twelve and had taken a stretch, so he was now taller than her. His face was full of hatred, and it reminded her of the way her uncle used to look at her before he took his belt to her. She cowered back from him, expecting him to strike her, but instead he burst into tears and shouted through his sobs at her.

'Well, I hope you're satisfied, Mrs Hepworth. My father only has days to live, and it's because of you. I hate you and I hope something bad happens to you.'

Her head became fuzzy, and she knew she needed to escape. She ran out of the class, leaving Mary and her other responsibilities behind. It was to be her last day at the school as Archie Campbell ran to tell Mrs McIver the teacher had left them on their own. It resulted in the community deciding she couldn't be trusted to look after the children anymore, so Elizabeth Macaulay took over until the new teacher arrived.

The last straw for Bunty came when her mother wrote to her again. Murdo had handed the letter to Mary who had torn it open before she could stop her.

'Uncle Charles is coming to visit us Mummy,' she said excitedly. 'Grandma says she wants to know how we're getting on. Do you think we'll be able to go home soon, mummy?'

Home. She thought North Uist would always be their home but now she might need to go back to Manchester. She burst into tears while Mary looked on, wondering what was upsetting her mummy so much.

CHAPTER SEVENTY-THREE

Although I knew Roderick was going to die, the boys didn't, and I kept things as normal as I could for them, well as normal as they could be with all that had gone on with Bunty and what was now common knowledge. So, they went about their usual routine of going to school. I'd heard from Flora that Bunty had been sacked and I wondered if she would take out her anger on my boys. When I asked them how she was being with them, they said she just ignored them and all the other children in the class.

'She just gives us some work to do, sits at her desk staring into space, and doesn't check it or anything,' said Roddy.

I thought it was strange behaviour and wondered what she would do now that she had lost her job. But I didn't care so long as she did it somewhere far away from North Uist.

Roderick's last days came upon us quickly, and he spent them in bed. I didn't get the chance to bring my mother along to help me tell the boys, as the time to tell them came when Roderick collapsed one day while they were at home. Although they knew the doctor had been coming to the house, they didn't realise how seriously ill their father was. They were terrified when they heard him scream with pain and asked me if he was going to die. When I said yes, they were bereft and cried for a long time.

Knowing that Roderick was dying was, in some ways, a blessing as it gave him, the boys, and me time to talk about our lives together and our love for one another. Roderick was keen to reassure the boys that he would be okay when he died, as he had seen how upset Donald had been after Colin died. So, we talked about what would happen to Roderick when he passed. As a Christian, Roderick didn't fear death and told the boys how much he was looking forward to being with the Lord and that he would see them again.

'You don't need to worry about me, boys. I'm going to a place where there's no pain or suffering and my saviour is waiting for me. Look after your mother. She's a special woman and God has blessed us by giving her to me as my wife and you by giving her to you as your mother.'

The boys clung to their father and cried when he said this. Then he spoke again.

'Your *mamaidh* has something to tell you now that is good news for this family and has sent me on my journey to the next world with a sense of peace and hopefulness.'

The boys looked at me expectantly.

'I'm going to have a baby. You two are going to have a little brother or sister to play with round about August or September.'

Neither of them spoke. They just smiled uncertainly, not sure if this was good or bad news. It also wasn't true that they could play with this new child as they would both be leaving North Uist at that time; Donald to go to school in Glasgow and Roddy to go to school in Portree.

We were all with Roderick when he passed and, if truth be told, his passing was a relief. He was in terrible pain and the doctor was constantly in attendance, administering morphine to give him respite. Roderick never found out what Bunty was planning in relation to Donald, as I never told him, nor did I tell him what the Laird was planning for Donald. I didn't have the heart to cause him more pain. Although it had been our intention to move in with my mother and father, Roderick died in the Factor's house before we could do so.

However, after his funeral, that's where Roddy, Donald and I would go until Roddy went to school in Portree and Donald went to Glasgow to stay with Victoria. The new baby inside me gave me some comfort, but I knew my life would change completely and prayed to God to give me strength to cope with what lay ahead. God works in mysterious ways as I had found out over the years and this time, as usual, he gave and then he took away.

208

CHAPTER SEVENTY-FOUR

As was their regular habit now, Bunty and Mary went to church every Sunday even although no-one spoke to them except Mrs Macaulay. Shortly after Mrs Macaulay had taken over at the school, Chrissie and the boys weren't at church, and she soon found out why.

'It is with great sadness that I need to tell you that Roderick Macdonald has passed away,' said the Reverend Macaulay in a sombre tone. 'Please keep Chrissie Macdonald and her two boys in your thoughts and prayers. His funeral will take place next week from the Factor's house.'

The worm in Bunty's stomach slithered and instead of feeling triumphant, all she felt was fear and as she listened to the Minister's words, her fear grew. His sermon was based on Matthew and the passage where Peter asked Jesus how many times he should forgive someone who had sinned against him.

Her thoughts went to Chrissie and what she had told her about what happened between Roderick and James Adams. It was her father who would have murdered Roderick had not Harold Winter intervened, so she had had nothing to take revenge on him for. It was true he had covered up her father's murder, but it would have made no difference to him being able to come back and save her from her stepfather. She had taken revenge on the wrong person, and she realised she was still taking revenge on her mother because she had never stood up for her against her stepfather. An image of her mother with bruised lips came into her mind and she realised she, too, had been subject to his cruelty. Why had she never noticed these things before?

The Minister's voice came into her consciousness again.

'*Beware lest there be among you a root bearing poisonous and bitter fruit* the bible says. This community has been turned upside down of late by a poisonous and bitter fruit and we have not reacted with compassion or understanding, only with gossip and retribution. There have been many allegations made against

Roderick Macdonald recently, some of which may be true, but I would ask you to think about the man you knew, the family that you know, and show them compassion and understanding. There is also someone else among us who needs your clemency, as this community needs to heal, and the only way is through forgiveness. We all make mistakes and if we are genuinely sorry and if we forgive our brothers and sisters from our hearts, God will forgive us. But if we continue to seek revenge and do not forgive those who have sinned against us, then we are bound for Hell.'

An image of fire and serpents came into Bunty's mind, and she pictured herself writhing in pain as God turned his back on her and threw her into the pit. She needed to show Him she was sorry for what she had done, and she needed to get Chrissie to forgive her, or she would be bound for Hell too. She grabbed Mary's hand and ran from the church. No-one tried to stop her.

CHAPTER SEVENTY-FIVE

The morning of Roderick's funeral, I had a miscarriage. When I awoke with cramps in my stomach and saw a bloodstain on my undergarments, I knew. To think I had Roderick's baby inside me, and it was now lost, broke me. I howled with anguish at the terrible unfairness of it all.

'Chrissie, Chrissie, what's wrong?' my mother called, coming into my bedroom where I sat, crumpled on the floor. Her terrified eyes stared at the carpet, which was slowly soaking up the lost blood and the lost life.

'I've lost it *Mathair*. I've lost Roderick's baby.'

Saying nothing, she sat beside me, took me in her arms and rocked me like her own baby. I was so grateful she had stayed with me the night before Roderick's funeral, knowing how difficult a time it was going to be for me. We didn't realise then how difficult.

Life had never felt so bad since the time Donald was born and we lost Heather. I remembered how sad and angry Roderick had been and how it had taken him a while to accept Donald. Now it was my turn to be sad and angry, and I didn't know how I was going to get through the day. People were gathering downstairs for Roderick's last journey, and I would need to greet them.

My mother helped clean me up, bringing a bowl of hot water, towels, and napkins to wear in case there was any more blood still to come. She helped me dress for the funeral, and I felt like a rag doll as she pushed and pulled my undergarments and funeral dress over my head, arms, and legs. My mind was blank as I stared at the bloodstain on the carpet, but my mother's voice brought me back.

'I could say you're ill and can't come to the funeral. I wouldn't be telling a lie.'

'I don't want anyone to know about the baby, *Mathair*. Please don't tell anyone.'

211

'I won't *mo graidh,*' she soothed. 'We don't need to say what you are ill with. People will understand. You've been under such pressure.'

'I can't let Roderick and my boys down. I'll come, but can you leave me for a little while? I want to be on my own.'

After she left, I went over to the window and looked out at the gathering mourners, dark-clad, sombre men, and women. People from our local area and from other parts of the island had come to pay their respects. Even the Laird was there. I was pleased for Roderick. Unlike Colin's funeral, there was no undertaker and no fancy casket. Lachie the joiner had made the coffin and my mother and some of the other women in our settlement had washed and prepared him, as was the custom. He was being buried in Kilmuir Cemetery over Balranald way, as that was where his family originally crofted. His oldest brother now worked the croft, and it would be passed on to his sons in the future. I looked at my two boys standing forlornly in their new funeral suits. What would I be able to pass on to them?

Donald and Roddy stood together, at last united. I thought Donald's friendship with Mary would end when we told him about Bunty sending the letters to the Laird and spreading the gossip about his mother being an Indian squaw. But when Mary told him she was his cousin, and she didn't care if his mother was a red Indian, they remained close, although he stopped going for tea. I was glad he was getting support from Mary, as the taunts and teasing from the other children at school about his heritage had taken its toll on him. I think he was relieved to be going to Glasgow to get away from it all. Victoria would send him to a local day school until it was time for him to go to boarding school. After that it would be university and perhaps military college like his father. I would miss him so much, but I could see it was in his best interest and his Aunt Victoria would be kind to him, unlike Bunty, who only seemed to know how to be cruel.

Roddy was a different kettle of fish from Donald. Outgoing and popular with the other children, he had never let their teasing upset

212

him and he had not experienced the shame that Donald had. He had never doubted his father's motives for what had happened in Canada and had constantly supported him. Roderick's death had left him bereft, but I knew my father would take him under his wing and help him come to terms with it. He loved working on the croft, so perhaps it would pass to him, and he would be the one to carry on our traditions. Like Donald, he would go away to school. For him it would be to Portree in Skye to get his secondary education and if all went well, then Roderick had always hoped he would go to University too. My fear was that once my boys left the island, like lots of other young men before them, they would never come back.

I looked at the bloodstain on the floor, bent to touch what was left of my baby, then said goodbye to what might have been and made by way downstairs. Although my heart was broken, I smiled and thanked people for coming while Flora put out pots of tea and sandwiches. My mother hovered nearby, obviously worried that I might find it all too much. When I got outside, it surprised me to see Bunty and Mary there. I was finding it hard to forgive her, but in the end, it was God's forgiveness she needed, not mine. I watched as they made their way over to Donald and Roddy. Mary held Donald's hand, but Roddy turned on them. He was a hot-headed boy who found it hard to cover his feelings, so I was unsurprised when he began remonstrating with Bunty and Mary.

Of course, it wasn't the time, and I could see the mourners frowning at his lack of respect for this solemn rite of passage. I felt relieved when my father went over and led him away, but his rage towards them was obvious for everyone to see. As Bunty and I exchanged glances, I wondered why I never learned my lesson. Why didn't I listen to my instincts? That first day I met her, I felt her evil eye on me, but I ignored it and trusted her. Just as trusting Colin had led to Heather's death, so trusting Bunty had led to Roderick's death.

Finally, it was time to say goodbye to Roderick. Kilmuir Cemetery was several miles away from Lochmaddy, so my father

and some other men lifted his coffin and placed it in the cart to be
carried for most of the journey. However, once it reached the
outskirts of the cemetery area, as was the tradition, the men would
lift it off and the funeral procession would begin, with the men
taking turns at carrying the coffin to the lair that the gravedigger
had prepared. We women did not go to the graveside, but we all
went outside to see the coffin being carried away. I cried as I
watched my two boys in their black suits joining the men; they
looked so young and vulnerable.

CHAPTER SEVENTY-SIX

After the coffin left, Bunty approached me. She was wild-eyed, and Mary looked a little scared.

'I need to talk to you, Chrissie,' she said, pulling my sleeve.

I drew my arm away and sent Mary over to stand with Flora. I didn't know what Bunty was going to say, but I didn't want Mary getting caught up in any argument that she might begin, but it did not prepare me for what she said next.

'I'm going to have a baby and it's Johnny's.'

What did she mean? How could she be having a baby? It was then I noticed for the first time how rounded her middle had become and guessed the worst had happened when she and Johnny had been intimate at the end of last year. So that was why my brother was so upset on the day he left for Canada. The witch had told him when he could do nothing about it. The sting of jealousy and resentment towards Bunty was overwhelming. Why was God giving her a baby and not me? I had always tried to do what was right while she had tried to do only what was wrong. I dug my fingers into my palm to stop myself from howling again.

I knew the women still gathered were watching us and thought it best if we moved inside, so I asked my mother if she would take Bunty and Mary into the house while I said farewell to the mourners. I was grateful for their support, but my mind was working feverishly, thinking that I would need to speak to Bunty and find out what her plans were. Eventually, everyone left, and I went into the house.

Bunty and Mary were sitting in the kitchen with my mother and Flora having a cup of tea and a scone. My mother's face was grim. As I looked at them, I wondered if Bunty intended to stay on the island and let everyone know Johnny was the father, or would she go back home? I would need to speak to my mother and father about it. Johnny's child would be my niece or nephew and my parents' grandchild. We had an obligation to support Bunty and

215

her child, as Johnny clearly couldn't. Was that why she was telling me now?

I took Bunty up to the study and, as soon as we sat down, she burst into tears. I watched as gulping sobs wracked her body. Normally, I would have tried to comfort her, but today I didn't have it in me. I wanted to say goodbye to Roderick without Bunty's spitefulness spoiling it. Eventually, she calmed down.

'Thanks for seeing me, Chrissie. I know I've done some terrible things, but I felt the baby move today and I needed to tell you.'

'I'm glad you've told me, Bunty. It's a terrible thing that you are having Johnny's baby and he's not here to support you. Does he know?'

'Yes. I told him on the day he left for Canada.'

I was right then. Poor Johnny.

'Why did you wait until then? If you had told him sooner, he may have stopped the wedding.'

She scoffed.

'And married me instead of Janet, you mean? I only realised I was pregnant on the day of the wedding and sent him a telegram asking him to come and see me. But he didn't. He made his choice, and it wasn't me. I just wanted to hurt him.'

I thought back to that day. I had told Johnny not to go and see her, so perhaps I was to blame, but I was in no mood for making her feel better.

'Yes, you're good at hurting people, Bunty. You've certainly hurt our family.'

'I know and I'm so, so sorry, Chrissie. I want to ask for your forgiveness. If you don't forgive me, you'll go to Hell. That's what the Minister said on Sunday.'

It took me all my time not to slap her. She was talking nonsense as I'm sure the Minister wouldn't have said such a thing, but Hell or not, it was way too soon for any forgiveness.

'I can't, Bunty and you have a damned cheek asking me on this day of all days.'

216

She rose from her seat, grabbed my hands, and knelt in front of me.

'Please, please Chrissie. I'm begging you. God will do something awful to us both if you don't.'

Her anguish was genuine, but my heart was hard. A surge of anger that she would come here on the day I was burying my husband to ask for forgiveness forced me to stand up abruptly. Her hands slipped from mine, and she fell back on the floor. I looked down at her with hatred in my heart.

'Get out of my house, Bunty. I cannot speak to you today. I will call on you by and by and we can talk about your plans for the future. But not today. I need to mourn my husband.'

And my baby, I said silently.

When she had left, I collapsed on the couch. I couldn't hold on to my anger any longer and, like Bunty, let out huge gulping sobs of pain. How I wished Roderick was here to steer me through the changes that were ahead and to share in the mourning of our lost child.

CHAPTER SEVENTY-SEVEN

Tears blinded Bunty as she and Mary walked back home. She knew Mary was frightened, but she felt incapable of doing anything about it. All her life, she had blamed other people for what happened to her, but she knew now that it was her fault. She was just bad. Her father was evil, and she was his bitter seed, producing rotten fruit that infected everything she touched, just as the Minister had said in church. No wonder her uncle had been cruel and had mistreated her. No wonder her mother had stood by and done nothing about it. All those years of dreaming that her father would come and save her were foolish delusions.

The baby fluttered in her womb, and she cried out. This baby would be evidence for everyone to see that she was an immoral woman who had encouraged a man to have sex with her. She would need to get rid of it. No-one could find out. Chrissie and her family needed protection. She had done so much to hurt them; she must cover up Johnny's sin so that no shame would fall upon them. It was then she heard his voice.

'Bunty, you're right. You need to get rid of that child.'

'But how, Johnny?'

'You know how to do it. Let your blood and it will drain away.'

'Mummy, why are you talking to yourself?'

She looked at Mary and smiled.

'I'm not talking to myself, chook. Can't you hear Uncle Johnny?'

'Is everything alright, Mrs Hepworth?'

She looked at Mrs McIver and nodded.

'It's just, you're not looking very well. It surprised me to see you at the funeral, I must say.'

She nodded again.

'I don't think my mummy's well, Mrs McIver. She's talking to Uncle Johnny and says he's talking to her, but he's in Canada.'

'He is indeed. Why don't you get your mummy home and I'll ask the doctor to call round?'

218

As soon as they moved on, Shona hurried round to the doctor's house and told him she thought Bunty Hepworth, the schoolteacher, had lost her mind.

'She's talking to Johnny MacIntosh, but everyone knows he's away to Canada. I'm worried about that wee girl, Mary. She shouldn't be on her own with that madwoman.'

The doctor was shocked at what he found when he arrived. Mary was crouching in a corner while her mother lay in a steaming hot bath, holding a sharp kitchen knife. He told Mrs McIver to get a towel, get Bunty out of the bath, and dry her off. He then told her to fetch the constable. Bunty tried to fight off both Mrs McIver and Dr McInnes, so he ended up having to sedate her. She had no recollection of going to Long Island Poorhouse, which was probably just as well. Dr McInnes took Mary home with him as the poor girl was distraught. His wife slept with her that night and comforted her when she woke up crying in the night.

CHAPTER SEVENTY-EIGHT

A few days after the funeral, I heard from Flora, who had heard it from Mrs McIver at the shop, that Bunty had ended up in the Long Island Poorhouse with a breakdown. Apparently, Mrs McIver had seen her and Mary walking home from the funeral and noticed she looked very upset. Poor Mary was looking scared and said her mummy had been talking to Uncle Johnny. Mrs McIver knew that talking to yourself meant only one thing. You had gone mad. So, she sent for the doctor, who certified her as mentally incapacitated and took her to Long Island Poorhouse. The doctor had taken Mary home with him and the police were trying to find Bunty's family.

When I heard this, I was troubled. I had so wanted to punish her for what she had done, but in the end, it was she who was punishing herself. Perhaps what I said on the day of Roderick's funeral had pushed her over the edge. I couldn't let Mary stay with Dr McInnes. She hardly knew him. My mother was hesitant when I asked her if it was okay for Mary to stay with us, but in the end, she said she could.

'It's not the wee girl's fault her mother is mad.'

Mary had been with us for a week when a man arrived with Dr McInnes at the croft and told us he was taking Mary and Bunty back to Manchester. He was tall and thin, wore a tweed jacket, plus fours and a cap. He looked like one of the Laird's guests dressed for a hunting trip.

'I'm Bunty's brother, Charles. I'm sorry to meet you in such sorry circumstances. I was coming to visit Bunty to check that her and Mary were okay, as we haven't seen them for three years. She upped and left without leaving a forwarding address and my mother only found out where she lived when she wrote to her requesting papers relating to her father. I had no idea this is what would greet me. Can you give me some idea of what's been going on?'

When I outlined Bunty's vindictive behaviour against our family, I could see how horrified he was at what his sister had done.

'My goodness, that's just the worst news to hear about Bunty. She's always been fragile, but I had no idea she was seeking revenge against your husband. I hope he hasn't lost his job because of her.'

'My husband is dead and I'm afraid I blame Bunty for that.'

His face paled.

'What do you mean? Did she harm him?'

'Not physically, no. But mentally, without a doubt. My husband was frail as he had TB a few years ago and her behaviour made it worse. He wasn't strong enough to cope with what she put us through.'

'I'm truly sorry for your loss. I'll need to contact my mother and find out what she wants me to do. Mary obviously can't continue to live here, so I'll take her home. She's missed that little girl so much. It was cruel of Bunty to take her away as she did. She'll want us to move Bunty closer to home as well, I'm sure, where we can check her care and recovery.'

I was relieved. Having been unable to shrug off the listlessness I felt about everything, I had neglected poor Mary. It was my mother who had looked after her and although she had done so with good grace; I knew Mary would be much happier with her own family,

'Oh, that's good news. Bunty will appreciate your support when she has her baby.'

'What do you mean, Mrs Macdonald, her baby?'

'Bunty is having a baby. Didn't you notice when you saw her?'

'She was in bed, so no, I didn't notice.'

'I thought the doctor would have told you.'

'He did not,' he said, scowling at Dr McInnes.

'It's as much a surprise to me as it is to you, Mr Adams. Bunty never came to see me about the baby. We better let Dr Graham know.'

'Who is the father?' asked Charles.

I hesitated and felt my cheeks grow pink. Although the reason Bunty was having a baby was my brother's shame, I felt that shame by association.

'No-one knows.'

'You mean she was not in a relationship with a local man?'

I shrugged my shoulders.

'Has someone molested her, do you think? Is that why she has ended up in that hospital?'

'I don't know. Although Bunty and I were friends, she never told me about a relationship or of any assault.'

My heart was beating fast as I told these lies, and I hoped God would forgive me.

'This changes everything. I need to discuss this situation with my mother. Do you know when her confinement will be?'

'I think it will be August or September.'

'Right. Thank you for everything you've done. Would you mind keeping Mary for a few more days until I can decide what to do about this new situation?'

'Yes, of course. We're happy to have her.'

CHAPTER SEVENTY-NINE

Bunty lay, she knew not where, drifting in and out of consciousness. She couldn't remember what happened, only that she was grateful for this somnolescent feeling as she lay wrapped in a medicine induced fugue. Unaware of the days and nights passing, she spent most of the time asleep. Until one day she heard a familiar voice.

'Bunty, can you hear me? It's Charles. I've come to take you home.'

At the word home, her stomach cramped with fear. She didn't want to go home. Her uncle would want to hurt her again. She wasn't strong enough. So, she lay pretending to be asleep. She needed more time in this safe place, this escape from life.

'What's wrong with her, doctor?' she heard her brother ask. If he was talking to a doctor, she must be in a hospital.

'She's had a psychotic episode, but we're not sure what's brought it on. We've given her some medication to subdue her, so that's why she's unresponsive. We'll reduce the dosage now that you're here and hopefully she will be more awake when you come back tomorrow.'

A psychotic episode. She felt a sudden wave of panic. That's what had happened when she had delivered Mary. Had she hurt Mary? What had happened? But she wouldn't think of it now. She couldn't. And relieved, she sank back down into the darkness.

When she next woke up, she felt less drowsy than she had been, and guessed the doctor had reduced her medication as he had promised her brother. Lying still, as she didn't want to alert anyone that she was awake, she squinted round the room. She saw she was in a medium-sized room with three beds lining the walls on either side. There were smallish windows on one side of the room, some of which were opened, allowing a fresh breeze to remove the smell of disinfectant. The other beds were empty and there was no-one at what she presumed was the nurse's desk, placed at the top end of the room.

Hearing a key being turned in the door lock, she closed her eyes. She wasn't ready to speak to anyone yet.

'Bunty, it's Dr Graham. Wake up, my dear.'

She felt a gentle shake and opened her eyes slowly. Her brother was standing over her and smiled when he saw her eyes open.

'Bunty! Hello! It's Charles. How are you feeling?'

She didn't respond, just looked at him, then closed her eyes again.

'She doesn't seem much more alert than yesterday, Dr Graham. When can I speak to her properly?'

'Well, I'm not sure when that will be, as we don't know yet if she has recovered from the psychosis. If she hasn't, then you won't be able to have a rational conversation with her.'

'I want to speak to her about her baby and propose that we put the child forward for adoption, but I wondered, em, doctor, whether there was anything medical that you could do to prevent the pregnancy from proceeding.'

'Do you mean abortion, Mr Adams?'

She could almost feel her brother's discomfiture.

'Well, I don't like to use that word, but yes.'

'I'm afraid the answer is no. It's against the law and more than my job's worth. Your idea concerning adoption is the only way to remove the child.'

Dr McInnes then spoke. 'The minister might be able to help you with that. I've referred several distressed families in your sister's situation to him.'

'Right, that's what I'll do.'

Bunty almost opened her eyes but realised she would need to think about things. She didn't remember being pregnant and wondered who the father was. Perhaps she was still psychotic and that was why she couldn't remember. She agreed with her brother, though. She would need to have the child adopted. There was no other way to protect her and Mary from the shame.

CHAPTER EIGHTY

When Charles Adams came to tell me he planned to have Bunty's baby adopted, I could only look at him in stunned silence. The baby was my parents' grandchild. Not that they were aware of that fact. No-one apart from me knew the truth.

'Mr Adams, I could look after the baby until Bunty is well, if you like,' I blurted.

He looked at me as if I were mad.

'Why would you do that? Bunty has done nothing but try to harm your family. You've recently become a widow and have sons of your own to look after. Bunty's baby would be better off being adopted into a family with two parents and no children.'

He was probably right, but the thought of our kin being sent away to an unknown family overwhelmed me with sadness. Our family would lose two babies if that happened.

'I believed Bunty to be my friend before I found out the truth, but from the way she looked after and clearly loved Mary, I would think that when she recovers, she will want to keep the child.'

'You misunderstand me, Mrs Macdonald. I wish the baby to be adopted because of the stigma, not because Bunty is ill.'

I could understand that. Hadn't Roderick and I pretended to be Donald's parents to protect him?

'But, as Bunty is so ill, she cannot consent to you taking her baby. You cannot take someone's child without their consent, surely?'

'I've applied to the court, and it will grant me power of attorney to act in all her affairs while she remains non compos mentis.'

He let me take that in, then continued.

'She will be told when she recovers from her illness that a family adopted the child. These things can be done quite informally, I believe. It is the only chance she has of living a decent life and finding a husband.'

I could think of nothing to say. He was her brother and was only acting in her best interests.

CHAPTER EIGHTY-ONE

The next few days were a blur to me. I had a restlessness in my spirit and often rode over to Clachan Sands to take walks by myself, hoping the rhythmic movement of the waves lapping the shore or battering the shore, depending on the weather, would bring me comfort. The boys stayed out of my way, and I could see my mother and father were worried about me, but I could do nothing about it.

Roderick filled my thoughts day and night, and I would go over and over the early part of our relationship when I had been unkind to him and suffered from the depression. I also remembered when my weak spirit had tempted me to enjoy the feel of a man's arm around me when I danced with Colin that night in Canada. Roderick didn't deserve to die. He had only ever tried to do good. That then made me think of Heather and all my grief at losing her struck afresh. I hadn't even been able to keep my promise to her to look after her son. To lose my baby so early was the worst of all, and now Johnny's baby was going to be lost to us, too.

As I lay on my back on the sand, staring up at the vast blue sky, I wondered if Roderick was up there somewhere. The gulls were wheeling high above, and I thought I heard a Corncrake's rasping call in the dunes. I wanted to lie here forever and not face up to the reality of life without him. No-one would ever brush my hair again or call me pet lamb or tell me how beautiful I looked. I would never hold a newborn baby to my breast again and feel its gentle suckling while I stroked its downy head. A rush of water as the tide came in washed over my feet and I got up. The sea was blue and beautiful today, so I stepped into it, hardly noticing the chill as my feet sucked and sank into the soft sand underneath. As I walked on, the thought struck me I could just keep walking and let the water take me. Who would care?

'*I would care, my pet lamb and your boys would care,*' said a whisper I could barely hear above the sound of the waves.

'Roderick, is that you?'

226

I looked round, searching for him, longing with all my heart that he would be standing there with his hand outstretched, waiting to take me back with him, but of course he wasn't there.

'There's another baby that needs looked after Chrissie.'

Another baby. What did he mean? What baby?

'You know, Chrissie. Johnny's baby needs a mother, and you need a baby.'

Suddenly, there was a clap of thunder, and the rain started. It poured down in huge, reviving drops and I laughed and cried with joy. Of course. I would need to find a way of getting Charles Adams to let me adopt Bunty's baby. It was obvious, but I had needed Roderick's gentle guidance to let me see. I knew then that Roderick would be with me and would see me through whatever the future would bring. I hurried home, oblivious to the state I was in, determined to find a way of adopting Bunty's baby. You can imagine my mother's face when I arrived home sodden to the skin, but she knew something had changed when I hugged her. She hugged me back and I could feel the sigh of relief as she let go of the tension she had obviously been holding on to.

CHAPTER EIGHTY-TWO

I slept fitfully now that I knew what I must do. The questions I ha
to find answers to were how I could convince Charles Adams t
let me adopt Bunty's baby and how I could avoid the stigma o
illegitimacy attaching to the child. People still talked about Sheon
Macqueen, who had a child without being married before I left fo
Canada, and Donald's parentage was still the subject of goss
because of Colin Donaldson. I wondered how his illegitimac
would affect the new life he was about to embark on, living, as h
would, among people with money and influence. While I la
ruminating, I realised the only way I could do it was to pass it o
as mine. But how? I would need to enlist the help of my moth
and father, but it took a bit of convincing before they accepted n
determination to adopt Bunty's child.

'For goodness' sake, Chrissie, why do you want to hav
anything to do with that baby after what its mother did to you ar
Roderick?' said my mother.

I hadn't told them yet that it was Johnny's child, but I wou
need to if I was to get them to help me find a solution for passir
the baby off as mine.

'There's something you don't know.'

'What don't we know, Chrissie?' asked my father, looking
me with exasperation.

'The baby is Johnny's.'

The two of them were speechless.

'He and Bunty had a brief affair before he got back with Jan
and this baby is the result.'

'Does he know?' asked my mother.

'Yes. She told him on the day he was leaving for Canada. Sh
wanted to hurt him and spoil his new life with Janet.'

'Well, we need to tell him Bunty is ill, and the baby is to b
adopted. It is Johnny's responsibility, not yours,' said my father.

'But it would wreck any chance of happiness that Johnny an
Janet have and, besides, the baby would need to live with the

228

stigma of illegitimacy.'

'Well, it will need to live with the stigma of illegitimacy if you adopt it too,' said my father, his voice stinging with sarcasm.

'You're a widow with a son of your own. How can you afford to look after it as well as him? The croft hardly sustains us,' said my mother, always practical.

I knew crofting life was hard and barely supplied a living for most people, like my mother and father. But I didn't have that problem any longer. After Roderick died, it surprised me to find I was quite a well-off woman. His careful spending, the saving on rent from working and living in the post office and the Factor's house, meant he had added to the lump sum from the sale of the farm in Canada. The money gave me more choices about what to do with my life.

'Roderick has left me comfortable *Mathair*, so I can afford to look after the baby.'

But money was not the only consideration. I knew that being a mother with a baby to bring up would ease the pain of losing my child and Roderick to the cancer. I needed this to keep me sane, and I continued.

'I need to do this, *Mathair*. You understand, don't you?' I pleaded. 'I just can't let strangers adopt that baby. Please say you agree and will help me find a way to do it without the baby's illegitimacy being discovered.'

My mother's face softened, but my father looked at me as if I were mad.

'What do you mean without the baby's illegitimacy being discovered?'

'I need to find a way of passing that baby off as mine.'

'But there's no way you could do that. Bunty's baby will be born in the asylum, and I can think of no way to cover that up to allow you to bring the baby home as yours.'

'The baby won't be born there, *Athair*. Charles will arrange for Bunty to be sent to an asylum closer to home. Apparently, it's not the first time she's been ill like that, so they know where to send her. The baby will be born there.'

'Okay. But you don't look pregnant. How could you suddenly appear one day with a baby? It's a hairbrained scheme, my girl.'

'Angus, I didn't tell anyone about Chrissie's miscarriage, so we could carry it off. You never saw Dr McInnes, did you, Chrissie, to get yourself checked over?'

'No,' I replied, suddenly feeling a flutter of hope that I could do this.

'We're the only people who know you lost your baby, so if you went away and came home with a child, no-one would think strange. We would just need to have a good reason for you going away.'

'Well, I have been depressed and Mrs Macaulay knows that as I spoke to her about it, so the reverend will know as well. We could just say I needed to get away to help my recovery. But where would I go?'

My mother grinned.

'I know someone with a lovely hotel on the Firth of Clyde who would welcome you, I'm sure.'

I laughed.

'Of course, Morag. Why didn't I think of that?'

'The problem is, if you were at the same stage of pregnancy as Bunty, you would show by now.'

I cried inside as I thought about how far on I would have been with my own baby. Perhaps I would have felt those little flutters life that had brought me out of my depression over in Canada when I was expecting Roddy.

'Maybe you could wear some padding round your waist make you look fatter till you leave,' suggested my father.

'But what about Roddy and Donald? I hate to leave them, but I couldn't take them with me. They must never find out the truth.'

'Don't you worry about Roddy and Donald. I'll keep them busy.'

All I had to do now was convince Charles Adams to let me adopt Bunty's child.

CHAPTER EIGHTY-THREE

Bunty's memory gradually came back, and thoughts whirled round her head as she remembered one thing after another. She recalled with shame all the trouble she had caused for Roderick and Chrissie. Although she hadn't killed him directly she was sure her vendetta against Roderick had taken their toll on his health and had caused him to have an early death. When she thought of Chrissie, she was even more ashamed. Chrissie had tried to be a good friend to her and all she had done was betray her. Her thoughts then moved to Johnny and the swelling in her belly. She remembered now that she was pregnant as she had heard her brother saying. Tears fell when she thought about Johnny and the day he left for Canada. How cruel she had been telling him she was having his child but that she would never let him have anything to do with it. If only things had worked out with him, she wouldn't be here now.

Her heart raced as she tried to push a memory away of what had happened after Roderick's funeral. How could she have thought about getting rid of the baby like that? Poor Mary must have been terrified. She needed to see her little girl and reassure her.

'Nurse,' she called. 'I need to see my little girl. Her name's Mary. Can you get her for me?'

'Don't upset yourself, Mrs Hepworth,' the nurse said when she came over. 'You seem much brighter. How are you feeling in yourself now?'

'I'm remembering things, nurse, and that's why I need to see my Mary urgently. I need to let her know I'm alright and to see that she's alright too. Will you get in touch with my brother and ask him to bring her in?'

'I'll need to speak to Dr Graham first and get him to assess you.'

'What do you mean, assess me? I'm fine. I'm telling you; I've remembered what happened.'

'Now, now, just lie back and relax, Mrs Hepworth. I'll see the doctor today and tell him what you've said.'

But Bunty couldn't relax. She needed to see Mary. Throwing the covers back, she jumped out of bed and inadvertently bumped into the nurse, who fell backwards. She let out a blood-curdling scream and shouted, 'Help! Help!' Before Bunty knew what was happening, several nurses surrounded her and forced her to the ground. As she looked up at their angry faces, she felt a needle pressing into her arm and sank into the blackness again.

CHAPTER EIGHTY-FOUR

When Bunty's brother told me she'd had a relapse, I felt sorry for her.

'What happened?'

'Apparently, she jumped out of bed and attacked a nurse.'

'Oh no, that's too bad. She must still be quite ill.'

'Yes she is, and I feel bad about leaving her, but I must go home so that I can make the arrangements for her removal from Long Island to another establishment closer to home.'

'When will you go?'

'We'll leave on Friday, so if you could pack up whatever belongings you have for Mary, I would be grateful. I've already arranged for Bunty's furniture and other bits and pieces to be shipped to my mother's home in Manchester. I will leave you her address just in case you need to get in touch.'

'May I take Mary up to see Bunty tomorrow, Mr Adams, if you are leaving on Friday? I think it might reassure Mary that her mother is alright if she can see her. She's been fretting.'

'I'm not sure if the hospital will let Mary in, but I shall ask Dr McInnes if he could arrange for her to visit Bunty in the garden. It might do Bunty a power of good as well. Apparently, she shouted she wanted to see Mary when she had her relapse.'

'May I ask you something before you go?'

He looked at me with curiosity.

'Have you contacted anyone about the adoption yet, Mr Adams?'

'Not yet, no. I was hoping to at least discuss it with Bunty, but she's not been well enough.'

'I see. You know I offered to look after the baby until Bunty was well again, and you refused, as you do not wish any stigma to fall on her or Mary. Well, I'm wondering if you would allow me to adopt the child.'

'You?'

'Yes. Losing my husband to cancer and my boys moving to school has been a huge wrench for me and I need something to keep me going, Mr Adams. I feel I could do a better job than strangers.'

'But how would you pass the baby off as yours?'

'I have a plan, Mr Adams.'

He didn't ask me what it was.

'I shall mull it over and let you know tomorrow. Bring Mary up to the hospital after lunch and I'll see if we can get her into the grounds to visit her mother before she leaves on Friday.'

Mary was excited when I told her we were going to see her mummy. She knew she was going back to Manchester and told me she was looking forward to seeing her Grandma again. I was glad to hear that. It would have been awful if she hadn't wanted to go.

'But I really want to see Mummy before I go.'

The resilience of the child surprised me. After what Mary had seen, you would think the last person she would want to see would be her mother, but she did.

We arrived at the Long Island Poorhouse just after lunch. The building was two storeys in height and built of grey stone, with several small windows looking out onto the courtyard. It looked quite grim despite the lawned garden and flower beds, and I wondered if the inside was more welcoming. As we looked through the gate, I could see several women sitting knitting on wooden benches outside the front door and several men working on the grounds. I assumed these were the people who lived there because they were poor and had nowhere else to live. Long Island still took in poor people and gave them board and lodgings for work, but they now took in patients like Bunty, who had lost their minds.

I realised that only God's grace had saved me from the same fate as Bunty. If Shona McIver had heard me talking to Roderic that day on the beach, she would have seen me as another candidate for the asylum. I thought it must be the worst thing

234

lose your mind, and I wondered why mental disorders affected some people and not others. From what Bunty told me about her uncle, she had not had a happy childhood, and perhaps that was why she had become so ill. I had been fortunate to be brought up in a loving family and I prayed my boys would gain some benefit from the love and care they had received in their early years, as the last few years had been very traumatic for them.

'Mummy,' Mary cried when she saw Bunty coming out of the house with Charles. As soon as they opened the gate, she ran towards her. Bunty stood with tears streaming from her eyes and held her arms wide for her girl to run into. I had a lump in my throat as I watched them. Charles and I and took a walk round the grounds while they chatted. Mother and daughter needed some privacy.

When we returned, a nurse came to take Bunty back inside but before going with her she turned to me and pulled me aside so that no-one could hear what she was saying.

'Thank you for looking after Mary and for bringing her to see me. It's more than I deserve.'

'I know I was harsh when I last saw you, and I'm sorry.'

'I deserved it, Chrissie. I'd tried to harm you and your family, and you had just lost Roderick. I hope you'll find it in your heart to forgive me eventually. I know I was wrong about Roderick and have asked God to forgive me.'

I thought she was becoming agitated and took her hand in mine which she grasped tightly.

'Chrissie, my brother plans to have my baby adopted.'

'Yes, I know.'

'I hate the thought of her or him going to a family who has no blood relationship. I'm anxious they might be unkind to them, the way my uncle was unkind to me.'

Her eyes filled with tears as she caressed her tummy, and I worried she might be having another relapse. Her next words and the wildness in her eyes told me she was.

'You need to steal the baby when it's born and take it over to Johnny in Canada. He'll look after it properly.'

'I wish I could, Bunty, but as you can see, I have my own baby on the way.'

I had begun to wear padding round my waist as my father had suggested, so people were getting used to thinking I was pregnant.

'I didn't know you were having a baby. Well never mind, I'll write to Johnny and tell him I'll bring the baby over to Canada for him and Janet to look after.'

Before I could say anything more, the nurse came over.

'We need to go in now, Mrs Hepworth.'

'I'm coming, nurse.'

I stood with Charles and Mary, watching her go back inside. She was clearly still unwell and not thinking rationally so she was in the best place. But somehow our conversation made me feel better about my plan to adopt her child. She wanted it to be looked after by family, and that's what I was. But I wondered what Charles would have to say.

CHAPTER EIGHTY-FIVE

Although only early in June, it was hot the next day, and the midges were out in force. By the time I reached the Lochmaddy Hotel, they had covered me in bites. It was a relief to get into the coolness of the hotel reception. Charles had asked me to bring Mary and her belongings to the hotel so that she would be ready to go home with him the following day. My stomach churned as I waited in reception, wondering what he would say about my proposal to adopt Bunty's baby.

'Mr Adams is waiting in the dining room for you, Mrs Macdonald. I am to take Mary and her baggage upstairs to her room while you have a chat,' said Rhona.

I smiled and went through, but noticed my legs were shaking a little. It felt like my life depended on whatever decision this man would make. He was drinking a cup of tea and reading the paper, but looked up when I came in.

'Good morning, Mrs Macdonald. Would you like some tea?'

'Yes, thank you. It's boiling hot today.'

He poured the tea, then looked at me.

'So, I won't keep you in suspense. I mulled over your request last night and have decided to let you adopt Bunty's baby.'

When I shook his hand, probably more vigorously than was necessary, he asked me what my plan was.

'I will go to Helensburgh to stay with my sister, who runs a hotel there, until I hear from you telling me Bunty's baby has been delivered.'

'But what I don't understand, Mrs Macdonald, is how you will be able to just turn up with a newborn baby? People will know it's not yours, so will still know the child is illegitimate. It's no life for any child.'

I put my hand on my stomach and his eyes widened. He obviously hadn't noticed my growing middle.

'This is padding Mr Adams. I was pregnant with my husband's baby before he died, but I lost it. No-one knows except my mother and father. They will tell people I've gone away for my health and will come back when the baby's born. Everyone will believe that it is mine and Roderick's baby.'

'I see. How will we arrange for the baby to be registered and handed over to you? There is no legal paperwork required to adopt a child so it will just be an informal agreement between us. I think the less paperwork there is for Bunty to discover, the better.'

'I agree. Shall we shake on it then?'

We shook hands and then I continued.

'I would like to have the baby registered in Scotland and I believe all that's needed is for the mother, father, or someone from the house where the baby was delivered to go to the registrar and tell them about the child. Would it be possible for you to bring the baby to me at my sister's house and I can register it as if the child were mine and was born there.'

'I'm not sure if that will be possible. Because the baby will be born in an asylum, we may need to register it there. I shall talk discretely with the doctor once Bunty is moved to the new establishment and see if I can arrange to do as you ask.'

'Thank you, Mr Adams. You don't know what this means to me.'

CHAPTER EIGHY-SIX

I sent Morag a telegram asking her if I could come for a visit because of my health and could she confirm by return that she had a room that I could rent. She replied, telling me not to be silly. I didn't need to rent a room as she and Michael had plenty of space for me to stay with them in their private apartments. Although Ian Fraser had told me all the correspondence through the post office was confidential, I could not take the chance of explaining anything further to Morag. I would tell her the full story when I saw her as I had no doubts that she would support me. That's what families do.

When I told Roddy and Donald I was going away for a while, they were full of questions and asked if they could come and visit me at Auntie Morag's, as they had so enjoyed their visit the last time. I said they could and that I would be back before they knew it to see them off to their new schools, although if Bunty had her baby late, I might not. As luck would have it, there were no delays, and I was home on time. I'll never forget the day I got the letter from Charles Adams telling me Bunty had given birth to a little girl.

Dear Mrs Macdonald

I write with great relief to let you know Bunty gave birth to a baby girl. There were no complications attached to the birth, but Bunty suffered another relapse when we took the child from her. She was reluctant to hand the baby over to me and when she was forced to do so by the medical staff, she screamed pitifully that the baby must go to Canada to live with her father. We had no idea what she was talking about as she had never mentioned the baby's father before and it seems strange that he would be in Canada.

We think it will be several months before she will be able to move home to my mother's house. Mary is happy to be back with her grandma and I believe she plans to write to Donald from time to time.

As we discussed the last time we met, I spoke to the doctor, and he agreed that I could take the baby to be registered in Scotland. I shall, therefore, be with you within the next few days.

Yours sincerely
Charles Adams

Although my heart went out to Bunty and the pain she must have felt when her child was taken from her, I cried with relief that the baby had been safely delivered and waited on tenterhooks for Charles to arrive. I thought he might have stayed overnight but he made his way back to catch his train immediately after handing Heather over. His voice trembled with emotion as he bade us goodbye.

'Thank you for taking the baby Mrs Macdonald. Bunty would not have had the resilience to look after her and Mary on her own. Although I have always advocated adoption, it has occurred to me just recently that she is my niece, and although we have only recently met, it gives me some reassurance to pass her care over to you. All the very best to you.'

As I held Heather in my arms, I knew I had done the right thing. She was just beautiful, with little pink cheeks and a shock of black hair. I was pleased to see she looked like Johnny, but I could see Bunty in her too. Hopefully, no-one else would.

CHAPTER EIGHTY-SEVEN
Lochmaddy, North Uist, August 1923

As I turn to Roddy and Donald, there is a huge kerfuffle behind me, and I look round to see what's going on. The Laird is there with several local dignitaries and is shaking hands with an important-looking man dressed in the uniform of the Cameron Highlanders.

'Who is that *Athair*?' I ask my father, but it's my mother who answers.

'Och, it must be that colonel who's unveiling the war memorial tomorrow. Our Lachlan's name will be on it,' says my mother proudly. 'It's a pity we shall miss it.'

'But we can't miss it, *Mathair*. We must go along.'

'But you've just arrived home. Are you sure you want to be out and about so soon?'

She looks at me meaningfully and I know she's worried about me mixing with so many of our neighbours so quickly.

'I'm fine *Mathair*. I wouldn't miss seeing my little brother's name on that memorial for anything.'

'Right, well, let's get you home.'

Before we move over to the cart, I smile at Roddy and Donald, who smile back.

'Come and meet your new sister,' I say.

So, they come over, stare into the pram, and scrutinise the baby. I hold my breath, but both turn to me with huge grins.

'She looks a bit like Uncle Johnny with all that dark hair,' says Roddy.

'I hope she's as much fun as he is,' says Donald.

I ruffle his hair and we set off for home.

When we get there, Murdo is waiting outside with a letter in his hand.

'Welcome home Chrissie and hello to you, Morag. It's been a while since you've been back home, is it not? I hear you've gone and got yourself married.'

'Aye, you heard right Murdo,' she says with a laugh.

241

He turns back to me.

'I've a letter here for you, so I thought I would wait until you came home. It's from Manchester, from a Hepworth and Sons Printers,' he says, squinting down at the ink stamp on the envelope.

My heart misses a beat at the name Hepworth.

'Do you think it's something to do with Mrs Hepworth, the schoolteacher? I hear tell she was pregnant when she left the asylum.'

'She never was,' I say, scandalised. 'But I think I know what this letter is Murdo. It's to do with Lachlan's diaries that he kept during the war. I've been trying to get someone to publish them.'

'Och well, it's good news that this Mr Hepworth is going to publish them. I'll be off now, and I'll see you at the ceremony tomorrow.'

When I open the letter, sure enough, it's from Bunty's father-in-law. He's writing to let me know he has been in contact with a publisher who is interested in Lachlan's diaries, but he's wondering whether I could write them up into a memoir as it would be easier for them to sell to the public. So, Bunty had kept her word and passed Lachlan's diaries onto her father-in-law. As for me writing up a memoir, I will need to think about that another time I have rather a lot on my plate just now.

The next day, we assemble at Clachan where the War Memorial is waiting to be unveiled. The Laird, who had chaired the Memorial Committee, begins the ceremony by mentioning the losses among the Cameron Highlanders at the Battle of Loos in 1915. I wonder if it was the carnage there that had caused Lachlan's breakdown. When he finishes, he introduces Colonel Cameron of Lochiel, who then takes over. We all stand in silence some looking at the Colonel, others looking at their shoes, as he speaks of the bravery of the men he had chosen from North and South Uist to lead the assault. He tells us he chose them because he knew they would win the battle for him.

'And they did, but at such a cost,' he says, his voice quivering

242